WROUGHT UPON US

Murphy O'Reilly

First published by Busybird Publishing 2023

ISBN:
Paperback: 978-1-922954-54-1

This is a work of fiction. Any similarities between places and characters are a coincidence.

Cover image: Kev Howlett, Busybird Publishing

Cover design: Busybird Publishing

Illustrations: Jack Howlett

Layout and typesetting: Busybird Publishing

Busybird Publishing
2/118 Para Road
Montmorency, Victoria
Australia 3094

www.busybird.com.au

"Unbelievable," a man muttered to himself, walking down an empty street, carrying his office belongings in a box. Pens, a mug, a fake plant, and a stapler he stole out of spite.

He was tall and slender, with shoulder-length brown hair tied back in a knot and light stubble he'd forgotten to shave that morning. He wore a light blue work shirt and a bland white tie, along with black pants and shoes.

"Five minutes. I miss the damn train by five minutes!" he muttered to himself, letting out an annoyed grunt. This day had been terrible from start to finish. Firstly, getting to work and having double the usual workload. Secondly, someone stealing his lunch from the break room when it had a label reading 'Kyle's Lunch. Do not eat!' stuck to it. And lastly, being let go due to downsizing.

Having missed his train, Kyle – the man in question – was on his way from the train station to a café just down the street. He resolved himself to wait for the next train, which was not due for an hour.

As Kyle walked towards the café, he passed an alleyway. He heard dull thuds and grunts coming from it. He turned his head to see a man being beaten by two attackers. One was holding the man in a full nelson lock while the other punched him in the stomach repeatedly.

"Think you're so tough now, huh?" the second attacker said. He kept hitting the man in the gut while laughing.

Kyle looked on from the edge of the alleyway, thought for a second, then kept walking.

As he neared the café, he thought to himself, *I can't just watch.*

Kyle sighed and turned around. As he got back to the alleyway, he put his box of belongings on the ground and stormed up to one of the attackers, shoulder-charging him to the ground. Then he hit the other attacker – the one holding the man – in the nose, and threw him next to the first guy.

The beaten man hunched over, clutching his stomach. He was dark-skinned, bald, and quite short. Blood dripped down from his nose and stained his green shirt.

"Are you okay, man?" Kyle asked, offering him a hand up.

"I'll be just fine," he said with a smirk on his face. "You should get out of here. It's for your own good."

"What are you—"

They were cut off as the attackers got up to fight back.

One of the attackers kicked Kyle in the groin, then punched him in the eye. The man Kyle had just helped was thrown against the wall by the second attacker and punched repeatedly in his face.

Kyle tried to fight back but couldn't find a window to punch. So, he was stuck blocking hits, which was already hard enough since the first attacker punched rapidly without taking a break.

Kyle managed to kick the first attacker in the shin, stopping him long enough to punch back, but his arms felt like they were about to break from blocking all those blows. His own punch felt hollow, and so he compensated by throwing the attacker against the wall. He looked at the other fight next to him, against the second attacker. The beaten man seemed to have gained the upper hand. He'd already broken his opponent's nose and arm and proceeded to kick him in the gut while he was crumpled up on the ground. Kyle decided this fight was over and threw his opponent next to the other. He pulled the beaten man away.

"Hey! You've done enough," Kyle said. "Let's just leave them here."

The beaten man took a second look at the two attackers on the ground. The one he'd faced was holding his right arm tightly while trying to get back up. And the one Kyle had fought was already on his feet, helping his friend.

"Okay. You wanna finish this?" the first attacker said. "Alex, stay back."

The second attacker with the broken arm – Alex – slowly backed away.

"Whatcha gonna do, Stu?" he asked.

Stu took out a switchblade from his back pocket. "I think it's high time we got to the fun part."

The beaten man looked at Kyle and smiled. "Okay. You've done enough. Just walk away. It's time to end this."

"No," Kyle protested, grabbing his arm. "*Enough.* Let's leave."

The beaten man grabbed Kyle by his collar and threw him to the front of the alley. He took a deep breath and exhaled.

His eyes glowed a deep blue and his teeth sharpened to a point. Claws grew from his fingertips. Deep black hair erupted from his body. Bones broke and extended. He let out a distorted growl as his face started to grow longer. His clothes ripped, unable to contain his ever-growing body. A tail sprouted from behind him. His feet burst from his shoes and his legs grew longer. In a matter of seconds, he had grown at least three feet in height.

Kyle and the two attackers were now standing in front of a large, grotesque wolf, staring down with a smirk, drooling at the sight of them.

He was a werewolf.

Chapter 2

"So," the werewolf asked Stu sarcastically, "you still wanna fight?" He spread his large arms to show off his size. He could almost touch both sides of the alleyway.

Stu dropped his switchblade, frozen in fear. His jaw was wide open in shock.

The werewolf swiped at Alex, slicing his abdomen and spilling his intestines. Alex fell to the ground, staring down at his emptying gut. The werewolf then grabbed him by the shoulders and bit his head off, spitting it out directly at Stu's feet. Stu did not get a chance to run before the werewolf lunged at him, next.

Then, from behind Kyle, a gunshot fired.

The bullet hit the werewolf in his left shoulder. The wound began to sizzle and melt his skin away. The werewolf clutched the wound and turned around, as did Kyle. The gunman pushed past Kyle into the alleyway.

"What're you doing, Damien?" he asked the werewolf. "You should know better, with your anger issues. Were you *trying* to get into a fight?"

"Stay out of this!" Damien, the werewolf, growled back.

The gunman didn't look threatening at a first glance. His short hair and neatly trimmed beard were white as snow, and his complexion almost matched. His face was covered in liver spots, and he looked extremely old; mid-eighties, possibly; but had no problems with his age slowing his movement. He was dressed in beige cargo pants and a black top with a dark green military field jacket over it. There was a sizeable cross tattooed on the right side of his neck. His pale blue eyes glared at the werewolf with anger.

"Stand down, Damien. You've already made too much of a mess. Maybe, if you're lucky, I won't have to kill you."

Kyle was stuck in the middle of this conversation. He tried to move towards the gunman.

"Stay right there!" the old man barked, pointing at Kyle. "I'll need to talk to you once this is over."

Kyle was frozen, not in fear, but in confusion. He's just seen a man transform into a werewolf and bite another man's head off. Then, someone waltzed into the alleyway and *shot* the werewolf. Now, they were arguing.

The werewolf growled and ran toward the gunman.

He was about to fire when Kyle intervened: he ran into the werewolf's path and kicked the creature as hard as he could in the snout.

"*Argh!*" The werewolf stopped abruptly to grab its nose in pain, which dripped blood. He glared at Kyle.

"Okay, *you're* dying first now."

The werewolf looked angrier than ever and was about to swipe at Kyle when the old man shot him once again, this time in the right eye. The werewolf fell backwards to the ground, gripping his eye and groaning.

"Get out of the way, idiot!" the old man yelled at Kyle, pushing him aside as he walked past.

"You're crazy, old man!" Kyle yelled back. "That thing would've torn you in half! You look a hundred years old! How the fuck can you even hold a gun upright?"

"Shut up and stay out of this!" the old man demanded.

During their bickering, the werewolf got back up, seething with anger. Kyle quickly took the gun off the old man and held it up to the werewolf.

"Stay back!" he said, his arms shaking.

The werewolf roared at Kyle; he could feel the hot breath blasting him in the face. Before Kyle could fire, the old man took the pistol back off him and unloaded the rest of the clip in the werewolf's chest. The creature slowly dropped to its knees, looking back up one last time before falling onto the ground. Then, he slowly turned back into a human.

"Stay there," the old man ordered Kyle.

He walked over to Stu, who was sitting on the ground, stunned in fear. He picked up the switchblade and stabbed Stu in the neck, then threw it beside what was once the werewolf. He then took out a phone from his pocket and texted someone. Once he was done, he turned back to Kyle.

"Come with me. We need to talk."

Kyle said nothing, unable to make sense of what was happening. He simply picked up his box of belongings and complied.

The old man escorted him down the street to a car, a black 1969 Pontiac Catalina, which they both got in.

"We have to get out of here fast," the old man said.

"Uh, yeah," Kyle replied, still very confused about what was going on.

The old man started the car and drove away from the scene. "It'll be easier to talk somewhere more private."

Kyle felt uneasy the whole trip. He'd fought a werewolf and won, albeit with some help, and now he was getting a ride with some old man to who knew where. The entire trip, there was no small talk. Kyle didn't know what to start the conversation with, and the old man didn't seem to be in the mood to chat.

They arrived at an underground parking lot. Luckily, there were only a few cars dotted around. They found a small, quiet spot in one of the corners.

The old man turned off the car and pulled his gun out, resting it on his lap.

"Okay, listen," he said sternly. "You stood your ground against a werewolf and then you stole my gun and threatened him. You could've run, or stayed put, but you chose to fight. So, I'm going to tell you a story, then I'll give you two options."

The old man straightened his back and cleared his throat. "I'm a Hunter. I track down the supernatural and keep them in check, making sure they don't reveal themselves to the rest of the world. Everything you're thinking is real. Heaven, Hell, God, Satan, vampires, werewolves, demons, ghosts, you name it. All real. I'm allowing you to join us because of what I saw tonight. Most people I meet who get caught up in messes like what you saw back then, I usually just kill. It's the easiest option, but one I'd rather not use. I got a good feeling about you. So, I spared you. Now, as I said, you've got two options. One; you can join me and become a Hunter. Or two; you can die."

The old man picked up the gun and held it to Kyle's head.

"We can't let the secret of the supernatural get out. So, what will it be?"

Kyle kept a calm demeanor and took in a deep breath.

"I—I have to choose now?" he asked, nervously.

"Yes," the old man replied. "This is the only option I can give you."

Kyle kept silent for a few seconds. He looked down the barrel of the gun, then back to the old man.

"What happens if I say yes?" he finally asked.

"Then we get to move forward and get to work," the old man replied. "There's a small place nearby that I can take you to. There, we can give you a full rundown and get you fully informed and trained. Judging by that box of things of you're carrying, you were probably fired, am I right?"

Kyle nodded.

"That's good," the old man said. "It means you can leave without having to explain why you're quitting. Now, how about your family?"

Kyle let out an exacerbated sigh and fidgeted with his necktie, pulling it loose so he could breathe. "Um, could you—could you maybe lower the gun, please?" he asked.

The old man complied. "Now, family?"

"I don't have any siblings, and my parents are still alive. They live in Maine, so I only see them around holidays." He hesitated. "What does, uh, what *does* happen at the place you wanna take me?"

The old man rubbed his eyes and lightly groaned. "Look, I don't have all day. Yes, or no?"

Kyle closed his eyes. He took a few deep breaths.

"I guess ..." he said. "I guess it does sound like it might be interesting to see what happens."

The old man finally lowered the gun and smiled. He held out his hand.

"My name's Ivan. Ivan Winters."

Kyle reached out to shake Ivan's hand. "I'm Kyle McManus."

"Good," Ivan said, putting his gun away and starting the car. "I'll take you home."

Chapter 3

It had been an hour since Kyle first met Ivan in the back alleyway. After a lengthy and awkward drive back to Kyle's apartment, he'd been sitting at his kitchen counter going over the events in his head. Not long earlier, Ivan had walked him up the stairs and to the door of his apartment, which was on the second floor – first door on the left.

"I gotta make sure that no one finds those bodies in the alley. I texted someone to help me clean up. So, I'm heading back to make sure everything's going okay. Just say here and don't let anyone in unless it's me," Ivan had said as he promptly shut the door behind him.

Kyle was stuck inside his own house. He thought about what was going to happen from here. He would occasionally get up and pace around the kitchen, then immediately sit back down. Ivan made it sound like police work, going around to 'protect humanity'. To *protect*. Protect what? What was there to protect? Maybe he was dreaming.

Kyle got up and paced his kitchen again. He only had a small kitchen space, so his pacing was about two steps in either direction. But it made him feel less anxious if he could walk around and think. His mind was conflicted. It was either join or die, which essentially made joining his only choice.

Maybe it would be fun. And he didn't exactly have much to stay for. Leaving could be a good chance for a fresh start. Maybe see a vampire or something.

He decided to leave the kitchen and head to his bedroom. It was down the hallway, on his left. He opened the door and turned on the light.

His room was simple. A single bed tucked in the back corner with a bland blue sheet on top. A dresser standing next to it with a lamp, and a wardrobe to the right of the door. A small trunk sat at the edge of the bed, and gray carpet lined the floor. Kyle sat on his bed and pulled his phone out of his pocket. He opened his contacts and called his mother.

"Hey, Mom," Kyle said.

"*Kyle, honey. How are you?*" his mother replied.

"Good. Look, um, I got fired today." Kyle started to rub his neck as he told her.

"*Oh no! Are you okay?*" she asked him, sounding concerned.

"Yeah, Mom, I'll be fine. I think I just need some time to think things over. I'm gonna be taking a few months off. I might go traveling or something. I'll probably be silent for a few months." He had stood up by now and opened his trunk, looking through it.

"*Do you want to move back in with us?*" his mother asked. "*We still have a spare bedroom you can use. And your father could find you some work.*"

"No, no, Mom. It's fine," Kyle said, pulling a few items from his trunk and laying them on the bed. "I just need some time to think things over. Maybe find a job I like. I'll call you in a few weeks, okay?"

His mother sighed. "*Okay, Kyle. I love you.*"

Kyle chuckled. "I love you too, Mom." He hung up and put his phone back in his pocket.

What he'd taken out of his trunk was an old gray backpack, which had been buried underneath clothes he hadn't worn in years.

He started to pack the bag with essentials. A few sets of clothes, a few books, and his laptop and charger. He then left his bedroom to return to the kitchen, placing his bag on the ground. His box of work belongings was there, which he emptied onto the counter. None of the items were of real value to him, so he simply left them there, and kept the empty box.

Kyle decided to leave his landlord a note, along with a check for the monthly rent. He pulled out a piece of blank paper and a pen from his office box and began to write.

Mr. Davies,

I've decided to travel the world for a while in a bid to rediscover myself. Sorry for the short notice, but it was a last-minute decision. I've left a check for my last month of rent. You can keep or sell anything that's left in my apartment since I won't be needing it any more.

Kyle McManus.

Kyle finished the note and placed it, along with the check and his apartment key, in an envelope, and sealed it. He pondered for a few seconds before returning to his bedroom to pack a few more sets of clothes, as well as a keepsake – a picture of his family taken a few years before, at his high school graduation – in the box. After packing everything up, he turned off the bedroom light and returned to the kitchen.

Kyle placed the box on the floor beside him, along with his bag. Then, he just sat there. Waiting for Ivan to return. Staring at the wall in front of him.

"What am I doing?" Kyle said to himself. "I can't go through with this, can I?"

He looked down at his bag and the box. That box was all he would leave behind if he was to go with Ivan. In truth, Kyle *wanted* to join the Hunters – his life sucked. He had no real passion for anything and landed a desk job to support himself while he figured out what he actually wanted to do. When he was younger, he'd wanted to be a professional baseball player but gave up on it after failing multiple tryouts and facing multiple setbacks.

Kyle tried to remain optimistic. He wanted to see what other monsters were out there. *If there are werewolves then there are definitely vampires*, he thought to himself. *Is Dracula real? He must be, right? What about Satan, and God? Could I actually meet them? How many monsters can there be?*

His heart began to beat faster. In his overthinking, he'd started to panic. He shot up and started to pace once more, frantically, around his house. He went to the bathroom and stared into the mirror for a few seconds, blinking hard and wondering if this was a bad dream. His breaths grew frantic. He went to the kitchen and grabbed a glass, shakily pouring himself a glass of water and downing it instantly. His mouth was still dry.

Can I do this? he asked himself.

Kyle ran his fingers through his hair and rubbed the back of his neck. *I can't do this! What the hell was I thinking?*

He carried his box back into the bedroom and pulled everything out, throwing its contents onto the bed, before sitting on the floor and taking a few deep breaths.

Kyle looked around his room. All the photos, the furniture, his wardrobe. He realized that none of it actually *mattered* to him. The clothing he never wore was still in the wardrobe. The pictures he framed were ones he bought to make the space feel more homely. The furniture he bought came from a thrift store. It was all just ... there. It didn't feel like he was choosing what was important to him anymore, but what he wanted to keep.

Kyle closed his eyes and regained control of the situation. "I can do this," he spoke.

As he repacked his box, there was a sudden, loud knocking at the front door. Kyle got up and went over to look through the peephole. Ivan was on the other side. Kyle opened the door to let him in.

"Ready?" Ivan said hurriedly.

"Hello to you too," Kyle responded sarcastically. "Yes, I am. Are we in a rush?"

"We are. I think I was followed here by the pack of that werewolf we killed." Ivan picked up the box Kyle had packed. "Is this all you packed? We should hurry."

Looking back at his apartment one last time, Kyle picked up his backpack, his box, turned off the lights, and shut the door.

He followed Ivan down the stairs.

"We have to go now if we want them to lose our trail," Ivan said, concerned. "Assuming they followed us here, of course."

"How many of them are there?" Kyle asked.

"Damien's pack? About thirty. A few of them spotted me as we were leaving the alleyway."

"Can you be sure his pack followed you?" Kyle asked.

"We just killed the alpha of a werewolf pack. So yeah, I'm pretty sure they're trying to kill us." The pair had reached the bottom floor and headed to Ivan's car. Kyle walked close at Ivan's heels.

"Wait," he said to Ivan. "If they're trying to find us, would it matter if they come after us now? Shouldn't they have noses like, well, wolves?"

"Werewolves have lives too, you know," Ivan said. "They could be IT specialists, or schoolteachers. I even heard one of the presidents was a werewolf. They can be anyone, anywhere, and you'd never know. You'll learn all of this when you get to the Farm. Now hurry up and let's get out of here. Better to leave before the scent gets picked up."

Kyle was ready to leave and start his new life. He put the letter to his landlord in his mailbox and placed his belongings – his backpack and his box – in Ivan's backseat.

"Ready?" Ivan asked.

"Yeah, we're all good here," Kyle replied.

Ivan then went to the back of the car and popped the trunk.

"I'm gonna have to ask you to get in the trunk. For security reasons, I can't let you know where we're going. Just for now."

Kyle looked perplexed. "It's a farm. How secure do you need it to be?"

"Sorry, not my rules," Ivan said. "Just wait until you meet the owner."

"How far are we going?" Kyle asked him.

"Can't say."

"Of course you can't," Kyle said, sighing. "Let's get this over with."

Kyle was about to get into the trunk when a group of women walked up to them.

"Hey, guys. Lovely night, isn't it?" one of the women said. She was casually strolling up to Kyle and Ivan with her hands in her pockets.

"Um, do you ladies need something?" Kyle asked.

"Well, I'm glad you asked," another one of the women replied as she ran her hand over the hood of the car. "You see, you two look a lot like the guys who killed our dear friend Damien." She narrowed her eyes while staring down Kyle.

"I think you have us mixed up with someone other people," Ivan said. "C'mon Kyle, let's go." Ivan walked up to Kyle and slowly closed the trunk.

"They're werewolves," he whispered. "I have an extra gun in the glovebox – try and get it out without them noticing."

Kyle nodded. He and Ivan walked to the front of the car.

"I'm sorry for your loss, but we honestly don't know what you're talking about," Ivan said nonchalantly as he opened the driver's side door to get in.

"I hope you catch the guy who did it," Kyle said, opening the passenger door and getting into the car. He immediately opened the glovebox and saw the gun Ivan said was there. A revolver, with a box of bullets beside it, as well as a first aid kit. He slid the gun into his lap.

Ivan started the car, but the gang of women walked up to the car, opened their doors, and threw them both out.

"Don't bullshit us," one of the women said, her foot planted firmly on Ivan's chest. "We know it was you two. We also know you're planning on taking *this* one to your hideout."

The woman's eyes started to glow a pale blue, lighter than Damien's. Her nails elongated to sharp talons and her teeth became razor-sharp. The second woman, who had thrown Kyle out, pulled him off the ground and held him in the air with one hand. Her skin slowly sprouted hair as she grew larger. She was starting to transform.

"You see," the first woman growled, "Damien was our alpha. He led us. Gave us purpose. Helped us out when no one else would. And you killed him like he was a mutt."

"Yeah, but he was gonna kill us," Kyle said. "So, technically, it was self-defense."

"Shut the fuck up!" screamed the woman who was holding him. "You had no right to kill him!"

"Oh Jesus," said Ivan. "We get it. We shouldn't have killed him. Now just fuck off. I'd rather not kill any more werewolves today."

Ivan pulled out a small gun he had strapped to his ankle. Kyle pulled out the revolver from the glovebox, and they pointed their guns towards the werewolves. Neither woman backed down. One of them lunged at Ivan, who he immediately shot in the leg. This sent the other woman into a frenzy, focusing on Ivan. She slammed Kyle into the ground and made a beeline for Ivan.

He might have looked like a frail old man but moved with the fluidity of a twenty-year-old. He was able to keep up with these werewolves despite their increased strength, speed, and stamina. He was as deadly in close quarters as he was from a distance. Ducking and dodging the swipes the werewolves were throwing, shooting any who got too close to him. He slid under a pair of legs and shot the first woman in the head from behind.

While Ivan fended off the first two women, three more lunged from the shadows. These three were already fully transformed and coming at Kyle fast. Ivan killed the last of the two he was fighting and moved so he was in between Kyle and the incoming werewolves. He aimed his gun and fired, killing two instantly with shots to the head. The third one received a shot to the chest, and kept advancing.

Kyle had been standing still the whole time, trying to take in the whole situation.

"C'mon!" Ivan shouted. "Last one's yours!"

Kyle snapped out of it just in time to dodge a swipe that would've sliced his gut open. The werewolf swiped a second time, and it went across his right bicep. Kyle grabbed it in pain.

"Shit!" he exclaimed. He dropped his gun on the ground. The werewolf grabbed him and readied her claws.

"Hmm," she snarled. "Looks like the old man made a mistake picking you. Weakling."

Then, Ivan put his gun in her temple and shot her through the head.

The werewolf's body dropped to the ground with a *thud*. Kyle was able to keep his footing, still grabbing his damaged arm.

"You're not very good under pressure, are you?" Ivan said. Kyle was still slightly shocked and stood there, staring blankly at Ivan. "Ah well, it doesn't matter now. We need to leave before anyone else arrives."

"Aren't you worried about the bodies? And the other two? And my arm? Can't the police trace the bullets or something?" Kyle asked in a panic.

"I used silver bullets. Can't be traced. We make them ourselves. You'll learn all about this when you start training. Now, hold still." Ivan picked the gun off the ground and put it back in his glovebox. He then took out the first aid kit next to it and examined Kyle's wound.

"Hmm. It's not that deep. You shouldn't need any stitches." Ivan bandaged Kyle's arm up. "It should be fine, but I'll get it better looked at later. Now get in the trunk."

Kyle let out an exasperated sigh and complied. Ivan smiled.

"It'll be fine. Just go with it for now," he said. "I promise I'll make it comfortable."

Ivan then shut the lid, started the car, and drove off.

Chapter 4

Kyle felt like vomiting. He didn't even know how long he'd been in the trunk. Maybe a few hours. His arm was still throbbing from the tightness of the bandage. All he could do is think over the events of the night. His entire life had changed in only two hours, and he didn't even get to change out of his work clothes.

Luckily, there weren't a lot of bumps, so it was bearable. He felt the car go off-road, possibly onto a gravel path, judging from all the rumbling. And it was slowing down. Then, he heard the engine turn off and Ivan opening the driver's side door to get out. The journey was finally over.

Ivan opened the trunk and the fresh air hit Kyle like a cold wind.

"Oh good, you're still awake," Ivan said as he helped Kyle out of the trunk. "Enjoy the ride?"

Kyle looked around, but it was pitch black. "Where are we?" he asked, hoping his eyes would adjust quickly. All he could make out was the path the car had driven down.

"This is the Farm. It's where you'll be training for the next month. Not too far from Aurora." Ivan patted Kyle on his shoulder. "C'mon. I'll take you inside."

Kyle's eyes were now slowly adjusting to the darkness. It looked like he was surrounded by woods. Two buildings were sitting at the edge of the woods in front of him. Ivan took him to the one on the right. Ivan walked Kyle to what looked like a bunkhouse. It had a single light hanging above to door, which was turned off.

"We made it without any problems after the rest of Damien's pack attacked us. As far as I know, anyway. Now you need to get some rest. You have a big day tomorrow. There are a few others who are already here, but they're probably asleep by now. Just find a spare bed and sleep." Ivan opened the door.

There were others in here, and as Ivan said, they all seemed to be sleeping. Ivan pointed to an empty bed by the door and Kyle sat down. Ivan slowly closed the door behind him.

Kyle kept pondering what tomorrow would bring. His entire world had been changed. And he knew that there was more to come.

The next morning, Kyle was awoken by a loud banging on the door.

"Get up, everyone!" Ivan yelled, waking up the room. "You've got five minutes before I'm back!"

The Bunkhouse itself was very open. Army-style beds on the left, with a small kitchen in the back right corner, and a small green couch with a matching armchair on the left. There was a large bookcase next to the couch, and a small desk next to that.

Kyle was finally able to see who else was there. There were roughly sixteen people inside the Bunkhouse with him. He counted ten men, including himself, and six women. All were wearing what they were presumably wearing when they were brought here and had their lives disrupted. A good eight people were huddled in a group near the kitchen speaking Spanish, seemingly arguing.

Kyle stretched and got up. He had not had a good night's rest. He thought about getting himself a coffee from the kitchen when the door swung open. Standing there was Ivan and someone else – a tall and dark-skinned man. He was bald, and sported a trimmed beard. He wore an old-fashioned suit: the coat was jet black with an open collar, along with black pants with black dress shoes. He looked like a socialite who came straight from the early 1900s.

His eyes were menacing. Darting around at everyone, examining them carefully.

"Follow me," he said gruffly.

The group was led out of the Bunkhouse and into the open. The Farm looked very bland in the daylight. There was one large, old-fashioned farmhouse to the right of the Bunkhouse, a small dining area to the left of the Bunkhouse, which included a grill and two large tables, and a barn far over to the right. The rest of the space comprised a vast open field enclosed by woods, almost in a perfect circle. In the middle of the field was Ivan. He stood still, watching as the group approached. Once they arrived, the bald man stopped in his tracks. He spun around and cleared his throat to speak.

"My name is Aaron Smith. I'll be helping you with your training. Now, first thing's first, I've been made aware that most of you were brought here hastily and weren't given much of a choice in the matter. You have had two days to think it over. Now, I would like to ask if there is anyone who doesn't want to be here? You've been told what's going on and what you'll be doing. So, we need to make sure everyone here is willing to do what needs to be done. Is anyone regretting their decision?"

The group was dead silent. Far in the back, one man raised his hand slowly.

"Let me through," Aaron said as he made his way past everyone and stood in front of him.

The man was short and had rough, tanned skin. He wore a gray hoodie with matching sweatpants and a trucker cap.

"Are you sure? You don't want to be here?"

"U-um, y-yes," the man stuttered.

Aaron looked him up and down. "I hope you have been told your options before, but I'll repeat them anyway. One, you can join us and become a Hunter. Or two, you can die. So, I'll ask you one more time." Aaron got closer to his face. "Are. You. Sure?" Aaron's eyes locked onto him. His glare was menacing.

The man was sweating bullets. But his mind was made up.

"Let's say we let you go," Aaron said sternly. "Let's say you were able to get to the closest town and you, for instance, decide to tell someone. *There's a small farm hidden in the woods. They're training people to kill werewolves and vampires.* I doubt anyone would believe you, but what if the person you tell is a supernatural? Then, they would know where we are and kill everyone here. Even if they weren't, you would be considered just another conspiracy theorist like the people who think the earth is flat or claim they were abducted by aliens. No one would believe a word you say, so shut the fuck up."

"I can keep it a secret. Really. I won't tell anyone. They wouldn't believe me anyway – like you said! I just wanted a way into the country," the man said, unable to stop himself from stumbling over his words. He looked like he was about to fall to his knees and beg.

Aaron pondered for a few seconds.

"You're lucky that I am lenient. I'll have Ivan take you into the closest town."

"Are you serious, Aaron?" Ivan exclaimed. "What if he talks!"

"It's not the first time I've let someone leave; nothing's happened."

Ivan grumbled and walked forward to approach the man.

"Okay. Let's go, buddy," he said, forcibly grabbing him by his arm and yanking him away from the group and into the woods.

"Would anyone else like to leave?" Aaron asked.

A few of the others looked around, but no one raised a hand or spoke up.

"Very well, let's start our training. In addition to basic weapons training, you'll be getting an education on everything we're fighting and protecting. You need to know the strengths and weaknesses of supernaturals if you want any chance of surviving. Some things you may already know from folklore or films; others may be different from what you thought you knew. Here, you will be given a fast-tracked training experience, something most recruits rarely get. That doesn't mean we will kill you, but you will feel like it. You will spend the next four weeks training to be Hunters."

Kyle raised his hand.

"What do you mean most recruits don't get this experience?"

"Not every person who becomes a Hunter winds up here. This is just a small facility we use as a safe house. I've known a few Hunters who discovered the supernatural when they were teens and trained in secret in their hometowns. All of *you* were brought here for one reason or another, which is good. It's far easier to teach you how to shoot a gun when there's no one around to hear the shooting."

Aaron continued a long lecture on the importance of secrecy and discrepancy; long enough that Ivan eventually returned. Aaron instructed him to open the doors to the Bunker. There were two metal doors in the ground right behind where Aaron was standing. Ivan opened them up.

"Follow me," Ivan said as everyone slowly descended the stairs.

○

It was an underground bunker. Quite spacious, but only as big as a small house. Each wall was covered top to bottom with supplies. The wall to the left was weapons, at the back wall was equipment, and to the right was canned food. It looked like a doomsday prepper's fantasy. The ceiling was draped with strip lights that made the room brighter than the outside.

Inside this room, at the very back, was a pale man with three large scars running across his face. He was dressed in a tight red shirt that showed off his muscles and surprisingly hairy forearms. He had a large black beard and long hair tied back in a tight knot. His eyes were as green as the woods outside. Aaron stopped the group in front of this man, who was sitting at a desk, putting together a gun.

"This is Marcus," Aaron said. "He manages the firing range and will be teaching you all about gun safety. We'll be meeting everyone before we start getting into actual training."

"It's nice to meet you all," Marcus said. His voice was very soft, despite his appearance.

Kyle spoke up.

"How did you get those scars?"

Marcus laughed. "I'll give you a hint." As he said this, his eyes glowed a pale blue – the same as a werewolf.

There was a still silence and one or two gasps from the recruits.

"He's a *werewolf*?" exclaimed a woman in the back.

"Calm down, he's not going to hurt you. There are some good werewolves," Aaron explained. "Some of them were Hunters before they turned, and some were born werewolves but decided to join up. Marcus was turned about fifteen years ago, sometime after he'd joined. It's things like this you will be educated about during your time here. Now, follow me."

Aaron walked past the group and back towards the entrance. There were two doors: one on either side of the room. The group was taken through the door to the left. Ivan opened it up and let everyone peer inside.

It was a medical bay. The room was a sterile white. It only had two beds, both placed on the right side. The left side was lined by a metal counter, beside which was a man wearing a lab coat, looking over papers. He was tall with long blond hair and clean-shaven. He looked up at the group.

"Oh, you're here already, Ivan," he said with an uncomfortably bright smile.

"This is Nick," said Aaron. "He's one of our resident doctors. We have two that take turns living here."

"Hopefully, I won't have to see you all in here. Please, leave me be for now. I have some work to go over," Nick said. It was an incredibly quick exchange, as they promptly walked back out of the room. Aaron and Ivan led the group to the opposite side of the room.

"How big is this bunker?" Kyle asked.

"Four rooms in total, including this one," Ivan replied.

The second room they were led into was set up with chairs in neat rows like a classroom. They all sat down, and Aaron took to the front.

"Now, anyone care to name every supernatural creature off the top of their head?" Aaron said, looking around the room. No one talked. Everyone looked around at each other, hoping someone else would answer.

"Anyone?"

One man in the back raised his hand, very timidly.

"Isn't it just vampires, werewolves, demons, monsters, and ghosts?"

Aaron gave a dry smile like he wanted someone to give this answer.

"Technically, yes. There are only five types of supernatural creatures. But there are also sub-types. Whilst vampires, demons, and ghosts are fairly standard, monsters and werebeasts aren't. Werewolves are not the only werebeast. Think of any land animal, and it probably has a were form. If you get bitten by a werewolf then you will either turn into a werewolf, a different werebeast, or die. There are two types of werebeasts: alphas and betas. The only difference between them is that an alpha will have darker eyes and a slightly larger form, and are stronger by far.

"If you get bitten by a beta werewolf, the chances of you turning are roughly fifty percent. If you don't die within the hour, you're a werewolf or another werebeast. If you get bitten by an alpha werewolf, you will turn one hundred percent – no death or turning into another werebeast. If, when a beta bites you, you turn into a *different* werebeast, you will be an alpha. You bite people, they become betas. If a beta werebeast bites someone, the same thing happens as when a beta werewolf bites someone and the cycle continues.

"Being a werebeast isn't exactly all fun. They have to deal with a constant bloodlust and will one day lose their mind and humanity, turning into their beast form one last time and unable to change back. Becoming a werebeast is a curse. The more violent a person is, the worse they are when they're a werebeast."

"Whereas with vampires," Ivan interjected, moving up to the front of the room, "you get turned one hundred percent of the time no matter if it's a thrall or a master vampire. Ghosts and demons are the simplest creatures to kill. Ghosts usually linger because they refuse to move on. Usually, they're in disbelief about being dead. Getting a ghost to move on can be fairly simple, unless they've gone feral and turned into a wraith. Then it gets hard. Demons are just as fragile as people, so killing them is very easy. Monsters are the hardest to kill, as they're so varied."

A woman in the front row raised her hand. "What happens when we die? Are Heaven and Hell truly real?"

"Yes, they're real," Aaron replied. "Unless you become a ghost. Then you're stuck here. We don't know much about Heaven or Hell, but what we can gather is that they're not exactly like how they're depicted in the Bible. The Bible isn't that reliable, honestly – God and Satan are real but that's pretty much it. Jesus isn't, surprisingly.

But you won't have to worry that much about them. God is more of an impartial observer and Satan is mostly harmless. Just don't ever make a deal with him."

The room went quiet. The woman who'd asked the question got out of her chair and went to the door; she was hyperventilating.

"I can't do this," she said frantically, tears streaking down her face and dripping to the ground.

"Marcus!" Aaron called out.

"Got it!" he shouted back. Everyone could hear her start to scream, which was quickly muffled as Ivan took her out of the Bunker. Aaron sighed.

"This isn't new. Most people have trouble handling all this new information all at once. We'll calm her down and talk to her privately."

A large man in the front raised his hand.

"Where's our stuff? You told us to take what we needed, and we haven't seen it since."

"Simple," Aaron replied. "You will receive your phones again once you've finished training. It's a distraction. We don't have much power here so there's no way to really charge your phones. Can't even get a signal, so even if you had them, there would be no point. It's better to be focused on this."

Aaron cleared his throat.

"Now, there's one more thing you should know and that's that we make most of our bullets here. Silver is a universal weakness for most supernatural beings, which is what we use. Of course, regular bullets can also work, it's just that silver is more effective. And untraceable.

Using them is better than regular rounds, but silver is expensive to get, so don't waste them."

The rest of Aaron's talk was very quiet. Kyle maintained his composure, taking in everything he could. He glanced at the man sitting to his left, who looked like he was about to pass out. He was covered in perspiration and his hair was either greasy or just wet from all the sweating he was doing.

Aaron finished up by talking about demons. He had given everyone in the room a basic rundown of what they could expect in any given geographical area, and not just for American states. The supernatural was all over the world, though the majority were in America and Eastern Europe.

"Okay, I think my introductory speech is done." Aaron promptly walked past everyone and left the room without another word.

No one was really able to focus as they were led back out by Ivan. The woman who ran out earlier was sitting next to Marcus as he tinkered away at his desk, putting together a gun.

"The shooting range is behind Marcus; he'll be teaching you how to handle weapons," said Ivan. "But for today, I'll be teaching you. Let's go outside."

Aaron stayed inside the Bunker to talk to Marcus. Once everyone was outside, Ivan pointed to the Bunkhouse.

"As some of you already know, that is where you'll be staying until you're finished training here. It's nothing fancy. There are only two bathrooms. One is in the Big House and the other is just behind the Bunkhouse."

He gathered everyone around him in the middle of the field. "I'll be teaching you all some basic hand-to-hand combat. Right here."

Chapter 5

Everyone spaced themselves out and listened to Ivan.

"You can't always rely on firearms. Especially if you're in close quarters or trying to sneak. You all need to have some kind of fighting knowledge. Which is why I'll be teaching you every morning when you get up and every afternoon before you eat dinner."

There was a slight laugh from the back of the group.

"You. Come here." Ivan pointed to whoever had laughed and beckoned him over with his finger. The snickering recruit was well over six feet tall and bulky, like a bodybuilder. He had neatly combed black hair with gray on the sides and a chiseled jaw covered with a strong beard. He walked up to Ivan.

"Name?" Ivan asked.

"It's Travis," he replied.

"You think I'm too old to teach you how to fight? Is that your problem?" Ivan asked.

Travis looked Ivan up and down and laughed again. "You look over a hundred. No offense, but yes."

Ivan smirked in response. Kyle knew what was going to happen next.

"Hit me as hard as you can," Ivan said, spreading his arms as wide as he could.

Travis quickly threw a punch, but Ivan sidestepped. He kicked Travis in the gut, who immediately groaned in pain and fell to his knees. Then, Ivan planted his foot square on Travis' chest.

"Rule one; don't underestimate your opponent," Ivan said, grinning as he pushed Travis to the ground with his foot.

There were a few snickers from the group, including Kyle, who held his mouth so he wouldn't laugh out loud.

Ivan picked up Travis and made him stand back with the others.

"Yes, I'm old. But that doesn't mean I can't fight. I have more experience than anyone here, which is why I'm teaching you. Today, I'm going to teach you the basics; learning how to punch and block. Pick someone to be your partner and let's get to it."

Kyle knew no one. Everyone had kept to themselves mostly. So, most people just picked the person next to them. Kyle looked to his left – the man standing next to him was the same man he had been sitting next to in Aaron's talk. He had short choppy black hair, a thin and patchy beard, bronzed skin, and was short in stature. He only came up to Kyle's chest. Kyle took the initiative and put out his hand. The man shook it, but his shake was limp, and his hand was clammy.

"I'm Kyle."

"Carlos," the man said softly.

Kyle and Carlos took their positions and faced each other, watching as Ivan instructed the class on defensive techniques. The first part was simple. Everyone was to take turns punching their partner's hands and then practice dodging each other.

Kyle seemed to have a better handle on it than Carlos. Carlos' hands were shaking slightly, and his hits were too soft. He had to dodge down – getting out of the was seemed to be his specialty. Kyle kept on telling him everything was okay, nobody expected to be good on the first try, but Carlos looked like he was about to cry. He seemed a lot younger than everyone else there.

"How old are you, Carlos?" Kyle asked.

"Eighteen," he said sadly.

"What are you doing here?"

"W-Well, I kinda joined a gang. Then left because I realized my mistake, and now they want me dead."

Kyle was astounded. "You joined a gang at eighteen?"

"Sixteen, actually."

"Six—Sixteen. And they never taught you to throw a punch?"

A smile tugged at Carlos' lip. "I didn't say it was a *good* gang."

"Well, it looks like you found a far better one. Now, hit my hands."

Kyle and Carlos continued with their drill, and Kyle got a glimpse of Travis out of the corner of his eye.

Travis had the body of a brawler and the ego of someone who was unstoppable. His partner's hands were completely red from his hits; he wasn't holding back. Ivan continued the lesson with simple stances and defensive tactics.

"Question," Travis raised his hand. "When do we get to learn more offensive moves? Like the one you did on me?"

"In due time," Ivan replied. "You will most likely be using defense more often, so we focus on that first. If you're in a one-on-one with a werebeast or a vampire and you have no weapons, defense tactics could save you. Whereas offense will probably get you killed sooner."

The lesson moved differently. Ivan had everyone working out; push-ups, sit-ups, jogging on the spot. It all seemed superfluous to Kyle.

This continued for a little while longer until someone walked out of the Big House and came towards the group.

This person was covered up from head to toe. Kyle couldn't see their face at all – it was covered by a ski mask. They wore what looked like ski gear to conceal their identity. They were well over six feet tall, as they easily reached the top of the doorframe. The parka they wore was white with black accents and a fur hood. They had thick black leather gloves over their hands. They wore black cargo pants with a pistol holstered to their right leg, as well as large black boots.

This mysterious person stood next to Ivan and tapped him on the shoulder. His size made Ivan look minuscule.

"Ivan. We're ready." Their voice was English and deep. It was muffled through the mask.

"Thank you, Neptune. Now you can stop everyone. He's ready for you."

Neptune then walked past the group and into the woods behind them.

"Who was that?" Kyle asked.

"Neptune. He's from England. I don't know why he keeps his face hidden so don't bother asking. And I don't know his real name. He's probably paranoid. But that's not important right now. Follow me."

Ivan took everyone into the woods opposite the Big House. The group walked a fair way in until no one could tell where they were. He stopped them somewhere in the middle, where there was a small clearing between the trees.

The woods were far denser the further in they went, and the thick tree line made it hard to see through to the field. The place where Ivan had stopped the group had a small wooden chair sitting up against a tree.

"Neptune will be teaching you stealth. It's important not just for sneaking up and staying undetected, but also for learning how to blend in."

"Where is he?" someone at the front said.

"I've been here the whole time."

Neptune was standing behind the group – how he'd maneuvered himself behind them without being noticed was anyone's guess. Then again, that was the point. Ivan went to sit down on the chair and pulled a book out from his jacket. Everyone turned their attention to Neptune.

"Today," he said, "I'm teaching you simple hiding and sneaking by using your environment.

"Firstly, you all need to learn how to walk softly. I was able to walk behind everyone without making a sound in the woods, and I'm in bloody boots. What I want you all to do is to try and walk in a straight line without making a sound."

Everyone stood still, looking bewildered. No one moved for a few seconds.

"We can do this at night if you prefer," Neptune teased. "It'll be a lot easier to not be seen then."

Kyle and a few of the others began to slowly walk forward. Kyle could hear the crunching of dead leaves and the snap of twigs under his shoe.

Neptune began to separate some of the more hesitant recruits from the group and spread them out, making sure everyone was doing their task. He would periodically pace around, leering over and pointing out flaws in their steps. He grabbed Kyle's foot before he could plant it and slowly placed it on the forest floor himself, without making any noise. "That's what you need to practice. Take your time. Lean forward when you step. It helps," he said, picking himself back up and moving on to another recruit.

Kyle was able to make it roughly five or six feet before he made a sound, as concentrating on moving slowly made him fall off balance. Carlos seemed to be better than most; he was able to walk more than ten feet before he would make a sound.

Neptune then stood in front of the group and called them to gather around him.

"Alrighty, you all have something basic to remember. Walk slowly and tread lightly. For now, I'd like you to try and sneak up on me. I'll be standing at that big tree behind you and, one by one, I want each of you to try and tag me. If I hear you, then you go back and do it again. And we won't be moving on until you *all* tag me."

Neptune made his way through the group and stood perfectly still in front of the tree. A few of the recruits whispered to each other. Kyle couldn't hear the words, but he guessed they were arguing over who would go first.

Kyle decided to go ahead and try his luck. He softly placed his foot on the ground, then started to walk almost heel to toe. Making sure to lean forward to reduce his sound. He was close, a few feet. If he got any closer, he could reach out and touch Neptune. But before he could touch him, Neptune said, "Back."

Kyle stopped in place.

"I said, back," Neptune repeated, turning around and shooing Kyle away.

"I wasn't making any sound," Kyle said.

"Then why did I stop you?"

Kyle didn't bother to argue. He simply walked back and waited for someone else to try their luck.

Kyle watched as everyone was unable to tag Neptune. Travis surprisingly got as close as Kyle, and Carlos ended up tripping over himself and smacking into the back of him. Neptune said it didn't count as a tag even though he technically didn't hear Carlos coming. Kyle tried again, and again. Each time getting close but not tagging Neptune.

Kyle thought, *What am I doing wrong?* Was there anything different about where he was standing? He looked at the ground; it seemed to be the same as the rest of the woods. Leaves and twigs were strewn along like crushed kindling. Kyle took a few intentionally loud steps, seeing if he could find any spots that could be stepped on *without* making a sound. He decided to hang back and watch the others, searching for a pattern or a patch of ground that was louder than the rest. All Kyle could see was that everyone was heading in a straight line, even though there was a whole forest surrounding them. He could try and sneak up to Neptune from the side, or even catch him off guard when he was distracted by another person.

Kyle looked at his shoes – the same office shoes he'd had on since leaving his apartment with Ivan. They weren't even comfortable anymore. Kyle took them off and took a few steps forward. He made less sound without them, even when walking slowly. He decided to go around rather than in front, ducking down behind a small row of bushes and making his way forward from there. He could see Neptune, standing still as a statue. He started using his hands to crawl closer, looking back at his feet so that he didn't tread on any leaves. He felt ridiculous, like he was imitating a cat trying to catch a mouse, but it was working. He had gotten as close as he did before, but instead of being directly behind Neptune, he was crouched down, hugging the forest floor.

He looked at Neptune's feet to see if there was anything that would make a sound if he moved. It all looked the same. He couldn't tell what was stopping everyone from tagging Neptune. Kyle didn't want to hesitate any longer – he crept as slowly as he could and reached out to tag Neptune on his leg. He extended his finger and poked him in his calf.

Neptune turned and looked down.

"Shit. You weren't meant to figure it out that quick."

Ivan guffawed from behind everyone. "That's five hundred!"

"Yeah, alright Ivan. Later."

"What's that about?" Kyle asked.

"I had a bet with Ivan that no one could tag me in the first lesson." Neptune helped Kyle up and he returned to the group.

"I'm not actually going to make you all tag me. I'll move on in a second, but before I do, can anyone guess how I was able to stop you?"

Carlos raised his hand. "You can hear really well?"

Neptune tilted his head as if to say, *Really?*

"No. Anyone else?"

Kyle raised his hand. "Echolocation?"

"He wishes," Ivan muttered loudly.

"No."

No one else raised their hands. Neptune pointed to a tree behind him, which had a small mirror hanging on it.

"I could see you behind me."

"That's cheating!" Travis said.

"Is it? Did you learn how to sneak more silently with each attempt? I'd say it's a job well done."

Travis huffed and crossed his arms disapprovingly.

Neptune moved on and showed the group some other simple stealth tactics, like how to hide in plain sight among a group. As well as how to follow someone without looking suspicious.

"You see, if you just slowly walk behind them then they're bound to notice. The best method of following someone is to keep a straight line of sight. Even if they look back, you can just walk past them and wait further up," Neptune explained.

Neptune took people individually and showed them a few quick tricks on how to blend in with crowds and environments. It was startling for a few people due to his size. Kyle's neck hurt after looking up to Neptune one too many times.

Carlos was good at this. Since he was small, quiet, and shy, he was easily able to sneak into large groups without them realizing it. Kyle seemed to be better at hiding using his surroundings: he kept hidden behind a large bush for five full minutes before someone found him. But stealth wasn't suited for everyone. Travis, for example. Big and burly didn't match stealth at all. He stood taller than all the other recruits, and because of his large frame, he could only just hide behind a tree.

Once everyone had a basic grasp on stealth, Neptune called the group back around him.

"You have one last challenge for today's stealth class: find me. I'll be within the woods around you. I won't be using another cheap trick so once you find me you can tag me. Once someone tags me, I'll be moving on. When you've found me, stay where you are until time is up. I'm giving you thirty minutes to find me. If you fail, you'll be getting some extra lessons tonight. When time is up, Ivan will blow a whistle. Follow the sound to make your way back here and we'll take you back to the Bunkhouse. I've heard that your lunch has been prepared."

Everyone kind of stood still. Not sure what to do.

Neptune walked back into the dense woods and was almost immediately gone from Kyle's line of sight.

"Your time starts now!" Neptune's voice sounded distant, like he was already on the run.

Kyle and Carlos stuck together. It was more like Carlos latched onto Kyle like a child with abandonment issues, but Kyle was happy to have the company. Making friends wasn't easy for him, so making one in an organization that kills supernatural beings was a good thing.

After a few minutes of walking in silence, Kyle finally opened his mouth to ask Carlos something that had been bothering him all day.

"Hey Carlos, why'd you want to become a Hunter?" he asked.

"Well, it was kind of a spur of the moment thing. Like I said, I was in a gang. And I messed up, so I ran. Neptune was the one who found me. I was planning on crossing the border into the States with some of the others who are here when a gang of vampires disguised as Border Patrol swarmed us. They were grabbing people and throwing them into vans or killing them then and there, sucking their blood out. I panicked and ran as fast as I could when Neptune came out of nowhere and saved what was left of the group. Neptune said he could get everyone some fake documents so we would be legal citizens, so that's why most of these guys are here; a free green card. I joined because Neptune said he thought I could make something of myself. Become braver and stronger. That kind of thing. And it was an easy way into America." Carlos let out a nervous laugh and rubbed the back of his neck.

"You joined because you wanted a backbone?" Kyle asked, laughing aloud. Carlos seemed embarrassed.

"And for the fake documents," Carlos added defensively. "Why did you join?"

Kyle thought for a second.

"Huh. I don't really know. My life wasn't going anywhere. Outta high school, I didn't want to go to college, so I moved to Illinois from Maine – thought I'd find something interesting there, maybe some direction. I started as a barista, then I did some interning. I even thought about becoming an artist and took a few classes for a while. But then I decided to put trying to find my 'dream job' on hold and picked up a job in an office. As for joining, I like all this supernatural stuff. I guess it was a spur of the moment thing as well."

"Art? Can you still draw?"

"A bit, yeah. Mostly sketches. Nothing major. I just do it for fun."

"What about your job?"

"Got laid off?"

"What did you do?"

"Taxation invoicing."

Carlos gave him a quizzical look.

"I input clients' tax invoices into a system so the company could keep track of spending habits. Like filing away documents, but with computers," Kyle explained.

"Oh, sounds like fun."

"Yeah, eight hours of looking at the receipts of rich people buying stuff like jet skis and five-thousand-dollar TVs sure is fun."

Kyle and Carlos continued to converse. They found they had a fair amount in common in the process.

"What did you do before this? Did you have a job?" Kyle asked.

"I was working in a warehouse for the gang. A lot of shady shit was going down there, selling guns and drugs mostly, but I kinda kept my head down. I just wanted some extra cash so I could come here."

"Yeah? You get any days off at the warehouse?"

"Only weekends. I grew up in an orphanage and we would play baseball all the time. So, I would play with my friends from there. We went to this park every Saturday and played for a few hours."

Kyle's eyes lit up. "I *love* baseball! I played in tournaments until I was seventeen!" Kyle started to smile widely. "What was your position?" he asked Carlos.

"We, uh, didn't have positions. We only had five people, so we picked a random batting order every week and a person would bat until they were out. We all picked a random position, too, and switched those positions during the batting change." Carlos rubbed his neck again. "It's a little lame. But I had fun."

"That sounds fun." Kyle put his arm around Carlos. "What matters most is having fun. Who the fuck cares if you didn't play an actual game?"

Carlos smiled at Kyle. "Thanks, man. It's nice to know I have a friend here."

"What about your friends back home?"

Carlos started to look uneasy. "A few of them came with me. And they died or were taken while we were running across the border."

Kyle could see Carlos was visibly upset, as his face started to drop.

"How old are you again, Carlos?"

"Eighteen," he replied flatly.

Kyle laughed and slapped his back. "You look easily in your twenties! You look great. Maybe clean up that beard and get some fancy clothes."

Kyle was trying his best to distract Carlos and cheer him up. He brought the conversation back to baseball, which seemed to help. The pair had completely forgotten that they were meant to be finding Neptune while wandering through the woods, enjoying each other's company. Then, they bumped into a female recruit.

"You guys still haven't found him?"

Kyle and Carlos went wide-eyed.

"Oh shit!" Kyle exclaimed.

The woman laughed. "I just found him so he shouldn't be too far. He should be back that way."

She pointed behind her. It was pointless, as the woods all looked the same. But Kyle and Carlos ran as fast as they could, hoping they weren't too far behind him. They stopped in front of a tree with boot prints going upwards.

"Look! He's in the trees!"

"Or he could be faking it, so we waste our time," Kyle said bluntly.

"We can't stop and think. Help me up."

Kyle helped push Carlos as he climbed the tree to get a better vantage. He looked around but couldn't see him anywhere.

"Maybe he's still on the ground?" Kyle said.

"If you look on the ground I can help from up here." Carlos gave Kyle a thumbs up and started to traverse through the trees. Kyle kept up by running through the woods. They were now constantly moving, only stopping to scan the area for any clues. After five minutes, Carlos dejectedly came down from the trees. They both knew that they wouldn't be able to find him in time.

"We might as well give up, man. He's too good," Carlos said hopelessly.

"That's the point," said Kyle. "He probably rigged it so that we have to use what he taught us. He wants us to test our stealth and detection skills; the only problem is we've only had one lesson. If we can hide, we need to make sure we can't be found. I think that's what he's teaching us now."

Kyle and Carlos doubled their efforts to try and find Neptune. Kyle searched for anything resembling a boot print in the ground and Carlos searched from the trees to see if he could spot him from a distance, but the density of the woods made it hard. After a few more minutes of searching, a loud whistle went off. That meant the time to find Neptune was done. And they had failed.

Kyle helped Carlos out of the tree and they walked back, defeated, with their heads down. Neither said a single word as they made their way back.

Carlos, Kyle, and Travis were the only three who had failed. Kyle and Carlos had only failed because they'd gotten too submerged in their conversation and lost track of time. Travis' failure was anyone's guess; he was probably still pissed off by Ivan beating him up. Everyone else had left with Ivan to get some food. These three, however, were told to hang back.

"Well, since you weren't able to find me in time, your punishment is simple. You'll be working the Graveyard shift," Neptune said.

"And that is?" Travis asked.

"We have a Graveyard behind the Big House – you'll be cleaning the graves. Aaron offered his time to the Graveyard shift for anyone who failed today."

Needless to say, they weren't so happy about this punishment.

"Now, you three are stuck here until you can actually track someone and find them." Neptune pointed at Kyle and Carlos. "This time, I'm splitting you two up."

"You only failed because you were together," Travis laughed.

"And you," Neptune said, turning his attention to Travis. "You were downright horrible at this. If you fail again, you're getting extra lessons and special attention in addition to the Graveyard shift. Now, the same time limit applies as before. So, you best hurry, lest you wish to spend more time with that bloody bore Aaron."

Neptune walked back into the woods and was gone again. The three wandered into the woods in different directions. Kyle went to the right. He knew the stakes this time: the Graveyard shift. It sounded a lot spookier now that he knew ghosts were real.

Kyle tried to find Neptune before time was up. He decided to go up into the trees again. Neptune could be hiding up there. He went from tree to tree, trying to see if there was any evidence of Neptune's presence. He looked onto the ground to see if he could spot him, in what little visibility there was. He felt hopeless. It had been probably twenty minutes by now. Time was running out. He knew that Neptune was a master of stealth, and this wouldn't be easy, but then he remembered something Neptune taught them earlier: hiding in plain sight. Kyle hypothesized that Neptune was waiting at the center of the woods and just sitting back at the bench. He'd never left. Kyle dashed back to the grounds, but he'd forgotten which way they were. He tried to go in a straight line, hoping it would take him in the right direction, and then he heard the whistle blow. It was too late; he'd failed again.

Kyle made his way back, and there was Neptune. Travis was already there, and Carlos wasn't back yet.

"I never left numpty," Neptune said.

"Yeah, I figured that out too late," Kyle said sadly.

"Good thing *I* didn't," Travis said smugly.

"You found him?"

"Yeah, I thought about what he was teaching us — about hiding in plain sight. So, I came back here, and he was sitting in one of the overhead trees."

Carlos finally arrived back from the woods, bent over and panting heavily.

"Did you guys find him?" he asked.

"Travis did. I figured it out too late. We both failed."

"Correct," Neptune said. "Now go get some food and rest up for tonight. You two," he looked at Kyle and Carlos, "are taking the Graveyard shift."

"Have fun, you two," Travis said.

"The Graveyard shift starts at midnight," Neptune said as he led them out of the woods.

The rest of the day was split between training with Ivan and receiving a lecture from Marcus about werewolves. Kyle couldn't keep focused since he probably wouldn't be sleeping that night. Carlos seemed to be nervous himself for the rest of the day.

After eating some dinner and washing up, everyone else had been told to return for the Bunkhouse. Most of the group were talking amongst themselves or relaxing on the small couch in the corner. Kyle found a book about vampires and decided to distract himself by reading through it. It was intriguing to learn more about what vampires were really like. It turned out that garlic was just an old wives' tale, and it was more just the smell that affected them than it was anything deadly.

Kyle managed to get through five chapters before Ivan walked in and called for him and Carlos. It was ten o'clock, which meant that he and Carlos would have to wait two more hours.

"Why'd you call us out this early?" Kyle asked.

"It's lights out for everyone else. You two get to spend some time out here with me before Aaron collects you. So, we're doing combat training."

"You couldn't just wait another two hours?"

"No. Now let's get to work."

Ivan took them to the center of the field and had them run through the fighting techniques they had learned earlier that day. It was hard at first until Kyle's eyes adjusted, then he could see better. Ivan made them do running drills, push-ups, and sit-ups for over an hour. He would make them run laps of the field if they complained and put his foot hard on their backs when they didn't do a push-up correctly. By the time he finally told them to rest, they were both exhausted. Kyle's arms felt like they were on fire, and Carlos didn't fare that well either.

"Okay, good," Ivan said, looming over the pair, who had collapsed on the ground, panting and huffing. "That's all for the warmup. I'll get you some water and call Aaron over."

"That was the warmup?" Kyle said. "What about the Graveyard shift thing?"

"That's what I'm getting Aaron for. This is just to kill some time before midnight. And it's also an effective punishment – better than cleaning graves."

Ivan walked into the Big House, leaving Kyle and Carlos on the grass in the dead of night.

"Hey," Kyle said. "Do you think we'll run into any ghosts?"

"Don't start with that, man," Carlos said, picking himself back up. "I hated ghosts when I was a kid. I'll have a heart attack if I see anything poking out of those graves."

Ivan came back with two large water bottles and put them on the ground.

"I'll be back with Aaron. Just wait outside the Graveyard until then."

Kyle got up and went with Carlos to the Graveyard, almost finishing his water within a few steps. The Graveyard was located just to the left of the Big House, behind the tree line. It was only just visible, but there were a few headstones poking out of the woods that were easy to see.

They'd both been waiting outside the Graveyard in the darkness for a few minutes. It was starting to get darker and colder. Aaron then came out of the Big House with Ivan, who had some cleaning supplies with him, and walked up to the pair.

"Put these back when you're done," Ivan said, abruptly turning back and into the Big House.

"Alright you two, let's go."

Kyle and Carlos followed Aaron into the Graveyard with their cleaning supplies. It looked like a proper horror film set. The graves were old and cracked, some had moss creeping up them, and some had even fallen over. A thin fog covered the ground and the air felt chilly. The Graveyard extended past the tree line and into the woods. It seemed to go on forever in the darkness. How many people were buried here?

"Okay you two, you'll be cleaning out the first ten rows of graves tonight. Now get going," Aaron commanded, standing at the edge of the woods, almost like he was guarding their freedom.

They both complied. Carlos was visibly more nervous than Kyle, probably because he was scared of ghosts. Kyle tried not to think about it. He decided to distract himself by asking Aaron a question.

"Excuse me, Aaron. Can I ask you something about ghosts?"

Aaron sighed. "You might as well. It's better than just standing around waiting for you to finish."

"Is the whole 'unfinished business' thing real? Like, how do you become a ghost?"

"I'm not too sure. You could become a ghost by having unfinished business. But I'd imagine the business must be something of great importance, not just any old business. For instance, someone who wanted to watch a film before they died. They wouldn't come back just so they could watch it. But someone who wanted to hand a loved one a letter or go to a specific location could come back. If the business doesn't get resolved for an extended period of time, or if the business involves a person who then dies, the ghost becomes a wraith. Like the ones you see in films attacking people."

"How long until a ghost becomes a wraith?" Carlos asked.

"It varies from person to person. Usually, a few months after their business becomes impossible to fulfill or if they lose hope. If their business is, for instance, to tell someone they loved them, we could get involved and tell them on the ghost's behalf. But if *this* person were to die, then the ghost's feelings couldn't be told. That ghost would then become a wraith, driven to insanity."

"Can a person who wanted someone dead become a ghost until that person dies?" Kyle asked.

"No. If that were the case, then there would have been a lot of ghosts in wars."

"Can everyone see ghosts?" Carlos asked.

"Ghosts can choose whether to be seen or not. Most of them choose not to because they don't believe they're even dead. It takes a while for people to even discover they're ghosts. Dying seems to give ghosts temporary memory loss, from what I've seen. But you will come across some ghosts. Most seem to trust Hunters to help them. We've helped a lot over the years. Just tell them you're one and they'll appear. Now that's enough. This is meant to be a punishment. Get cleaning."

Kyle and Carlos kept cleaning the graves. Moving from one to another. Kyle thought to himself, *If the supernatural is real, and if some folklore is real, then ...*

"Is that Van Helsing guy real?" he asked Aaron, who seemed more annoyed than before.

"He was, yes. He's been dead for over five hundred years. And no, he's not a ghost. He was known as a great Hunter. Not the first, but one of the best. He primarily hunted vampires. There were a lot in Romania in the 1400s, thanks to Dracula. Now get back to it or I'll have you here until sunrise."

Kyle went back to cleaning graves and kept his mouth firmly shut. He and Carlos managed to get through five rows when he came across a familiar name. The headstone read:

Aaron Smith
c.1844~July 16, 1888

"Excuse me, Aaron. This gravestone has the same name as you."

Aaron walked over to Kyle and leaned in.

"Ah, yes. That was my great-great-grandfather. He was the first in my family to become a Hunter. I was born into this profession. It's not unheard of but it's also not that common. He was born a slave but killed his master and went on the run. He ran into some Hunters and became one of them. He was also part of the Civil War, fighting for the Union. In case you're interested, the Confederates had a large number of vampires on their side. Vampires were mostly slave owners back then. An easy supply of blood for them, and the emancipation proclamation threatened their easy life."

Aaron leaned back up and walked over to Carlos to check on him. Carlos was lightly spraying pesticide on some graves. Something seemed off about Aaron to Kyle. He wasn't usually this forthcoming. He was usually to the point and grouchy. Maybe he had taken a liking to them? Could he have lowered his defenses while he was alone, away from the other Hunters? Kyle had no way of knowing, except for asking him. But he'd probably snap back to his old self if asked. Maybe it was because his great-great-grandfather was here. If he'd been born into this life, then his entire family may be buried in this Graveyard. That might be it, but then why would he have offered to take the Graveyard shift? Kyle decided to speak up.

"Are all Hunters buried here?"

"No. Most will be buried in regular graveyards unless they're close to this location. We bury most of the dead in a local graveyard if we can. If a more well-known Hunter dies, then we almost always bury them here. It's something of a formality."

Kyle was about to ask another question when Aaron interrupted him by putting his hand up to stop.

"I think I've been lenient enough with the questions. After this, you'll be going through some night-time stealth lessons with Neptune. And then maybe you can get an hour or two of sleep."

"But isn't this the Graveyard shift? Not the night shift?"

"You asked too many questions. This is meant to be a punishment. Not get to it," Aaron snapped.

And Aaron was back to his old self again. Perhaps that was the question he wasn't meant to ask, or maybe Aaron didn't like the idea of having to be out here. Kyle kept his head down and went on with the cleaning.

As he went on, he tried to find another Smith name, but there wasn't any. Could they have died out in the world? He tried to keep it out of his head and continued to clean graves. No notable names came up. He found the grave of some who had died a few years ago, but not much else. They finished around one o'clock.

"Good, now stay put. I'll get Neptune. Tomorrow, or this morning more like, you're doing gun training."

Kyle and Carlos packed up the cleaning supplies and put them on the porch of the Big House. They then waited patiently for Neptune to arrive and give them more training.

"Let's never do that again. Right, Kyle?" Carlos said. He sounded exhausted.

"Maybe Neptune will be in a good mood and just let us sleep instead," Kyle replied, slumping down to the ground. Aaron came back out of the Big House with Neptune.

"Right, you two are lucky I can't be bothered to do proper training with you. I'm just too buggered. So, I'll limit this to an hour. Now follow me."

Neptune sounded very tired and angry. He ushered them back into the woods. It was a lot harder to see anything at night through the trees. Kyle kept tripping up on fallen trunks and large roots. And the training was arduous. Kyle and Carlos spent the hour doing stealth drills. It was getting colder and colder. Kyle could barely feel his hands. Neptune had them crawling on their bellies, trying to not make a sound, learning how to climb trees and practicing stealth takedowns, which Kyle enjoyed. They took turns to yank each other's legs and pull them to the ground. It hurt his chest when he fell, but it was far better than what *could've* been done.

Luckily, Neptune eventually called it a night and let them stop. He led them back out of the woods and to the Bunkhouse. Kyle's arms were bruised, and his hands were turning purple. They felt like they had been in a freezer. Before Neptune let them in to the Bunkhouse, he held out his hand to stop them.

"Don't let this shit happen again. I hate having to do this."

Neither Kyle nor Carlos said anything. They just waited for Neptune to open the door so they could go in. When they did finally enter, they both slumped into their beds and fell asleep almost instantly. The next thing Kyle felt was being awoken by a fellow recruit.

"Wake up, we have another session with Ivan and then we got weapons training."

Kyle got himself up, ate breakfast, and headed outside to meet Ivan again. Kyle was looking forward to seeing him lay out Travis again, as long as he was still obnoxious.

As Kyle was making his way outside, he saw Travis shoulder-check Carlos.

"Watch out, short stack," he laughed as moved to the front of the group, looking back to sneer at Carlos. Kyle leaned into Carlos.

"Don't worry, I'll see if I can get Ivan to lay him out again."

Ivan eventually emerged from the Big House and walked up to the group.

"We're learning some attacks today. I'll be pairing you off."

Kyle was unfortunate enough to be paired with Travis. He was easily a head higher than Kyle; he was like a hairless werewolf. He even huffed like one. And Kyle would know.

Ivan continued with his lesson.

"After your opponent attacks, quickly deflect it and try to hit the center of their chest. This is simple stuff. It can help you get away in a hurry, or as the start of an attack to take someone down. In your pairs, one will do a basic punch while the other will block the punch, deflect it to the side, then hit their partner's chest. Don't hit too hard – or you'll be getting *me* as your partner."

It felt like he was talking to Travis directly. But Kyle knew Travis wouldn't go easy on him.

"I'm going first," he said to Kyle. He took a deep breath and pushed his chest out. "Alright. Hit me."

Kyle sighed and gave a light punch. Travis slapped his hand out of the way and hit him in the chest. He didn't even hide the fact that it was a real punch. Kyle felt like he couldn't breathe for a few seconds.

"You good, scruffy?" Travis asked sarcastically.

Kyle took in a deep breath. "Scruffy?" he asked.

"That pathetic excuse of a beard of yours," Travis replied harshly, stroking his own beard as he did so. "It's scruffy, as are you."

Kyle gave a disgruntled look and brushed it off.

"Yeah. I'm good," Kyle replied harshly. He tried to take a breath, but his chest was throbbing from the punch.

It was Travis' turn to attack while Kyle blocked. Travis, instead of going for a quick jab, wound up and struck Kyle. Kyle wasn't able to block and deflect in time. Another hit to the chest. He staggered back slightly, grabbing his chest, air shooting directly out of his lungs. He felt like his sternum was about to break.

"You gotta block in time, scruffy. How are you gonna survive out there against a real werewolf?" Travis was purposefully pushing his buttons. He even tried to give Kyle a love tap on his chin, which Kyle slapped away.

He took a deep, painful breath and exhaled, trying to catch his breath.

"I've fought a real werewolf before. That's where I met Ivan. His name was Damien. I punched him straight in his fuckin' nose and broke it. While he was in his wolf form."

Travis stopped looking so confident as his eyes widened in disbelief. He stood up straight, marched up to Kyle, and grabbed him by the collar.

"Bullshit. You're just making that up." He sounded more agitated than normal. Maybe Kyle had gotten to him.

"You can ask Ivan, he was there." Kyle smirked, seeing an opportunity to humiliate Travis. But Travis simply clenched his fists and got back into a fighting stance.

"Nope. You're just trying to sound bigger than you are. If it were just you, me, and a werewolf in a room, I'd be saving your ass while you sat in the corner pissing yourself."

He was trying to sound tough again – he even started jumping on the spot like a boxer. But Kyle had broken his façade. Travis doubled his effort to hurt Kyle. Harder hits, more insults, anything to break him down. He wasn't pulling his punches anymore. Kyle fought through the pain and tuned out Travis' insults. His chest felt like it was going to break on the next hit and his arms were starting to bruise. They were beet red from the relentless hits.

Ivan walked past everyone to see their progress.

"Okay, the next move is a sweep. After defending a strike, duck down and swing your legs. Go easy on your opponent still. We don't need any broken bones."

Kyle knew this was it. Travis was going to break him this time. He could just let it happen. Travis would get punished, but he'd end up worse for wear. Maybe fight back? He'd just get punished again. It seemed like a lose-lose situation. Of his options, Kyle thought that fighting back seemed like the easiest option.

"Try not to let those little legs of yours break, scruffy." Travis started to shadowbox. His eyes narrowed, and his face reddened. Veins popped out of his forehead as if he were trying to hold back from screaming in Kyle's face.

Kyle gave a light strike to the chest; Travis smacked his arm out of the way and went for the sweep. But Kyle simply jumped over his leg.

"You gotta sweep in time. How else are you gonna survive out there?" Kyle said smugly; something he instantly regretted. Travis got back up and just stared at Kyle. He looked like he wanted to break every bone in his body. Travis looked Kyle straight in the eyes.

"Let's do it again – properly this time," Travis said, fists clenched. He used a stern voice, talking down to Kyle as if he were a five-year-old. Kyle knew he was done for.

If he was going to get beaten up, he might as well put up a fight. Instead of a light blow to the chest, he went for a left hook to the jaw. Travis wasn't ready for the strike and didn't block in time, taking the hit directly. But his body didn't even move. He slowly turned back to Kyle, rage building up in his face. Without a word, he went to punch.

Kyle managed to move out of the way just in time and went to punch Travis again, this time in his chest. He managed to land the hit, but it felt like he hit solid concrete.

"Ah, shit."

Kyle flicked his hand a few times to lessen the pain. Travis stood still for a second. A few of the recruits nearby saw what was going on and stopped to look at them. Travis slowly walked up and looked at Kyle with a fire in his eyes. Kyle swore he saw his eyes glow for a second, but it was probably just his mind freaking out about what was going to happen next. Travis grabbed Kyle by his shirt and held him high in the air. He punched Kyle in the gut, then immediately dropped him. Kyle almost threw up from the force. Travis pulled Kyle back up and punched him again, directly in the face, as hard as he could. Kyle fell to the ground, clutching his nose and screaming.

"Fuck!" Kyle yelled through his cupped hands around his nose. He moved one hand down to his mouth. None of his teeth fell out but they did hurt, and he could taste blood. There was no turning back at this point. He jumped up and charged at Travis, kicking him in the groin for starters. Then, he punched him in the nose, right where he'd been hit. Travis barely flinched with either blow, but blood started to drip from his nose. Kyle couldn't help but smirk.

Ivan started to run over. "Hey! Break that shit up! Now!"

Kyle pushed Travis over and got on top of him, then started to punch his face repeatedly. Kyle maybe got in five hits before Travis had been able to block a punch and grab Kyle by his throat. Then he turned Kyle over by slamming him into the ground. He punched Kyles's face three ferocious times. The first hit completely wrecked Kyle's senses, the second stopped him from feeling any more pain, and the third almost made him black out. Even though Kyle could barely tell where he was or what was going on anymore, he could feel his head was a lot softer than before.

Through blurred vision, Kyle saw Ivan grab Travis by his arm before he could strike again and break it at the elbow. Then, he threw him off Kyle. The last thing Kyle heard was the sound of Travis' scream at the snap of his bone before he faded into unconsciousness.

Chapter 7

Kyle woke up in the medical bay. He could feel a bandage tightly wrapped around his head. Ivan was sitting next to his bed, casually reading a book, before noticing he was awake.

"Good. You're up. You're head's fine. Just a small fracture and a concussion. Although, you did get your nose broken and you lost a few teeth. Your ribs and arms were close to breaking, too. Until those injuries heal, you're sticking to theoretical studies. So, I guess you're the lucky one."

Ivan closed his book and put it in his pocket. He then pulled his chair forward so he was closer to Kyle, his eyes narrowing.

"Now, tell me what the fuck happened back there."

"I—I don't know. I remember we were training, but I don't remember what happened after we gathered around you."

"You should be fine for now. It's not like you almost died. Just think. *What happened?*"

Kyle was still a little bit dazed, but he managed to gain some focus and tell Ivan what had happened. That Travis was antagonizing him, thinking he was better than everyone, and trying to push every button he could. And that it had gotten the better of him and he'd ended up instigating the fight.

"Hmm, I see. Travis said that you just snapped. That you got carried away with the fight and he was defending himself. He's not the best at lying. We won't kill him over it, as much as I want to, but he's on the Graveyard shift for the next month. He's also not permitted to do any practical training, either. Aaron insisted we let him stay and try to get him to cooperate in the future. We get recruits fighting now and then. Over time, you'd be surprised."

Ivan got up and left the room. "I'll go get Nick. He wanted to see you when you woke up. Nice sweep, by the way."

Kyle laid back down, his head throbbing from the pain. He knew he needed his rest, so he tried to close his eyes and get what little he could before Ivan got back.

Ivan returned momentarily, along with Nick, and Carlos hiding behind them.

"Ah, good to see you back so soon," Nick chirped, unwrapping Kyle's bandage and examining his head.

"Hmm, everything looks fine. Just need to do a few checks."

He took out a penlight from his pocket and shone it in Kyle's eyes.

"Good, all good. Sit up, please."

With help from Ivan, Kyle sat upright on his bed, watching Nick put a small bag on his desk and take out some tools.

He gave Kyle a hand strengthener and told him to squeeze as hard as he could. Kyle squeezed it as hard as he could.

"Good enough?" he asked.

"Yes, yes. Very good. Now for the last test – you should like this one."

Nick took out a rubber hammer and knocked Kyle's knee, which shot upwards.

How original, Kyle said sarcastically.

"It's necessary to see if you have suffered any nerve damage," Nick explained.

"From a hit on the head?"

"A grade-two concussion. You're lucky that Travis didn't hit you a fourth time. Your skull could've caved in. You would have died."

"How long was I out?"

"About two hours."

"Huh. Could've been worse, I suppose."

Nick told Kyle his head was mostly fine for now, but he'd have to wait a few days to do any practical exercises. That sucked, as Kyle was looking forward to weapons training.

"Shooting weapons was awesome!" said Carlos.

"I thought you were in a gang?" Kyle asked.

"I just did dead drops. Anyway, I gotta get back. I'll see if I can get you in the shooting range and show you the cool stuff we learned with weapons later tonight."

He was about to leave when Ivan put a hand on Carlos' shoulder. "He can catch up later. The last thing we need is more injuries. We can't afford to lose any more Hunters. Waiting a week won't hurt you as much as *I* will if you disobey."

Carlos was silent, but he understood and left promptly.

"Is there anything I can do?" Kyle asked.

"We're doing a lesson on constructing weapons and ammunition in the Barn. You should be fine with that. It's not like we're having you use the shit you make. Will you be fine? Or do you want to rest?"

"Yeah, I'll be fine. Let's go."

Kyle got out of bed slowly, Nick helping him stand upright. He made sure Kyle could walk before letting him leave and follow Ivan to the Barn.

"You're lucky this isn't going to be a long lesson," Ivan explained. "You'll be learning about how to make various weapons and silver bullets. Just be careful. Fumes might night you out."

Ivan stopped at the entrance to the Barn and let Kyle continue on his own.

The inside of the Barn looked a lot different than Kyle expected. It was like a giant workshop. Kyle could see that everyone was huddled around a giant smelter with someone at the far end, so Ivan let him go and he walked up and entered the group. The instructor was a woman this time. She was short, maybe just over five feet tall. She had long blonde hair tied up into a plaited ponytail. She wore rounded glasses, a leather jacket over a gray hoodie, baggy gray pants, and big black boots.

"Good, he lives!" she exclaimed. She had a southern accent. And her voice was honeyed. And she seemed to be more upbeat than anyone else Kyle had met at the Farm.

"We only just started. Now, as I was saying. When a vampire dies, they burst into flames and turn into a pile of ashes. The best thing to do is to spray flame retardant on yourself before you go into a fight. Garlic ain't one of their weaknesses. It's just silver and stakes. Crosses don't work on them unless they touch them, so they're only useful at short range. But today, we'll be making simple stakes and I'll show you how we make silver bullets. Now get going, people."

The group walked off to one of the two available workstations positioned at either side of the Barn. The instructor pulled Kyle aside before he had a chance to move.

"You gonna be alright today, hun? There's a small risk of fumes from the flame retardant and some items at the forge. If you feel dizzy, let someone know. But for now, just focus on making stakes. You and the kid said you were good enough friends, so you can work together."

"I'm eighteen, actually. I'm technically an adult," Carlos said from his workstation. But the instructor didn't seem to hear it.

Kyle and Carlos got to one of the available workstations. There were some blocks of wood, sanding paper, chisels, mallet, hammers, and a lathe for turning wood, allowing for easier crafting. Kyle looked and saw Travis in the corner at the far end of the room. His right arm was in a sling, and all bandaged up. His left eye had a small bruise under it that looked like it was almost done healing. He had a partner, a guy who looked like a US marine: he had crew-cut brown hair, bulging biceps with visible veins, and a strong chin covered in stubble.

Travis caught Kyle looking at him and immediately turned away. He was clearly in a dour mood.

Kyle kind of felt bad for him. So, he decided to walk over to him.

"Look, it's gonna be awkward one way or the other. Let's just try and be friendly from now on, okay?"

Kyle offered his hand. Travis looked up at him with a blank expression, then eventually shook his hand.

"Whatever. Just leave me be."

Kyle walked back over to his station and got to work with Carlos. There was an instruction booklet on every table with steps for how to make various weapons. The first one was a stake. After that, there were more complex weapons. One that caught Kyle's eye was the MVK; the Master Vampire Killer; and an illuminated cross made of silver. He focused on just the stake and flipped back to page one. He got to work. It was a simple design: saw your block of wood in half and use the lathe to get a cylindrical shape. Then, use the sandpaper with the lathe on the end to sharpen the wood to a point. The purpose of this was to familiarize yourself with the tools in the workshop. A beginners' lesson.

Carlos seemed to have a hard time with the saw. He kept stopping to shake his hand.

"My hand keeps cramping, man. How do you keep this up?"

The instructor walked up to Carlos.

"Extend your index finger. It'll help stabilize the saw. And push forward with the saw. You'll get more out of it."

"Hey, didn't catch your name, kid," Kyle asked the instructor.

"It's Adelaide. Adelaide Parker. Try to remember it, Mr. McManus. And I ain't a kid. I'm twenty-six," she said, pouting.

Adelaide looked like she was trying to be authoritative. From this close up, Kyle could see the neat row of freckles strewn across the bridge of her nose. He had to stop the urge to laugh. She was literally acting like a kid trying to be an adult. The size difference between the two made Kyle wonder if this was how Neptune saw everyone else.

"You're older than me?" he asked.

"Damn right, *kid*." She punched Kyle playfully in the arm and walked off, giggling to herself.

Kyle got back to his work. He and Carlos were able to saw their wood better, thanks to Adelaide's help. It was simple enough for them. Place the wood in the center, start it up, and shape it. The problem was they needed to use chisels against the spinning wood to chip it down quickly. Carlos was hesitant and Kyle was just as scared. Adelaide walked over again.

"It's not scary, fellas. As long as you don't jab it in, you won't get hurt. Just ease it in slowly and hold tight."

Adelaide held Kyle's chisel over his hands and guided him into the wood. It was only just barely touching, and he could hear the wood chip away. He was still a little nervous about using the lathe, but Adelaide kept her hands wrapped around his and aided him in making a few inches of progress.

"See hun, if you're holdin' back, you're gonna get hurt. Just move slowly and you'll be right."

Adelaide moved to help Carlos, as he was struggling more than Kyle was – he hadn't started to even *try* to chip the wood.

Kyle continued his work. He was able to chip down the wood to a cylindrical shape, then he moved onto the front. He took his sandpaper out and got to work. He held the lathe over the wood and pushed down. The wood slowly went down, splashing sawdust over his workstation. He pushed it forward to form the point. When he was done, he turned off the lathe to see how he'd done. It looked mostly alright. Maybe a little bit too thin at the top. He took it to Adelaide to check.

"Not too bad for a first-timer. Sand around the top to get a good point and make another one. You did well today, kid."

"You're not gonna let that go, are you?"

"Afraid not." She smirked.

Kyle went back to his workstation and sanded the top to a point, then examined his work: a six-inch wooden stake with a wonky pointed tip. Carlos was close to finishing his and showed it to Kyle. His stake looked a little bit thinner, like a large pencil. Probably used the chisel for too long, but Kyle wasn't in the position to criticize. They were both beginners. Kyle got to work on his second stake; he felt a lot more confident with the lathe this time. It was still not perfect, according to Adelaide, but she seemed to admire Kyle's craftmanship. Carlos' turned out a little bit too thin again, but otherwise alright.

The time to make stakes was over shortly after, but Kyle wanted to stay longer. He'd found something he liked to do for once, but it was time to move on. They were to try their hands at making silver bullets. Adelaide gathered everyone to the smelter at the back of the Barn. There was an array of tools on the wall behind it, including a small table with a set of casings for different types of bullets. They were labeled and arranged from smallest to largest. The group stayed back as Adelaide got the .22 caliber casing bullets. She had already started to melt some silver down. All that was still needed was to melt the silver into the molds. This was still difficult and required proper protective gear. If any molten silver got onto you, it wouldn't exactly be nice. Adelaide was showing the class how to pour the silver into the molds precisely.

"Remember people, silver's a universal weakness. Almost every supernatural is weak to its effects. Works best on vampires and werewolves. Never go into a fight without some silver on you."

The group watched as she slowly poured the silver into the .22 casings without spilling a drop. Ten glowing orange spots, like small suns, lighting up their faces. Kyle could feel the heat from where he was standing, about two feet away.

Adelaide put the casings in a large bucket filled with water, which fizzled and sent steam into the room.

"There's no need to go fast with these," Adelaide said. "You'll just get molten silver everywhere. You don't have to move at all. The silver will fill in all casings – just make sure you don't go overboard and put too much in. Now, you won't be doing any smelting, probably ever, but you need to know how it's done so you don't whine about it taking forever to get your bullets."

Adelaide showed everyone the finished silver bullets once the casings had been cooled down.

"There's one for each of you. A little souvenir from me. Once I get these into working bullets I'll hand 'em over. Give me a day."

The rest of the lesson was focused on weapons that could be made with wood. It was getting boring for most of the group, but Kyle was keenly interested. Eventually, the lesson was over, and everyone got some food by the pavilion.

Kyle took his food, hot chicken soup, back to the Bunkhouse, along with Carlos.

They were sitting on their beds, eating and chatting.

"Why are you so scared of everything?" Kyle asked Carlos unexpectedly.

Carlos looked up, pondering the question.

"Because of what's gone on around me growing up," he finally said. "I was raised in an orphanage – I got beat up a lot because of that. I'm kinda small, too. I joined a gang to get tough, then I was treated like a rat. So, I decided to run away when I was old enough. Then

I watch a bunch of my friends get killed by vampires. Those of us who survive come here and almost watch someone die because they had second thoughts. We've been told that practically everything religious is real. The supernatural is real. Hell is real. Heaven is real. All this new information is overwhelming. I'm afraid if I screw up, whether it's during the training or out there, I'm going to get killed. How can *you* stay so calm?"

Kyle gave it some thought. "I like to focus on the fun side of things. Werewolves are awesome. Ghosts are awesome. Vampires are awesome."

"You get used to it." Adelaide had overheard their conversation as she walked into the Bunkhouse. "I was just like you Mr. Alirez. Look at me. I'm five feet tall. I'm a tiny little thing. I was born into this, but it doesn't mean I wasn't still scared growing up, knowing all this. My parents were both Hunters. I was raised here. When I was fifteen, they took me out for my first real assignment. Vampires. Unfortunately, the vampires had the upper hand – Dad didn't make it, and a lot of the others didn't, either." She sat down next to Carlos on his bed.

"I was scared shitless during that attack and just watched as people were torn apart by those vampires. What I eventually learned was that there's no point in being scared because it makes you an easy target. You freeze up and stop thinking 'bout stuff. Show some backbone and you already have an advantage; you show you're not gonna back down. Even if you have to fake that backbone, just looking tough is enough to fool some people. One day you'll find your backbone. But until then, just take it easy."

"You seem very eager to share," Kyle said.

"The kid sounded like he needed to hear it." Adelaide said as she reached up to pat Carlos on the shoulder. "Don't sweat it, honey, I was a lot like you." She gave Carlos a caring smile, then walked away to check on the others.

"That was ... enlightening," Carlos said.

"Could be worse. She could be a tiny Ivan."

Kyle and Carlos finished their food and joined the others at the pavilion, where they had also finished eating. Everyone was given a few hours free to do as they pleased before training with Ivan again; something Kyle was now exempt from, which meant that he could go down to the Bunker with Carlos and do some shooting.

Carlos excitedly dragged Kyle towards the Bunker but stopped when he saw Ivan walk out and look directly at them.

"What'd I say?" Ivan snapped.

"You, uh, you—uh. You said—"

"He needs more time to heal. It's only been a few hours."

"But—"

"Nick said wait a week before doing anything serious. That means he's benched for combat training. I'm not letting him down there until Nick clears him. Could be tomorrow or next week. Just find something else to do."

Ivan remained at the entrance to the Bunker and folded his arms.

"Shit," Carlos muttered to himself. "C'mon, Kyle. Let's go find something else to do."

Kyle followed as Carlos walked back into the Bunkhouse and slumped onto his bed.

After some reassurance and a quick talk, Kyle was able to keep Carlos from getting too frustrated and they instead spent their time reading in the corner – their only real option to kill time – but there were some interesting books, at least.

Three books in particular caught Kyle's eye. One was titled *Werebeast Index* and featured illustrations of various werebeasts and explanations for how they differed. Another was called *Demonology: Seven Deadly Sins*. It talked about how each deadly sin was able to manifest in certain humans and possess them if the connection was strong, and detailed they manner of possession for each demon. Kyle was somewhat fascinated by the illustrations for pride and sloth demons. Pride was a hulking mass while sloth was more like a blob of goo. But the book warned that these were the deadliest sins, and advised killing the host immediately if possession could be confirmed; as that would send the demon back to Hell.

Kyle spent the remainder of his afternoon with Adelaide in the Barn. He'd wanted to try and make a new stake and it would give him something to do.

Adelaide was still at the forge, hammering out the silver bullets out of the casing she'd made earlier.

"Hey, Adelaide," Kyle said, walking up to her.

"Oh, it's you! Whatcha up to?"

"I'm bored, and Nick said I can't do much until my head heals. Do you mind if I kill time here?"

"Sure, hun! I could use the help anyways. Go ahead and fire up the lathe. I could use some good stakes."

"What do you need them for?"

"Someone will always need stakes. They're simple to make, so it's good to have a lot of them around. If you want to make a few crosses as well, you can go ahead. Just make sure to use the maple wood – doesn't burn as quick when vampires grab at 'em."

"Crosses go up in flames if a vampire grabs them?"

"Sure do! It's why we usually stick to metal or silver; they just get hot. But wood is just as fine. You can whack 'em with it after, anyways."

Kyle went to a workbench and got to work making stakes. It was quite relaxing. He still made a few short or uneven, but he was able to get five done in twenty minutes. Adelaide came over to check on his progress.

"These do look nice and fine." She poked the tip of each one. "They should go nice and easy through a heart. I'll varnish 'em up later. You're really good at this, Mr. McManus!"

"You can just call me Kyle."

"Maybe, if I feel like it." She smiled at Kyle playfully and took all his stakes away from the table.

Kyle tried to make a few crosses but ended up breaking them whenever he tried to cut around the corners. He was able to cut to the outline and instead made a few in advance so he could practice getting it right. Adelaide eventually joined him and showed Kyle how to properly cut a cross.

"You shoulda been usin' the jigsaw blades, not the saws, dummy," she cackled.

"Is there any way to actually make you unhappy?"

"Nah, too busy havin' fun."

Adelaide had taken over and shown Kyle how to cut crosses correctly. They both continued for an hour. But it only seemed like a few minutes to Kyle. He'd found a great way to kill time doing something he loved.

Chapter 8

Kyle spent most of his afternoon away from the rest of the group, in the Barn with Adelaide. She'd let him stay as long as he liked; something he was grateful for.

Adelaide was more down to earth than any of the other Hunters that Kyle had met whilst living on the Farm.

"What's wrong with likin' Bon Jovi?" she asked. They're a good band."

"Because," Kyle replied, "they had like two good songs. AC/DC is one hundred percent better."

Adelaide let out an exasperated sigh. "Another AC/DC fanboy. I'm gonna need to strap you to a chair and glue some headphones to your head."

"I dunno – you'd have to beat me in a fight to do that. I reckon I could win."

"Considering how your last one went, I could easily win."

Adelaide eventually shooed Kyle out as she had some important work to get on with by herself. By this time, Ivan was already coming over to grab Kyle.

"Nick wanted to get you looked at again before you eat dinner. Let's go."

○

Nick examined Kyle for a few minutes, just like he did before.

"You seem to be well, for now. I don't want you doing any combat training for another week, but you should be fine for weapons. I'll let Marcus know; now go eat and get plenty of rest. It will help."

Kyle followed the doctor's orders; he didn't want to risk anything. He even stayed in bed a while longer after he woke up the next morning to get as much rest as possible before weapons training.

Kyle was excited about trying out weapons. He'd missed out on the other lesson yesterday after Travis knocked him out. The group made their way to the Bunker, where Marcus was waiting for them. Marcus was at the back of the room, sitting at his small desk in front of a door. He greeted everyone.

"Nice of you to join us today, Kyle," he said gruffly. Marcus opened the door behind him and led them inside. Kyle hadn't seen what was behind this door the last time he was in the Bunker. It was a large shooting range with enough space to fire without worrying about hitting someone. There was also an arrow target range off to the right of the room with wooden dummies, painted with targets on their heads and torsos, and beyond that, a smaller space with punching bags and what looked like crash test dummies strewn up in poses. Marcus gathered everyone around him.

"Today, we'll be opening up the moving targets. You're to only use pistols at the firing range. For those who want to try the blunt objects on the training dummies, you can use the bats and knuckle dusters today. People who want to use the arrows, remember to only fetch arrows when no one else is firing. Get moving, people."

The recruits went to their desired stations and got their equipment. Marcus stopped Kyle before he could walk off.

"Since you missed out on the last lesson, I'm going to tail you around. I want you to start with the shooting range. I'll turn off your moving target for starters."

Kyle was happy he was able to use a gun. He'd always had a distant fascination with them, though he'd never fired one before. Carlos was at the arrow range using a crossbow, firing one after the other. He was pretty good at it. Kyle got a pistol, a pair of goggles and some headphones, then got into position at the firing range. Marcus stood behind him.

"Don't tense up your hands. Make sure your arm is aligned with the gun to reduce recoil. Breathe out when you're about to fire and make sure your breathing is controlled. You'll eventually get used to firing a gun and the recoil won't affect you as much."

Kyle kept repeating those instructions in his head; *don't tense, align your hand, control your breathing.* He took a sharp breath in, let it out, and fired. He missed the target. The recoil flicked back his wrists and hurt him slightly. He winced.

"Ah well, not everyone's good at firing the first try. A few of the others missed as well. Have another go."

Kyle aimed the gun and repeated the instructions; *don't tense, align your hand, control your breathing.* He took a slow breath in this time, and let it out as he fired. He didn't hit the center, but he got within the second ring. At least he hit *something* this time. Right in the neck. Kyle smiled gleefully.

Marcus patted him on his shoulder. "Good, now do it again."

Kyle aimed, thought of the instructions, and fired. He got the bullet in the second ring again.

"Reload."

He ejected the clip and reloaded it.

"You have twelve shots in a semi-automatic pistol magazine. You don't get the luxury of taking your time to fire out there. Imagine that target is running at you with speed. Unload the whole clip this time."

Kyle looked at the target down the sights of his pistol, lining it up. He then unloaded the whole magazine at it. He couldn't count how many of the shots landed on the target, but he'd hit a bullseye. Marcus took out some binoculars and counted the bullet holes.

"Seven out of twelve. Nice shooting. Let's see how you do with a moving target."

Marcus grabbed a lever next to him and a werewolf-shaped target with small targets on its head and chest dropped down. It moved from side to side at a medium pace, like it was waving at Kyle. He reloaded his pistol and aimed.

"Shoot at where it's going to be, not where it is. If you time it right and keep your aim steady, you can score a bullseye with every shot."

Kyle aimed down the sights and slowed his breathing. He lined his aim up with the chest bullseye. He fired, and almost got a bullseye. It was just over an inch above it. He kept his aim firm and fired a few more rounds in succession. No bullseyes, but they were close to the center. He unloaded the remaining rounds and saved the last for a headshot. Out of those twelve rounds, the only bullseye he got was the headshot.

"I think you got him." Marcus chuckled. "Your aim is decent for a beginner, but this is just a pistol. Over the next month, you'll be using a range of other weapons. But take it from me – stick to pistols. They're small and concealable, and easy to shoot. Now follow me."

Kyle followed Marcus. He took him to the training dummy section. There were a few people there attacking the dummies with blunt weapons, including Travis – five people in total. The weapons available were wooden and metal bats, maces, knuckle dusters, nightsticks, and various other miscellaneous household items that could be used as weapons, all contained in boxes lining the wall.

Kyle was about to pick up a metal bat when Marcus stopped the group.

"Okay, you lot. I have a surprise for you today. *I'll* be your training dummy. Grab a wooden bat or a nightstick and go all out on me. I want to test your strength."

"Are you sure?" Kyle asked.

"Yeah, yeah. Just go for it."

Marcus took off his shirt and pants, then transformed in front of them. The sound of his bones breaking and elongating was like the crackling of a bonfire. A few of the other recruits from the shooting range looked over their shoulders to watch him transform – some probably hadn't seen a werewolf transformation before. Marcus' wolf form looked different from the last werewolf Kyle had seen. Marcus' fur was jet black and his eyes were a light blue. He seemed to be leaner than the other one, too.

"You can go all out on me," he said, his voice sounding distorted. "Wooden weapons don't deal much damage to us in this form. Our durability is higher while we're like this. Line up and hit me. Like a piñata."

Kyle walked up and was first in line. Being this close to a werewolf made him uneasy. He'd faced one, but he'd had help that time. Now, with a werewolf standing right in his face, it felt alarming. Marcus breathed heavily with excitement and stared down at Kyle.

Kyle decided to go for Marcus' right knee. He swung the bat as hard as he could into Marcus.

Marcus dropped and grabbed his knee.

"Ha! Good one! You have a good swing, Kyle. Next!" He seemed to enjoy the feeling of pain.

"Are you getting off on this?" Kyle asked.

"No. I haven't left this place in years – it's nice to finally put this form to use is all!"

It seemed a good enough reason, but Kyle felt a little put off. Was he being kept here because he was a werewolf? Had he done something wrong?

He went to the back of the line and watched as everyone attacked Marcus. Marcus laughed as each one hit him in various places, commenting on their good work and asking the next to hit harder. Travis hit Marcus multiple times in the chest with a baseball bat until the wood split and broke. Even with one arm in a sling, he was strong.

When it was Kyle's turn again, he swung straight for the jaw – on Marcus' insistence. There was a loud *crack* when he made contact. Marcus grabbed his jaw and let out a muffled scream. He let his hand down to show the damage. His jaw wasn't broken but it was dislocated, hanging to the side like a wonky smile. He gave a thumbs up and readjusted it.

"I good clean dislocation! Very good if you need a moment to catch your breath in a fight. A break will also suffice against a werewolf, but it'll be hard for any of you to break a bone in this form. Next!"

This kept going on, Marcus sounding more and more aggressive with each hit. Then Kyle heard the door open, and Ivan walked in. He immediately saw Marcus and screamed.

"Marcus! Out of that form, now!"

"Why should I, Ivan? I've been holding back all these years. It's nice to get out once in a while!" Marcus laughed maniacally. Ivan pulled out a pistol and aimed it at Marcus.

"Get out of that form *now*." He sounded a lot calmer than before; more collected.

Marcus huffed. Ivan wasn't having it. He shot Marcus in the knee. Marcus clutched his knee and fell. Then, he looked up at Ivan and snarled. Ivan flipped his pistol around and hit Marcus around the head with the butt of his gun. He then grabbed the hair on Marcus' head and pulled him down, so they were face to face.

"Change. *Now*."

The anger on Marcus' face subsided as he slowly started to transform back. The hair over his body receded. His body shrank. His face became flatter. And then he was once again back to being human. His knee was still bleeding. He could barely hold himself up, and hit the ground with a *thud*. Kyle could hear him whimpering.

Ivan picked him up.

"He'll be out of commission for the next day. Just get back to what you were doing. I'll look over the rest of his lesson," he said as he walked out of the room with Marcus over his shoulder.

Everyone was silent for a few seconds, not sure how to process what had just happened. But eventually, the group resumed what they were doing. Travis then leaned into Kyle.

"He's pretty weak, don't you think, scruffy?"

Kyle ignored him and put the equipment back, then moved onto the archery range.

Kyle was adept at archery and had little problems, due to there not being much recoil with a crossbow. He would sometimes miss the target completely, but when he did hit, it was always close to the center. Eventually, time was up, and Ivan called everyone to him.

"Well done, everyone. Today was a good day for you all. Keep up your target practice daily and you'll eventually never miss the targets. Now go get some food. I heard that your next session is with Aaron. Probably history or something. Get going, people."

Kyle and Carlos got back together and headed off to lunch. They were a little concerned about Aaron's upcoming class. Mostly because he seemed to drag speeches along like he was delivering an award-winning monologue.

"What do you think we're learning with him?" asked Carlos.

"Ghosts? I'm hoping ghosts. Sounds like they're pretty easy compared to everything else."

"My guess is demons. We haven't learned anything about them yet. They could be fun to learn about."

Once they had finished eating, the group made their way back into the Bunker and to the room on the left. Aaron was already standing at the front of the room, and Ivan was standing at the back as usual. Everyone took their seats and waited for Aaron to speak.

"Today, we're learning about vampires."

Chapter 9

"What is a vampire?" Aaron asked the class. No one answered. "A vampire is someone who was cursed to live as an abomination forever. Whilst we don't know the real reason for how they came into fruition, we do know that they date back as far as Ancient Greece. Vampires aren't exactly how they're depicted in movies and shows. Does anyone want to tell us something they know about vampires?"

The class was silent. Kyle decided to raise his hand.

"They can't go out in sunlight," he said sheepishly.

"Correct. Probably the most famous trope. Anyone else?"

"Drinking blood," someone at the back said.

"Yes. Vampires drink blood because it helps to keep them looking frozen in time. It's also their only source of nourishment. Too long without blood and the looks start to fade and they start to starve."

Carlos raised his hand. "They can only be killed by a stake to the heart?"

"No. There are several ways to kill a vampire. Decapitation, silver bullets, stakes, and sunlight, to name a few. The stakes are reserved for master vampires. I'll touch on that later."

Someone else raised a hand. "They turn you by biting you."

"Yes. When you get bitten by a vampire. You will begin to transform immediately. Once it's complete, your soul will leave your body, and you will become undead. But there's another way. The ways to become a vampire include getting bitten by a vampire, and then drinking human blood; or to be drained of blood and offered the blood of a vampire. If a vampire just drinks some of your blood, then you won't turn. Nor will you transform. We don't know why really, but we call this transformation the 'three-day vampirism'. If, after three days, you haven't consumed any human blood, you will become human again. But these three days are horrible. An insatiable appetite, along with some other vampiric traits, can drive you mad."

Aaron straightened his tie and continued to lecture.

"There are two types of vampires. There are thralls, and then there are master vampires. Master vampires are the heads of their 'families' – their fancy way of saying 'group'. A master vampire is stronger, faster, and tougher than a normal vampire. If you can kill a master vampire with a silver stake shaped like a cross and covered in holy water, it'll turn everyone that vampire is bitten back into a human. We can make those weapons. We call it the MVK: Master Vampire Killer. This is the recommended way to kill a master vampire if you want to save lives. A normal vampire is fair game with any weapon. Are there any questions as of now?"

"Garlic is bullshit," Kyle said. "I read that in one of the books in the Bunkhouse."

"Yes, though you expressed it quite vulgarly. Garlic is indeed a false weakness."

Someone in the front row raised their hand. "Is Dracula real?"

"Yes. Dracula was known as Vlad the Impaler, and then the knowledge that he was a vampire surfaced from various myths and rumors. But in actuality, the rumors are true. Vlad became a vampire sometime during the fifteenth century and used his power to create an army and conquer his enemies. But most of his vampire army was decimated and he went into hiding. We don't know where he is today, but we know he's probably been biding his time to create a new army. The last sighting was in the 1800s. He was a slave owner in Louisiana. That's all we know for now, unfortunately."

The rest of Aaron's lecture was mostly a history lesson on what vampires had done in later years. They'd been slave owners during the 1800s, as it was easy to access to blood. Some had been wealthy business owners in the Industrial Revolution, or generals in the Civil War, fighting for the Confederacy. Overseas, vampires had always maintained an air of wealth, and some had been reclusive royals all over Europe. The cons outweighed the pros when it came to being a vampire, but Kyle thought to himself it might be interesting to *experience* being one, if just for a day. The lesson finished with Aaron listing all weaknesses to vampires.

"Listen, everyone, this will be important. Notes can always help you in the long run. Tomorrow, we will be talking about demons and monsters. Now you can do whatever you want for the rest of the day. Make use of your time by using the shooting range or studying the books in the Bunkhouse."

The group disbanded and went off to do what they wanted. Kyle and Carlos went back to their bunks to have one of their (usually long) conversations about their lives and their interests, but there was a present waiting on Carlos' bunk. It was a baseball bat and ball, along with two gloves. There was a note on the baseball bat:

> Overheard you two in the woods. Found these in the attic.
>
> Have fun,
>
> N.

Carlos smiled and laughed.

"This is awesome! We can have games like I did back in Mexico!"

Kyle picked up a glove and put it on.

"Shame there isn't a left-handed glove here. I guess I can make do. Hey, we can ask around and see who else wants to play," Kyle said.

Turning around, he saw only one other person at the end of the Bunkhouse, doing push-ups beside his bed. He had thick, curly brown hair and a five o'clock shadow. Veins popped out of his biceps. He was the man who had been with Travis in the Barn earlier. Kyle slowly walked up to him.

"Busy?" Kyle asked sheepishly.

"A little," he replied, inhaling sharply with each push-up. "What's up?"

"You wanna play baseball with us?"

He didn't answer right away. He did a few more push-ups, then got to his feet. When standing, he was almost a head taller than Kyle. He wiped the sweat from his brow.

"Sure, just let me finish this set, yeah?"

Kyle stood there blankly, staring at his size – he was almost as tall as Travis, but his biceps were bigger.

"Oh, yeah, sure. We'll be just outside."

"Nice. I'm Andrew, by the way." Andrew extended his hand for a handshake. Kyle complied.

"I'll leave a glove at the door for you."

Kyle quickly turned around and went back to Carlos. The pair left a glove for Andrew and went outside.

"He looked pretty scary, huh?" Kyle said.

"Just a little. I just hope he doesn't throw as strong as he looks," Carlos replied. "C'mon, let's find a good place to play."

The two looked around. The Farm was enclosed in an oval by woods. They didn't have any real options other than to play off to the side, out of anyone's way. Carlos started to walk out towards the edge. He walked in a few circles and tapped his bat to the ground now and then, kicking the dirt and stirring small dust clouds. He looked up toward Kyle.

"This looks about right! Stand over there!" he shouted, pointing with his bat.

"What was with pounding the ground before?" Kyle asked as he passed him.

"Just checking where the ground's hardest. It's so I can keep my footing."

Kyle was impressed. This was the most confident he'd ever seen Carlos. It was almost like talking to a different person. Baseball seemed to calm him more than anything else. Carlos guided Kyle to a reasonable spot to pitch from. Carlos swung the bat a few times.

"Okay, give me a few test throws," he said to Kyle.

Kyle threw the ball as limply and as softly as possible. The ball started to fall. Carlos corrected his stance and managed to hit the ball upward. It was a perfect pop-fly. Kyle didn't even have to move; he simply raised his arm and the ball fell into his glove.

Kyle threw the ball again, this time with a little more force so it wouldn't fall. Carlos hit it dead on. The ball headed straight to Kyle's chest. Again, he didn't need to move. He simply raised his arm and caught it.

"That's some crazy good accuracy you got there, Carlos. How long did it take you to hit that good?"

"I've been doing this almost every day since I was about six," Carlos replied pridefully. "It's just practice."

This was the first time Kyle had seen a genuine smile on Carlos' face. For a brief moment, it seemed Carlos had forgotten where they were and what they were doing – he was just playing baseball with his friend. They continued practice throws until Andrew showed up.

"Sorry I'm late. Had to finish my workout," he said.

"Don't worry about it, we're just warming up," Kyle replied. "You can just find a spot behind me and we'll get to it."

"Fine by me," Andrew said, walking past Kyle and standing a fair way back from him.

Kyle turned his attention to Carlos. "Okay, ready for a real ball this time?"

Carlos got into his batting stance. "If you can pitch properly," he said, grinning. Kyle threw the ball as hard as he could. Carlos was able to hit it with ease. The bat made an audible cracking noise as it made contact. The ball flew over Kyle and went straight to Andrew. He jumped and was only just able to catch it.

"That's a pretty insane hit you got!" he shouted as he threw the ball back to Kyle. Carlos gave a thumbs up.

"Stand a little farther back. Let's see how good you can catch!"

Carlos did a few practice swings. Kyle threw a fastball, and Carlos hit it again, with another *crack* of the bat. It sped past Kyle. Andrew had to run so he could catch it. The ball was low to the ground, but Andrew was fast. He dove to catch it before his body hit the ground.

"Are you okay?" Kyle asked. Andrew got up with the ball in his glove, holding it up high.

"You're out!" he said. Laughing and mimicking a referee.

Carlos smirked. "Damn, I haven't had this much fun in ages!"

Carlos gave Andrew the bat and he took to the pitch. Kyle went into the outfield. Andrew was pretty good with a bat. He was able to hit almost every ball Carlos threw. Most of them tended to land in front of Kyle. He couldn't hit it nearly as fast and hard as Carlos did.

"So, how did you get here, Andrew?" Carlos perked up the courage to ask him.

"Travis and I were out, celebrating me coming home. Ran into something weird. The girl in the Barn helped us kill it and she brought us here. I think she said it was a demon."

"What were you celebrating for?"

"I was in the army," Andrew answered. "Two tours before I was discharged, so the gun stuff isn't exactly new to me."

"Well, can I ask why you were discharged?" Carlos asked.

"Of course. IED." He lifted his right pant leg to reveal a prosthetic leg below the knee. Carlos' intrigue had slowly faded into a bland, sad face.

"I, um, I—"

"You don't have to be sorry, it's not like it holds me back."

Carlos clearly still felt bad for asking.

"C'mon. Let's get back to baseball!" Andrew said enthusiastically.

Carlos got back to pitching, with Andrew hitting his balls consistently. Kyle was able to catch a high-flying ball eventually, meaning it was his turn to bat.

Kyle's strategy was power. Always was. Andrew wound up his pitch and threw the ball. Kyle swung as hard as he could. This strategy paid off as the ball flew into the air. Carlos was crazy fast and caught it immediately. Kyle felt defeated and dropped the bat disappointedly. As everyone switched positions, Kyle gave Carlos a playful punch to his shoulder.

"Next time let me have at least two hits," he said, smiling at Carlos.

Carlos laughed. "Sorry, man. Got caught up in the fun. I'll make sure you can have more batting time."

Carlos took to the batter's position again. Which meant Kyle was back to pitching. He decided to throw a harder pitch this time, a screwball. Carlos wasn't fazed by this, though. He was still able to hit the ball perfectly. Both Kyle and Carlos watched as the ball flew into the air and well into the woods. Even Andrew couldn't see where it would've landed.

"Shit, Carlos, I think that's game," Kyle said, laughing at the situation.

Andrew jogged over. "I don't think we're getting the ball back. You know if there are any more?"

"I don't think so, sorry man," Kyle said. "I wish we could've at least had a few more hits."

"Don't worry about it," Andrew replied. "We can find something else to do another time. Don't be shy." He handed Kyle back his glove and walked to the workshop. Kyle saw Andrew walk over to Travis and strike up a conversation, as he and Carlos went back to the Bunkhouse to return the bat and gloves to Carlos' bedside before heading to the firing range. Both needed to improve their aim. When they got there, there were a few others already using it. Kyle and Carlos took out some pistols and got to work. Neptune and Marcus were there, supervising those who showed up, and engaged in a casual conversation. Marcus was sitting down in a chair. His skin looked pale, and he seemed only half awake.

"Are you okay?" Kyle asked Marcus. "Ivan said you got some kinda mental issue with your werewolf form."

"I'm not so big on talking about it. Sorry," Marcus said softly. "Just remember, this is still a curse."

Kyle focused his attention back on the shooting range. He was slowly improving. Able to land almost all twelve shots on the target this time. Carlos landed about seven.

"You need improving, Carlos," Neptune said as he walked over. He handed him a silenced sniper rifle.

"Try this. I want to see how you are with a scoped, long-range weapon. Enough with the pistols. You need to know your other guns."

Carlos was reluctant to take the gun. But when he did, he almost dropped to the ground from its weight. He heaved it up and plumped it on the table. When he picked it up again, he leaned backward so as to not fall over. As he got accustomed to the weight, Carlos pulled it up to his eye line. He looked down the scope and aimed at the target.

"Remember; slow breaths and exhale before you shoot." Neptune stood right behind Carlos, holding the rifle with him to help him stabilize it. Carlos took in a deep breath, he kept the rife steady, exhaled, and fired. He almost got a bullseye. Hitting just off-center.

"Damn, nice one, man!" Kyle exclaimed. He went over and gave him a hefty pat on his shoulder. It looked like Carlos could hardly believe it himself. He'd barely gotten close to the center of the targets before.

"It seems that you might be better off with scoped and long-range weapons," Neptune said. "Of course, that was a stationary target. But you should still try to get proficient with a variety of weapons. Sticking to one isn't the best option."

"What weapons do you use, Neptune?" Carlos asked.

"I stick to rifles, SMGs and shotguns. Shotguns are best if you're in close quarters with a small gang of enemies. But sometimes fists do the job just as good," Neptune answered, cracking his knuckles.

"That's easy for you to say," Marcus chimed in from his chair. "You're taller than everyone here. We short people have to use guns. Nothing beats a good pair of semi-automatic pistols. If you've got plenty of silver bullets, you're practically unstoppable. As long as you can keep yourself at a safe distance, you can win any fight." He sounded like he was fighting to stay awake. The toll of his transformation had not subsided yet.

"What's the best melee weapon?" Kyle asked the group.

"Knives," Marcus and Neptune said in unison.

"Easy to conceal. You can jab someone with it if you need to get away. Perfect weapon if you've got no guns. If you don't have a stake, using a silver knife can finish a vampire just as quickly. Doesn't even have to be in the heart," Neptune explained, making a stabbing motion as he did so.

Kyle looked behind Neptune to see that Marcus had fallen asleep. The three continued to talk about various weapons while Kyle and Carlos used the firing range. Eventually, the allotted free time for recruits was done and they were recalled by Adelaide for dinner and night lessons. Today's night lesson was another stealth class with Neptune, which was a lot harder at night than it had been the last time – the previous exercise had at least been at sunset. Of course, this one was harder; not just for Kyle, but for everyone involved. Travis seemed to be better at night-time activities than everyone else; he had completed everything easily this time around. By the time the lesson finished it was close to midnight. The group was sent to the Bunkhouse. It had only been a week and Kyle and learned so much. He'd been knocked out by a brute, made a new friend, and learned how to shoot and sneak all in a small amount of time. He still had three weeks to go until the training was done.

This place feels like boot camp, Kyle thought to himself. *I just hope we can get this over with soon. I miss going to bars.*

There were some good things, like learning about vampires and ghosts and other monsters. But there were also bad things, such as killing, or his own life now being on the line. Now that he knew that Heaven and Hell existed, he thought about what he could do to *not* go to Hell. He didn't know what was true and what wasn't.

Not the best thought to go to sleep on, but Kyle had an early day tomorrow, and he needed all the rest he could get.

○

Over the next three weeks, Kyle learned how to shoot various weapons with great accuracy, make his way through an area without alerting anyone, set traps such as wires and bear traps, make his own bullets and weapons, fight bare handed, basic first aid, and grasped a general knowledge of supernatural creatures. His aim had improved marginally with guns. He still had a little trouble with long-range weapons such as crossbows and snipers. Kyle's hand-to-hand combat was steadily improving, though his first week had made him evasive to the subject. His stealth was brilliant, as was Carlos', who had become great friends with Kyle. However, with all this training, his body felt horrible. He was sore almost all the time from workouts and training – but it had been worth it. He'd gained some muscle and was starting to show signs of abs.

He'd also started to get on well with some of the other recruits. Like Andrew, who was a great guy to have a chat with – after the initial awkward and short baseball game they'd had together, Kyle had started to talk to him more. Andrew was a great shot with the crossbow and the most proficient with guns of everyone. Then there was Charlie, who was a shy girl, but when she warmed up to people she never shut up. And Maya, who was very carefree and tended to make nice with everyone. She, like most of the recruits, had been with Carlos the night he was rescued by Neptune. Her English wasn't all that good, but Carlos would come by and translate if she needed it.

Carlos hadn't made as much of an improvement as Kyle in terms of friends, but he'd had his own victories: he stuck close to Neptune and learned how to use snipers and daggers. Neptune had commented that Carlos was easily a great sniper and could probably take out anyone he could see in a scope. There was still some nervousness around him, but it seemed a lot better than when he'd arrived. He was no longer scared to try something new or learn about monsters. Carlos' facial hair had grown from a few small hairs on his upper lip to a patchy goatee – he was still only a teenager. But he was proud of anything he could grow.

Travis, on the other hand, hadn't made any real improvement. He'd gotten the Graveyard shift almost every night since he'd knocked out Kyle in the first week. And his arm was still in a sling. He was always distant from everyone else and seemed to be disinterested in everything, only ever talking to Andrew; usually to argue with him. The previous night, he was caught trying to break into the Big House, where they kept the recruits' belongings. Apparently, he'd been trying to use his phone to call someone. And he was almost killed for it, had Andrew not practically begged Ivan not to.

It was decided that Travis would be forced to leave the Farm with Andrew by the end of the week. And to top it off, his phone was destroyed. Andrew was also punished as compensation for siding with Travis – barred from all remaining lessons and sworn to absolute secrecy about where he and Travis had been for the past month.

Travis had been on edge ever since then and gotten a lot more agitated. Andrew seemed to be the only one able to calm him down whenever he was on the verge of an outburst.

It was late afternoon and the last lesson of training. Travis had been asked to go back to the Bunkhouse instead of attending. The lesson was to simply pass a quick weapons test. But something seemed off. Considering all the training they'd been put through, shouldn't the final exam be more ... extensive?

The group entered the Bunker's firing range. Standing there were Ivan and Marcus.

"This is your last test," Marcus said. "You simply need to show you have proficiency in various weapons and combat. Like every other time you've been here, you will be at the shooting ranges or with the dummies. We will be assessing you throughout."

Kyle raised his hand. "Is that it?"

"Something wrong?" Ivan asked.

"Well, it just seems to be a little simple, considering this is what we've been doing for the past few weeks."

"Were you expecting a written test? This is what ninety percent of your job will be. This is what counts. Now get going," Ivan answered, as everyone went to grab a weapon and start.

Kyle went to the archery range first and fired a few shots at his target. Aaron was standing at the back, slowly walking past everyone. He didn't say a word; he just looked at them, then moved on. Kyle kept his eyes on the target and ended up getting ten arrows all on target, close to the center. Aaron came up to Kyle and leaned into him.

"You're good to go. Grab a gun."

Kyle did what he was told. He put down the bow and walked to the guns. He saw that Marcus was manning this one. There were two guns for everyone. A simple AK-47 and a Glock. Marcus walked up to Kyle.

"You're to use one magazine with each. I don't need you wasting bullets."

Kyle picked up the AK-47 and aimed. The target was moving from side to side. He unloaded the clip. Most seemed to hit, but he wasn't fully able to stabilize the gun without using a burst fire method. He then put it down and picked up the Glock. He aimed and fired. All ten rounds managed to hit the target, with one exactly on the bullseye. Kyle was proud of himself for the improvement he'd made with shooting. He put the Glock down and walked to the dummies. Neptune was there and everyone present moved into a single file line. They were to fight Neptune, close quarters. This was probably because fighting against a real person was a lot easier to assess than fighting with a dummy.

Kyle calmly got in line behind Maya. He felt a tap on his shoulder. It was Charlie.

"Nervous?" she asked.

Kyle gave a small laugh. "Yeah, a little. I think I'd rather fight Travis than this guy."

Ivan was standing off to the right of Neptune, evaluating everyone. Next to the start of the line was a bucket with blunt weapons. Even still, this seemed like a futile exercise. Neptune was almost seven feet tall. His towering stature made him look like a statue had come to life. Armed or not, the recruits were going to have a very hard time taking him down.

The line was short to begin with; only four people. And when they were done, they just moved on to something else. When it came to Maya's turn, she was knocked off her feet almost immediately. She had chosen a baseball bat, which Neptune snatched off her and broke in two. She'd managed to get a few hits in, after which point Neptune pushed her down with ease. She slowly got up and looked at Ivan.

"You're good. Just go." And she did. She walked off to the archery range.

Kyle was next. He picked up a mace. It was only wooden, but it felt heavy like a real one. He decided to charge at Neptune. But instead of hitting him, he threw the mace. While Neptune went to block, Kyle slid and went for a leg sweep. But, due to Neptune's massive stature, all he did was kick his leg and stop. He quickly got up and punched Neptune in the gut. He only got in three hits before Neptune picked him up by the collar. He held Kyle above him with just one arm, dangling him in the air. Kyle didn't let it faze him and he started to punch Neptune's mask. Neptune responded by dropping him. Kyle got back up, but before he could attack again, Ivan stopped him.

"That's enough!" Ivan almost shouted. Kyle froze in place. Ivan composed himself. "You're good."

Kyle left. That was all he could do. He was done. He saw Adelaide at the exit.

"Finished already?" she asked.

"Yeah, what do I do now?"

"Wait here. The second part is happening soon."

"Second part?" he asked.

"Yeah. You'll see. Just wait here for now."

Kyle stood beside Adelaide and watched as everyone else continued to train. He watched Carlos try and fight Neptune. He'd used a baseball bat as well. Carlos swung at Neptune's knees instead of his face like everyone else, which made Neptune drop. Carlos took the opportunity to kick him down onto his back. This move was met with praise from the other recruits and approval from Neptune, as no one had been able to floor him before.

"You have a very bright future ahead, Carlos," Neptune said, getting back onto his feet.

"Still got other work to do," Ivan said. "But yes, good job. Next."

Carlos moved quickly on. And eventually, the last person finished up. Then, they all gathered around Ivan near the shooting range. Neptune, Ivan, and Marcus were talking amongst themselves quietly. Neptune then moved to leave the room.

"We have one last task for all of you. Sit tight," Ivan said as Marcus walked up to everyone with a box of pistols. Everyone took one out as Neptune returned. He was wheeling a large cart with what looked like scarecrows in them and placed one in front of each of the shooting range targets. Each scarecrow had a crudely drawn face with fangs on it.

"Pick a lane and aim!" Neptune instructed.

Everyone quickly got into line and prepared to fire.

"These are vampires," Ivan explained. "We're using this as an opportunity for you all to get some experience with what it would be like to kill one. You'll all do it eventually."

Ivan called for everyone to take fire. But no one shot.

"C'mon! Start shooting!" Ivan barked as he walked up to everyone and shook them back into reality. Kyle aimed his dummy.

Don't tense, align your hand, control your breathing, Kyle thought to himself, remembering his training. He took a deep breath in, let it out, and fired.

He hit his dummy in the middle of the chest. Blood started to pour out of the bullet hole.

"What?" Kyle said.

"They're full of fake blood," Ivan said. "Makes it a little more realistic."

A few others started to fire. Andrew shot his dummy right between the eyes. Kyle turned his focus back to his dummy and fired again. He shot it in the throat, and blood spurted from the wound. He kept firing, shooting the dummy five times before the head was covered in blood and it fell over. He dropped his gun and backed up.

Carlos was still having trouble hitting his dummy. Andrew walked over to the two of them.

"Hey, Carlos. Come on. Just don't think about it. Slow breaths." He was right behind him and held onto his shoulders.

Kyle just stood back and let Carlos shoot the dummy.

Everyone else slowly started to fire. Except for Charlie. She seemed to be at odds with what to do. She eventually broke down in tears and dropped her gun.

"I—I just can't do this anymore," she said, wiping the tears away from her eyes. "It doesn't feel right."

Adelaide walked over to help her up.

"It's okay, honey," she said softly. "I know it's hard. Just don't think about it."

Everyone stopped and watched as Charlie slowly got back onto her feet.

"Is there no other way?" she asked Adelaide.

"No. This is what you gotta do sometimes. Everyone will eventually have to shoot someone."

Charlie's face fell, tears streaking down her cheeks. "But—but it feels wrong. I can't. I just can't!" she said, doubling over and falling to the floor, sobbing uncontrollably.

Adelaide knelt and offered her hand. "C'mon, let's get you out of here."

Charlie took a few seconds before finally accepting Adelaide's hand. She was still crying.

"I ... I want to leave. Please! Just take me somewhere I can get away from this and forget all about it!"

Adelaide pulled her in and hugged her, patting her back gently. "It's okay, hun. I'll take you to the closest town."

"Alright, everyone!" Ivan said. "Lesson's over!"

Everyone immediately started to fall in, dropping whatever was in their hands. Marcus led them back outside the firing range.

Marcus gathered everyone around him at the exit.

"I can understand how some of you are feeling. It's going to be hard, this life. I want to make sure everyone here knows what they are getting into. I hate seeing all this going to waste. What we need is Hunters. People who aren't afraid to get their hands dirty to keep this world safe. Just like any job, it will take time to learn."

Marcus looked out to blank faces and started to sweat.

"Look, uh, just remember to not get too frightened or overwhelmed when you're out there. You all did well today." He forced a smile before retreating and letting everyone out of the Bunker.

Ivan was waiting topside. He ushered everyone to the Bunkhouse, where Travis was sitting on his bunk, mulling over his thoughts. Kyle and Carlos stood with everyone while Adelaide joined Ivan, Marcus, and Neptune at the front of the room.

"Tonight is your second last night in the Bunkhouse," Ivan spoke. "It *was* meant to be your last, but we'll be taking tomorrow to talk over some subjects and make sure you're all properly prepared. We will also be taking anyone who wants to leave into town tomorrow night. So, Adelaide offered her time to give you all one last chance at the end to change your mind. Anyone who stays will be receiving their first assignments and leaving the morning after. So, go get your rest. Day after tomorrow is the beginning of your new lives as Hunters."

Ivan, Adelaide, Marcus, and Neptune then all left the Bunkhouse. Everyone went back to their normal monotonous routines. Those close to Charlie were with her, trying to help her stop crying.

Kyle and Carlos sat at their beds and started to converse.

"So, that seemed fun," Kyle said.

"Yeah, I feel kinda bad for most of these guys, though. We're all here for one thing and that was a promise to get into America – none of us signed up for all this secret stuff."

"Yeah, I get you. But you've had fun here, right?"

"Oh, yeah. Totally. I'm ... I'm just feeling like this decision was made for most of us."

"You holding up okay?"

"Yeah, I'll be fine. Don't think Charlie will. I imagine most of these guys will be leaving tomorrow night."

"Do you wanna get out and play some baseball?"

"Nah. It'll be dark soon. We won't be able to play long."

Andrew walked up to Kyle, seeming panicked.

"You got a minute, Kyle?" he said, sounding urgent.

Kyle nodded and got up. "Sure, what's up?"

"Come with me," he said, grabbing Kyle by the wrist and dragging him outside.

Andrew shut the door and took Kyle behind the Bunkhouse, looking around to see if there was anyone nearby.

"You need to leave," he said bluntly.

Kyle was in disbelief. "Why? What did I do?" he questioned.

"No, you didn't do anything. But you just need to leave. Get Carlos and the others and run." Andrew sounded increasingly worried. "The exit is right there." Andrew pointed to a small gap in the tree line at the opposite end of the Farm. He grabbed Kyle and started to pull him towards to exit. But Kyle pushed away.

"Wait. What are you doing?" he said, slowly backing up towards the Bunkhouse.

"Just—Just trust me. It's Travis. He's not dealing with everything so well. You need to get out of here before he snaps. He's going to kill someone soon."

Kyle groaned. "Why do you care so much about Travis? You're the only person I see around here who willingly spends time with him. If he has a problem, just tell him to back off for me," he said angrily.

Andrew sighed. "Travis – he's my older brother, okay? That's why I spend so much time with him. He's a loose cannon and I'm the only one that knows how to deal with him. But it's starting to get out of hand."

"You're brothers?" Kyle asked, astonished that someone as calm and friendly as Andrew could be the younger brother of a brute like Travis.

"It'll take too long to explain everything. You need to leave. If you don't—"

Andrew was cut off by a large hand firmly placed on his right shoulder.

It was Travis.

"Excuse us, Kyle. I need to have quick chat with my dear brother," he said with a grin. "C'mon, Andrew." He pulled Andrew away with him into the center of the Farm. Andrew didn't even put up a fight. He conceded and hung his head low as he was led away. Kyle wanted to intervene, but he knew it wouldn't end well. Kyle, knowing he couldn't help, returned to the Bunkhouse.

When Kyle woke up, it was the very early morning. He could see the dimness of the night slowly fade into the pale blue morning sky. Since he had finished all his training, there was nothing for him or the other recruits to do. Kyle decided to do something productive. He got out of his bed and went for a jog around the Farm.

The crisp morning air made it a good morning to get the blood pumping. Kyle liked doing laps in the morning – it gave him time to think and clear his head. He was usually up before anyone else and would do laps most mornings. The sun would slowly rise above the trees and hit the Farm. It made Kyle feel like he was living in a secluded forest, like a hermit. He got a brief hit of warmth as he passed through the sunny area.

After ten laps, Kyle stopped. He'd worked up a good sweat and was starting to get tired. He stopped just outside the workshop. Out of curiosity, he looked inside, and heard footsteps on hardwood flooring, but there was no one in sight. Kyle looked up and saw half of the ceiling was covered in flooring. Adelaide was on a second floor he'd never noticed before. It seemed like she lived in the workshop. Kyle decided to walk in and say hello.

"Adelaide. You awake?" he asked, trying to find a ladder to climb up.

"McManus?" she asked. "What are you doin' in here?" She peered over the edge of her flooring to see him looking around.

"I was jogging by and thought I'd say hi. You, uh, got a ladder or something?"

"Oh yeah! Hold on." She scuttled back out of sight and returned quickly holding a ladder, setting it down so that Kyle could climb up.

When Kyle did climb up and looked around, he saw that Adelaide's bedroom looked like a teenager's. There were miniature lights strewn above her bed at the far end – a single mattress with floral sheets. She had a desk with pictures all over it along and a large black book in the center. She had a band poster of Bon Jovi next to her window that overlooked the clearing. Her wardrobe was a large chest in the left corner, with a standing mirror right next to it.

"So, runnin' again?" she asked him in a cheery tune.

"Have you been watching me run in the morning?"

"Kinda hard not to when you go right past me."

Adelaide grabbed a chair from the corner covered with clothes and threw them off. She also got her desk chair and pulled them both up to the window, and then beckoned Kyle to sit.

"So, how you doing?" she asked him earnestly.

"Okay, I guess?" Kyle was a little confused by the question. "I'm a bit tired."

Adelaide laughed. "So silly. About last night. How are you doing?"

"Oh. That." Kyle sat upright. "Well, it's still a bit shocking. I don't think everyone's coping with this well. I don't know Charlie that much, but she's clearly in a bad shape."

Kyle started to fiddle with his thumbs.

"What about you? Holding up?"

Adelaide sighed. "I'm just glad she didn't kill herself. It's not the first time I would have seen someone kill themselves over this. But you gotta keep movin' on."

Adelaide put her hand on Kyle's shoulder. "You tell me if you're not feelin' good, honey," she said softly. "I'm always here if you need to talk."

"I'm fine, Adelaide, honestly," he said, pushing her hand away. "You should probably be talking to Charlie more than me. Maybe a few of the others, too."

"I've had words with her. She's goin' later tonight, along with Travis and Andrew."

Kyle looked outside the window and gazed out at the silent Farm. The sunlight almost fully engulfed the clearing now, meaning that Kyle would need to head back to the Bunkhouse soon.

"It's a good view, isn't it?" he said.

"Never gets old," Adelaide replied, resting her elbow and the window and looking out with admiration.

"You live here full time?"

"Nah, I have a house in Fresno where I stay for most of the year. I just come here for a few months at a time to help with training and stuff. Pick up an assignment or two. I'm gonna head back in January after finishing some things here. It's a really nice house, too. Got two spare rooms if you wanna swing by one day."

Kyle laughed. "Sure. If this is what your temporary room looks like I can't wait to see what your whole house looks like."

Adelaide giggled. "It's definitely *not* what you're picturing in your head right now, I can tell you that. It ain't no fancy mansion. It's a lovely, two-story Victorian house. Sticks out. And It's got a really big backyard for my workshop, so I got plenty of space and privacy to do what I want without the neighbors peerin' over."

"I'm sorry, I can't imagine you in a big house. Unless it's eighty percent empty," Kyle joked.

Adelaide laughed and gave him a playful kick to the shin. "Hey! My house looks brilliant on the inside! Not a space wasted. I can assure you it looks pristine."

Kyle snickered. "Well, I'll just have to see for myself. What about a job? I don't suppose this pays well."

"I'm a sculptor. Mostly do chainsaw carvings. Sometimes some metalwork on the side."

Kyle snorted. "Yeah, that sounds about right."

"It's a good cover. Means I can make weapons at home, and no one bats an eyelid. I always say it's for some fancy competition, or that I'm testing myself."

Kyle looked out at the field, stuck in thought. Then, he noticed a tattoo on Adelaide's ring finger: the word 'DAX'.

"Who's Dax?" he asked.

Adelaide looked down at her hand. "Oh, this? I'm married. Don't do rings. They get in the way of work. So, we got each other's names on our fingers instead."

"You're married?" Kyle sounded downhearted by the news.

"I'll have you know I have a charming personality," Adelaide said matter-of-factly.

"I don't doubt that. I just haven't met anyone here called Dax."

"Dax isn't a Hunter. Plus, I gotta have someone at our house to make sure no one steals all my equipment from the workshop."

"I see," Kyle said, turning his attention away, back out the window.

He got up out of the chair. "I better go. Thanks for the talk."

Adelaide smiled kindly. "You're like the dumb little brother I always wanted."

Kyle smiled back and left to go back to the Bunkhouse quickly.

Opening the door quietly, he saw that everyone was still asleep apart from Travis. He was already sitting quietly on his bed, staring blankly at the floor. He paid Kyle no notice. Almost like he was in a trance.

Kyle sat on the edge of his bed. He turned to Carlos,

who was still sleeping. He decided to tap him on the head to wake him up.

"Get up," he said in a whisper. Carlos groaned. Kyle lightly patted Carlos' face repeatedly until he slapped it away.

"Alright, I'm up," he said, slowly rising until he was upright. He scratched his head and ruffled his hair.

"What time is it?" he asked Kyle.

"Not sure. But the sun is up. So, morning." Kyle pulled Carlos' sheets away quickly. "C'mon. Get up."

Carlos then stood up and stretched. "Any other way to give me a wake-up call?"

"Unless you wake up on time, no," Kyle said, smirking.

Everyone else was slowly starting to wake up.

"I'll get us some coffee," Kyle said.

When he returned with the coffees, Kyle and Carlos sat on their beds, slowly waking up.

"So," Carlos said, "last day, huh?"

"Yeah, been a fun month. I can't wait to get back to society. It felt like summer camp here!" Kyle joked.

"Really? I thought summer camp was going to a lake and pulling pranks. But that's what I got from movies."

"I've never been to one, so I can't answer. But I doubt it's exactly like that."

Ivan entered the Bunkhouse.

"Alright everyone. Breakfast is ready. You also have the day off. Make the most of it by going down to the shooting range if you want. We still have some stuff to work out on our end. Starting tomorrow, you will be leaving once and for all."

As quickly as he'd entered, Ivan left.

"Hmm," Kyle said. "I guess we can go down there. Wanna?" he asked Carlos.

"Sure. Better than nothing," Carlos replied. "Let's eat first."

They went to the eating area next to the Bunkhouse and sat down. None of the recruits ever saw food being prepared; they were all busy with training to ever notice someone cooking food on the grills, but they were always supplied with food. They almost had the same meals every day. For the past three days, breakfast had been scrambled eggs and toast. Kyle and Carlos always sat at the end of the table closest to the Bunkhouse. Each seat already had a plate and utensils on it. The food was being brought out by Marcus and Adelaide on large platters for everyone to take what they pleased. Kyle grabbed enough food to feed two people, whilst Carlos had only gotten a small spoonful of eggs.

"What's the matter?" Kyle asked, pointing at Carlos' plate with his fork. "Not hungry?"

"Nah, it's not that. Just kind sick of eggs every day." Carlos was picking at his food.

"C'mon, last day. Eat and let's see if we can play some baseball later. We could even get a full game going if we ask around."

"Yeah, that sounds like fun," Carlos said, smiling.

Kyle wolfed down his food as fast as he could. He'd always had a big appetite and eggs were something he loved to eat. Carlos managed to eat everything off his plate at the same time Kyle had finished his.

"How is that even possible?" he asked.

"Always been a quick eater," Kyle replied. "Mom used to pester me about eating the food on my plate, and if I took too long, she would throw it in the trash. It kinda stuck with me. Now, grab your bat and get the gloves. I'll see if we can get a game going. Let's see if you can break a window this time." He smirked.

Carlos laughed. "Maybe. If I try, I could get it through the workshop's window."

Carlos left for the Bunkhouse.

Kyle started to ask around the tables to see if anyone wanted to play. Everyone declined. Most were quiet with their responses. He even asked Adelaide, who was sitting with Ivan – she replied that she was busy with work in the workshop. And Ivan wasn't remotely interested. He'd given Kyle a staunch "No" without even looking at him. He looked around for Andrew but couldn't find him anywhere. Kyle knew that asking Travis wouldn't be the best idea. He decided to give up and headed back to the Bunkhouse to see Carlos.

Carlos was just coming out of the Bunkhouse with his baseball gear when Kyle caught up to him.

"Hey. Looks like it's just us for today, buddy," he said, trying to stay positive.

"Oh. What about Andrew?"

"Can't find him. But we can still have fun. Maybe just play catch."

"Uh, yeah. Sure." Carlos looked defeated as he handed Kyle two gloves. "I'll put the rest back next to my bed," he said, slowly turning around and going back inside.

"Fuck," Kyle muttered under his breath.

Kyle walked to the middle of the field and waited for Carlos, who appeared shortly after. And the two started to play a game of catch. Carlos' throws were slight off-center and weak. His arm was limp when throwing, seemingly disinterested.

"Are you doing okay, Carlos?" Kyle asked, throwing the ball towards him.

"I don't know, man. I just thought we'd be able to play a real game," he replied, limply throwing the ball back.

"Hey, c'mon. Don't feel bad. Would you rather be here by yourself or with me? You got one person right here that'll always be there for you. That's better than ten people who *might* show up if they feel like it."

"Huh, I guess I never thought about it like that. But still, I haven't played a real game in months. I was prepping for the border cross for weeks and didn't get the time to play. I just miss it, you know." Carlos was starting to throw the ball properly.

"I'll tell you what. Once we're out of here, we can try and see if we can go to a batting cage or join a local team. Maybe go to a game."

"You mean it?" Carlos said with hope.

"Yeah, why wouldn't I mean it?"

Carlos smiled. "I've never actually been to a live game before."

"Ah, I see. I can take you to Wrigley Field in Chicago. There should be a game there soon. My treat."

"Awesome, man! Thanks!" Carlos was starting to cheer up.

The two threw the ball back and forth for what felt like hours. Talking about what they might face and hope they had enough courage when they left the next morning.

"I kinda wanna see some vampires again," Carlos said. "Maybe I'll go back to where I crossed the border and find the guys who attacked me. Show 'em who's boss. What about you?"

"Werewolves are where it's at. I met one the night I met Ivan, and then there's Marcus. I think it'd be nice to see some more werebeasts, too. Being one might be fun."

"Maybe you should ask Marcus to bite you," Carlos joked.

"Nah. He'd probably get mad or something. Even worse if I die, then who's gonna look after you?"

"If you die you'd probably crawl out of Hell just to play baseball with me."

"I promise the first thing I'll do when I die is come back as a ghost and haunt your ass until we play one last game. That is my unfinished business," Kyle said, putting his hand on his heart as he spoke.

"I'm holding you to that."

"First person to die has to come back as a ghost for one last game. Deal." The two burst out laughing. Carlos was bent over, hand on his knees.

"Bahahaha! Oh! I needed that!" Carlos let out a few wheezes as he tried to compose himself, and stood upright again.

"Okay. Show me how fast you can throw it at me," Kyle said, bending his knees and holding his gloved arm. Preparing for a hard shot.

They both continued to play catch until midday, at which point both their muscles were sore and they could barely lift their food without pain shooting through their arms.

"You wanna check out the shooting range after this?" Kyle asked. "I wanted to try out some of the machine guns."

Carlos' mouth was too full of food to answer. He just looked at Kyle and nodded. Their lunch was sausages and mashed potatoes, something they both loved immensely. Kyle had, once again, a lot on his plate. Carlos had almost the same amount as Kyle on his. Both of them scoffed down their food and made their way to the shooting range.

When they descended, Marcus was sitting at his usual spot behind his desk, writing in a book.

"Afternoon, Kyle. Carlos," he said, not even looking up.

"How can you tell?" Carlos asked.

"Heightened senses. If a werebeast spends enough time around someone, they can get familiar with a person's scent."

"Interesting," Kyle added. "What do I smell like?"

"Lavender."

"Really?"

"No," Marcus said bluntly.

Kyle and Carlos walked past him and into the shooting range, which was empty.

Each stall had a few guns to select from initially. Kyle picked up the machine gun at his station and started to practice with it. Carlos was next to him, using pistols. Kyle's proficiency with firearms had gotten increasingly better throughout the weeks he was at the Farm, favoring pistols. Carlos had shown to be good with crossbows and snipers. Both decided to try and get better with a larger range of weapons to expand their arsenals. The two were alone at the firing range for an hour, with only Marcus entering to monitor them occasionally.

"How are you feeling, Marcus?" Kyle asked him.

"A lot better, thank you. You only feel shit for about a day after transforming. Still feel a little dizzy today."

"How does it feel to transform?" Carlos asked.

"It hurts," Marcus said, crossing his arms. "All your bones break and grow out, hair shoots out of your body, and you can feel your muscles tear. But once you fully transform, it's like removing a splinter. That good type of pain and relief. That's where the rush comes from. Becoming a werewolf gives you immense strength. It makes you feel powerful, indestructible even. And it's also our biggest hurdle – stopping yourself from getting hooked on the euphoria of power."

"Hmm. Interesting. Are you an alpha or beta?" Kyle asked.

"Beta. Gotta kill an alpha to take its power. Or just be a natural leader or something, I don't know."

"Were you ever offered a place in a pack?" Carlos interjected.

"A few times, yeah, before I came here. But I'm happy being on my own. Now, let's get shooting."

Marcus moved to an empty station and joined Kyle and Carlos in shooting targets. They all conversed during their time at the range. Marcus checked his watch and his eyes widened in surprise.

"It's almost four o'clock. You two should get going. Maybe check if there's anything else to do around here. Adelaide might want some help in her workshop."

"Yeah, that sounds like a good idea," Kyle said, placing his gun down.

Kyle and Carlos headed over to the workshop. They could see Ivan holding a sparring session with a few recruits just outside the Bunkhouse. It looked like they were a bit disinterested. Adelaide was in her workshop, melting down silver for bullets.

"Hey, Adelaide!" Kyle called out to get her attention. "Need some help?"

Adelaide took off her protective mask to see who was there. "Ah! Of course, it's you two! If you wanna do somethin' then grab some wood and start to make me some stakes," she said, pointing her head towards a pile of wood.

"Might as well. Better than training with Ivan," Carlos joked.

They got to work on making stakes. Kyle loved to whittle away and make them. It felt relaxing. He could make them quickly. Although, the fumes from the melting silver were starting to make him feel dizzy.

Carlos' stakes were a little crooked. He always somehow made the point uneven. It was easy to see which were his and which were Kyle's.

Adelaide had started to finish up with her silver bullets. "Hey! You wanna check these out?" she asked them.

"Sure," Kyle replied, putting his stake down.

Adelaide showed them the table where the silver bullets were. They were still in their molds, waiting to harden. These bullets were a lot bigger than any of the other bullets she'd made. At least the size of a finger.

"Woah," Carlos exclaimed. "What are these for?"

"Sniper rounds for Neptune," Adelaide said. "He always asks me to make a few for him before he heads out."

"He's leaving?" Carlos said sadly. "When?"

"Dunno. But probably within a week." She shrugged. "He never tells me anything."

Carlos' face fell. Adelaide gave him a hearty pat on the back. "Don't worry, silly, you're going with him! He told me he wanted to take you."

"Really?" Carlos replied hopefully.

"Same goes for you with Ivan, Kyle."

"Huh. Interesting," Kyle said, intrigued.

"Most people usually spend some time outside with the person who brought them here. Like a guide. Still, I'm surprised with Neptune. He brought a whole truckload of people with him. Thought he'd just dump 'em and leave."

"What happens to everyone else?" Kyle asked.

Adelaide thought for a second. "Hmm. Probably we'll send them out to meet with another Hunter to provide backup. Or keep 'em local for a while. Don't have enough people here for everyone."

"You're not gonna take someone?"

"Ha, nah. I don't think I'd be good. Now get goin', you two. Probably got somethin' out there to do." Adelaide shooed them out of her workshop and closed the door behind them.

Kyle looked over the Farm and saw the sparring practice with Ivan wrapping up. Andrew was there, looking sad. Kyle jogged over and called out to him. Andrew seemed disinterested, turning away, trying to leave.

"Hey, Andrew. What's wrong?" Kyle asked him, grabbing onto his arm to stop him from leaving.

"I'm sorry, Kyle," he said in a monotone voice. "I—I just can't talk to you." He shrugged Kyle's arm off. "You should leave."

"Why? What's with the rush? Are you scared of Travis?" Kyle put his hand on Andrew's shoulder. "I can help."

"No, Kyle, that's not it. It's—It's just not safe. You can still go. Just do it tonight. With everyone else that's leaving."

Kyle was started to feel concerned. "Okay, Andrew. I'll see you later." He saw Ivan starting to enter the Big House. So, he ran up and stopped him.

"Ivan! Need to talk to you."

Ivan turned his head. "What is it?"

"I think Travis is going to kill me."

Ivan looked puzzled. "What? Where'd you get that idea?"

"Andrew. He keeps telling me to 'leave while I have the chance'. And, last night, when he was trying to physically get me to leave, Travis showed up and stopped him."

Ivan thought for a few seconds, staring at Kyle.

"Okay. I'll check it out." Then he disappeared into the Big House.

There wasn't much else Kyle could do apart from staying away from Travis, wherever he was hiding. It was going to be dark soon, so Kyle and Carlos returned to the Bunkhouse to read at the study.

Everyone had returned to the Bunkhouse after what was a slow day. No one was talking, either. Adelaide opened the door.

"Alright, everyone! Follow me!" she said, quickly walking out of sight. Everyone followed suit. She led them to the eating area. There was a large spread of food on the center table, along with a few choices of alcohol.

"I wanted to have a little graduation party of sorts," Adelaide explained. "So we decided to throw a little party!"

Ivan, Neptune, and Marcus were the only Hunters in attendance. Everyone slowly grabbed some food and drinks. It took a while before people started to talk and liven up, which was helped by Adelaide's electric personality.

Carlos had pulled Kyle aside to talk to him privately.

"Hey man, I just wanted to say thanks."

Kyle laughed. "For what?"

"For being my friend. I was kinda scared I'd be by myself while I was here, but I'm really glad I met you."

Kyle smiled. "I'm glad I met you too, buddy. Friends for life."

Kyle and Carlos hugged each other and went to the table to grab some drinks. Ivan saw Kyle and walked up to him.

"Hey. Just wanted to say, nice job. I'm happy to see you made it through. I just hope all goes well out there."

"What does that mean?" Kyle questioned.

"You've seen what goes on around here. There are two rules you gotta follow once you're out in the rule world: keep your head down and don't shoot everything you see. The last few people I've recruited ended up dead. Cocky little bastards forgot rule two. I try to focus on restraint when I teach specifically so no one goes through what they did. But I have a good feeling about you, Kyle. I feel like you're going to surprise me."

Kyle didn't know how to take that compliment but managed an uncomfortable smile.

"Well, thanks for thinking I was cut out for this. Can I ask you something?"

"Sure, what's on your mind?"

"The day we met. What did you see in me?"

"You stood up to a werewolf. Simple as that. Most people just stand there, scared shitless. There wasn't much other than that. I probably would've just left you there if that had been the case. I'm sorry if you thought it was something special. But you've changed a lot since then, and that's what I like about you. You might just survive out there. So, here's to you."

The pair clinked their drinks together and drank them whole. Kyle went on to mingle with the others. Ivan went around and talked to people individually, giving them feedback on ways to improve. Kyle was talking to Neptune about stealth tactics. Carlos was asking Marcus for tips to improve his aiming. The small party seemed to be going well. Everyone was having fun; the recruits were relaxed for the first time in a month. Even Carlos seemed excited to finally put his training to use. Travis and Andrew were not in attendance – Kyle could see them both behind the Bunkhouse, talking silently. Travis would peer around the corner constantly, trying to see if anyone was eavesdropping.

Of course, the party eventually ended. Kyle had one too many beers and felt a little tipsy. Adelaide ended up drinking thoughtlessly and apologized to Charlie and a few others who had decided to leave that night. She said she would take them first thing tomorrow morning. Neptune had wandered off halfway through the party and no one knew where he was. When asked, Ivan said he was busy packing, preparing to leave, and had probably gone back to his room.

Everything had been packed up and the recruits were left in their Bunkhouse for their last night, except for Kyle. He had unconsciously followed Ivan into the Big House, wanting to ask him a question he'd already forgotten. He was tired, so Ivan put him on a couch to let him sleep. No harm was done in that.

Kyle laid down, half-drunk, clumsily flinging his shoes off. Carlos was also in there, standing at the front door. He stumbled in and sat in the corner near a bookshelf. He hadn't had as much alcohol as Kyle, but he didn't seem to leave.

"Whatcha up to?" Kyle slurred.

"I was gonna grab you and take you to the Bunkhouse," Carlos whispered.

Kyle shooed Carlos. "I don't wanna. I'm comfy here."

"C'mon, we're not allowed in here."

"So? No one will really care, right?"

"I mean … I guess?"

Kyle smiled. "Then grab a chair and get sleeping. Big day tomorrow."

Carlos shrugged and followed Kyle's instructions. He pulled a chair next to the couch and sat as comfortably as he could.

"Goodnight, Kyle."

Kyle waved his hand in the air. "Love ya, buddy." He grinned.

He laid his head down and closed his eyes. He'd done it. He'd made it through training. Tomorrow was the first day of his new life as a Hunter.

Chapter 10

Kyle woke up to darkness and a crashing noise. His head felt like it was spinning, and his eyes were sore. He saw a lamp nearby and turned it on. His eyes took a while to adjust. He looked at the clock beside the lamp.

It was two o'clock.

Carlos was next to him, still asleep. Kyle saw a window next to the door, so he got up and looked out of it. He could see the Bunkhouse. Someone was moving around in there. There also seemed to be a large stain on one of the windows. Kyle noticed that there was a kitchen just behind the couch he was sleeping on. So, he went to get some water. He downed two large glasses to clear his head and try to sober up. Then he headed back to the couch to get some more sleep, when he heard a scream from the Bunkhouse. He decided to check it out.

Kyle walked out of the Big House and over to the Bunkhouse.

He opened the door and approached cautiously. At the foot of the door was someone's body, lying sprawled out.

It was Andrew.

His eyes were wide and his face was frozen in shock, with a large gash over his chest and his guts sprayed out across the floor. His blood coated the Bunkhouse door.

Kyle was shocked wide awake. He immediately ran back to Carlos in the Big House and shook him until he woke up.

"What's up, man, why'd you wake me?" Carlos groaned, not even opening his eyes.

"*Shhhh!*" Kyle said quietly. "Andrew's dead. I think we're under attack."

"What?" Carlos got up and walked over to the window with Kyle. He saw the large stain on the window of the Bunkhouse, which Kyle could now identify as blood. Kyle dragged Carlos outside and pointed to Andrew's corpse. Carlos was about to scream when Kyle covered his mouth.

"Run and get help. I'll stay here and check it out. Hurry."

Carlos nodded and ran into the Big House to find someone. Kyle went back to the Bunkhouse and stepped inside.

He turned on the lights. After his eyes adjusted, he wished he hadn't.

Everyone was dead.

There was blood and bodies everywhere. There wasn't a single person who hadn't been torn to pieces. There was no point in checking to see if anyone was alive – no one could have survived this. He saw Charlie, but only her torso. Maya's head was on the other side of the room, separated from her body. The floor was almost completely covered in blood.

The culprit was at the back of the Bunkhouse, a werewolf, staring angrily at Kyle. This one had mouse-brown fur and deep blue eyes. It was an alpha; so tall it nearly reached the ceiling. The werewolf started to walk towards Kyle.

"I was hoping you wouldn't have woken up yet, scruffy," the werewolf said with its distorted voice.

"*Travis?*"

The werewolf laughed. "Yeah, I was saving you and your friend for last. Since you killed Damien, I wanted to leave you until then. Savor the revenge. It's just luck that we're here at the same time."

Kyle started backing up outside. He looked around the sea of bodies – the pools of blood – and breathed heavily.

"Why are you here?"

"Well, Andrew and I were sent here to infiltrate and get some info. I was meant to contact my pack once I had everything I needed, but they took our phones away. When I finally got to them the other night, they thought I'd died. But they were able to track my signal and find out where we are. They're all outside waiting for the signal to burn this place down."

Kyle tripped over Andrew's body.

"What about Andrew? He's your brother!"

Travis looked down at his brother's corpse, pushing it out of the way with his foot. "He had to go," he said remorselessly.

Kyle got back up and started to run for the Big House, with Travis chasing after him.

"Ivan! Carlos! Anyone!" Kyle screamed.

Travis tackled Kyle before he could make it in. He pinned Kyle to the ground with one hand, leering over him. Kyle could feel Travis' hot breath as he leaned in. It smelled horrible.

"I'm going to make you watch as I gut your friend, then I'll call my pack down and we'll all take turns slicing you up bit by bit." He growled, running the tips of his claws down Kyle's face. "You're going to pay for what you did!"

Kyle tried to squirm free, but Travis put more pressure on his chest and snarled at him.

"I'll make your suffer," Travis said as he dug his claws into Kyle and slowly dragged them across his chest.

"*Arghhhhh*!" Kyle screamed. Blood poured out from his wound. It felt cold dripping down his body.

"Get off him!"

Ivan was standing in the door with Carlos. Both held pistols aimed at Travis.

"Oh, I'm sorry. Did you need him?" Travis said sarcastically. "This is good. Now he can watch as I kill you both."

Travis grabbed Kyle by his ankle, swung him around, and threw him towards the Bunkhouse. Kyle hit the Bunkhouse wall and fell to the ground. Satisfied, Travis then walked toward Ivan. Both Ivan and Carlos opened fire, but the bullets seemed to only graze his skin. Unscathed, Travis grabbed Ivan by the throat, holding him high in the air, and pushed Carlos out of the way. Travis readied his claws to sink into Ivan when Carlos shot his knee.

"*Argrrg*!" Travis screamed as his knee buckled and he dropped to the floor.

Still holding Ivan, Travis slammed him into the wall then threw him aside like a ragdoll.

He went to swipe at Carlos, but Carlos quickly picked himself up and got out of the way. Before he could fire another shot, Travis grabbed the gun out of Carlos' hands and threw it away. It landed near Kyle.

Kyle saw this as an opportunity.

He picked himself up, grabbing his chest to avoid blood loss. He powered through the pain and, bleeding thoroughly, got up, and walked over to the gun to pick it up.

"Hey!" he called out. "Your fight's with me, idiot! I'm gonna put you down like I did with that asshole Damien!"

Travis stepped away from Carlos and stared at Kyle menacingly.

"You keep pushing like that. I can torture you for months without killing you."

Travis again lunged at Kyle. He galloped toward him on all fours. Kyle rolled to the side and evaded. It was pretty hard to do with his chest bleeding – he didn't roll so much as he *fell over*. Kyle quickly tried to pick himself back up. Travis slammed into the Bunkhouse wall and went straight through it, creating a large opening in the side. He seemed a little dazed from the impact.

Kyle backed up to Ivan and Carlos. Ivan had picked himself up. He was slumped against the wall of the Big House as Carlos tried to keep him upright. But it was no use. Ivan was out for this round. He held his chest tightly.

"I think he broke some ribs. Finish the job, you two," Ivan huffed. "Carlos, back Kyle up. I can get inside and get some help." Ivan made his way inside the Big House.

Carlos got the extra gun from the ground – the one Ivan had dropped – and Kyle checked the rounds in his. Almost empty.

"How many rounds, Carlos?"

"Two. You?"

"Three. We need to make these count."

"Agreed."

Travis regained his composure and stared at the pair.

"My pack is right outside, ready to slaughter everyone here! It's all over! Just die!"

"I don't see any backup for you, Travis," Kyle said. "C'mon, where are they?"

Travis laughed and let out a howl. It was terrifyingly loud. Kyle had to cover his ears.

"Shit," Kyle said.

"Give it a minute," Travis said.

Travis started to come towards them. Kyle charged him, and Carlos strafed left. Carlos opened fire and hit Travis in his side with both shots – it didn't stop him. Kyle slid underneath Travis, but he stopped Kyle and stood on his chest, pressing on his fresh wound. The pressure stopped Kyle from breathing.

"Predictable. You're too easy to read. Maybe consider a different strategy in your next life."

Travis picked up Kyle by his throat and readied his claws once again. Carlos threw his empty gun at him.

"Hey! Back off my friend, *coño!*" Travis snarled at Carlos. This gave Kyle enough time to shoot him. He fired two of his three shots into Travis' chest. That was enough to get him to drop Kyle as he grabbed his chest in pain.

Kyle was losing too much blood. It splattered over the ground. He tucked his gun into his pants and quickly staggered into the Big House to find the kitchen. There must be a first aid kit in there.

Meanwhile, Carlos was stuck with Travis. He wasn't doing much. The bullets had slowed him down enough. Carlos was shouting at him in Spanish.

"*El burro sabe más que tú!*" he screamed. "*Hijo de las mil putas!*" He spat on the ground. "*Espero que te folle un pez!*" Carlos grabbed his crotch and rubbed it vulgarly.

"What was that about a fish?" Travis asked.

"Oh shit. He knows Spanish." Carlos ran past Travis and followed Kyle into the Big House.

"Come here. I've been waiting to kill you," Travis said, casually following behind them.

Carlos had started to sweat profusely. Kyle made it to the kitchen, but he couldn't see the first aid kit. He opened up a top drawer – it was just cutlery. But he could still use that to his advantage.

Carlos ran into the kitchen to join Kyle. He was by the dining table.

Travis burst into the Big House, tearing a giant hole where the door once was and sending splinters flying. Carlos quickly ducked to avoid the debris, while Kyle could only shield his face. Carlos kept his distance from Travis. Travis stood between the both of them. He chose to go after Carlos, glancing at Kyle as he made his way over.

"I told you I'd make you watch me kill him," he growled, pointing with his claw.

"You sound exhausted. Those bullets really did a number on you," Kyle retorted.

Carlos tried to make a run for it, but Travis stopped him. Instead of doing anything, he just stood in front of Carlos. He knew the fear that Carlos was feeling would be enough to ground him in place. Travis grabbed Carlos' face and threw him into the kitchen counter.

Travis had started to breathe heavily. His wounds weren't healing as fast as the others did. He was still bleeding from his chest, blood dripping onto the ground.

"I have enough energy to finish you both off," he said, staring down at Kyle.

"You could," Kyle said, starting to pant himself. "But I won't let you win."

Kyle used his remaining strength to run at Travis. Travis picked Kyle up with no effort and held him high. Kyle just smiled.

"What's so funny? Travis asked.

Kyle pulled a knife he'd taken from the cutlery drawer out from his pocket and stabbed Travis in the throat. Travis immediately dropped Kyle. He fell backward, grabbing the knife, pulling it out, and clasping his throat. Blood pooled in his mouth. Kyle took out his gun – there was one bullet left. He looked down at Travis. It looked like he wanted to say something.

"I'll ... see you ... in Hell," he sputtered through gasps of blood and air.

"Oh, just shut the fuck up already," Kyle said coldly as he shot Travis between his eyes.

Travis immediately stopped gurgling. His eyes widened, his arms relaxed, and he died.

Kyle took a deep breath before falling to the ground.

"Grab the first aid kit, Carlos! It's in the bottom drawer under the sink," Ivan said as he walked down the stairs and came towards them. He knelt next to Kyle and tore off his shirt.

"Congrats on your first kill. Now sit back and rest. We got you from here."

"What about you?"

"It's just a rib or two. I've had worse."

Carlos walked over with the first aid kit. He and Ivan got out the bandages and wrapped up Kyle's chest. Travis had done a great deal of damage with his claws. And Kyle had lost a lot of blood.

"You're gonna need stitches. A lot of them. Let's get you to the Bunker."

Ivan made sure the bandages were tight and Carlos helped Kyle to his feet. The bandages were already soaked a deep red as he rose. Carlos put Kyle's arm over his shoulders and the three walked out of the Big House.

Adelaide ran over to them from the Barn, which was on fire.

"I heard howling. How bad is it?" she asked Ivan.

"Never mind us – what happened with the Barn?" he said, pointing behind her.

"Oh, that? A buncha werewolves torched it. Don't worry, I killed them. And the fire should die down soon. Just need an extinguisher. Now, how bad is it here?"

"Pretty bad. There are werewolves everywhere. That howl of Travis' was the signal for his pack to attack."

"Travis?" she asked, confused.

"He was a werewolf," Carlos explained. "He and Andrew came here to kill us but Andrew chickened out, so Travis killed him and now he's also dead and—" Carlos paused, as though he'd just realized something. "Andrew ... was his brother. The bastard killed his *brother*. He killed our friend! Everyone! *Why*?"

"She's got the point, Carlos," Ivan interrupted. "I saw them coming through the woods from upstairs. It's a full-on assault. Get Kyle to the Bunker. Nick can take care of him."

"What about me?" Carlos asked Ivan.

"I need ammo. Carlos, you get to the shooting range and grab as many weapons and ammo as you can carry. Kyle, you're still injured. I don't want you out here. Stay in the med bay with Nick. Adelaide, stick with Kyle and make sure he doesn't die."

Adelaide was already set. She had a large shotgun strapped to her back. The three headed to the Bunker's entrance while Ivan ran back into the Big House and upstairs. Carlos put Kyle down at the edge of the doors on the top of the staircase leading down into the Bunker, then he ran inside for the shooting range. Adelaide waited with Kyle, taking out her shotgun and cocking it. It was pitch black. Kyle could barely make out the tree line. He could hear gunshots, growling, and screaming in the distance around him; the others fighting back. Adelaide looked around, trying to see if there were any werewolves nearby. Kyle held his chest wound, putting pressure on it to slow the bleeding.

"How bad is it?" Adelaide said.

"I was able to kill Travis with a butter knife. So, I guess I'd say mild to moderate."

Adelaide giggled. "You're pale as a ghost, honey. As soon as Carlos returns, I'm leaving to help and you two are staying put here."

"But Ivan said—"

Adelaide blew raspberries. "Ivan says whatever. You two get inside and I'll grab the rest of the recruits. Y'all are safer down here."

"Yeah, everyone else is dead."

Ivan returned from the Big House. He ran up towards Adelaide and Kyle. "I only got one magazine. Tell Marcus we need to restock topside."

Adelaide could see someone approaching the Bunker from the Graveyard. "Hey. Is that Aaron?"

It was indeed. He was casually strolling up to the Bunker's entrance, his hands clasped behind his back.

"Nice night for a walk," Aaron said calmly. "Why are you three waiting here?"

"Ivan's out of ammo," Kyle said.

"Ah, well. I can stay with Kyle here while you go get more."

"Carlos is already getting more for me," Ivan replied.

"Even better. I'll wait with you, then."

"Hey Aaron, do you have any spare ammo?" Kyle asked.

"I never carry anything on me." He sounded too calm about the situation.

"Shouldn't you?"

"Hmm. Perhaps."

The four couldn't do much. Kyle was gravely injured, Ivan was almost out of bullets, Aaron didn't have anything on him, and Adelaide seemed to be the only one who was prepared. She ended up running back to her workshop to grab some spare weapons. All they could do was keep their heads down and wait for Carlos to get back.

"Where the hell are those werewolves?" Kyle asked.

"In the woods," Aaron replied. "Neptune and Marcus are trying to slow them down."

"Carlos should be back by now," Ivan spoke up.

"He can't be dead, right?" asked Kyle.

"No. There are no werewolves in the Bunker. Something's holding him up."

Just then, Carlos came running out of the Bunker. He was carrying a large box and had an assault rifle slung on his back.

"Sorry. I didn't know how much ammo we needed. And Marcus isn't there, so I had to grab all this by myself." Inside the box were some pistol and rifle magazines, two hunting knives, three spare pistols and a flare gun. He and Ivan were sorting through the ammo box when they heard someone.

"Can I get some help here!" Adelaide shouted as she ran from the workshop. She was being chased by two werewolves. Both had deep brown fur and pale blue eyes. They were around the same size as well. Carlos fired at their knees to give Adelaide enough time to reach the Bunker. Ivan took out a magazine and reloaded his pistol, then grabbed a second one. The two werewolves slowly walked up to them.

"Good to see you two again. Long time no see," one of the wolves said. The voice was feminine and sounded familiar.

Kyle took a second to think.

"Are you one of those women who tried to kill us outside my apartment?"

"Glad you recognize us," the other said, laughing.

"You're in bad shape, human. Looks like we get to finish the job."

One moved toward Carlos, but he whipped his assault rifle around and unleashed the full magazine into her. She fell over, instantly dead. The other werewolf, now angrier than before, pounced to attack. Carlos ducked out of the way. Ivan fired, but he missed. She swiped at Aaron. He dodged perfectly. He kept his hands clasped firmly behind him, maintaining his composure.

"Well?" Aaron said. "Is that all you got?"

The werewolf let out an angry howl and lunged at Aaron again. She was about to swipe through his face, but then something interesting happened.

Her claws went straight through him, as his body seemed to turn into smoke and dissipate before regaining its form.

Carlos looked dumbfounded, frozen in confusion.

Adelaide ran at the werewolf and attacked, shooting with precision. But the werewolf wasn't going down: it grabbed Adelaide by her leg and swung her in an arc, throwing her far out of the way. She then turned her attention to Kyle.

Ivan reloaded his gun and attacked, killing the werewolf with ease.

He then ran over to help Adelaide to her feet.

Kyle was shocked at what had just happened.

"That grave I saw ..." he said to Aaron. "It was yours, wasn't it?"

"Indeed it was, Kyle," Aaron said, smiling.

He had been a ghost all along.

"Why aren't you a wraith, then?" Carlos asked. "You said that if a ghost's unfinished business takes too long to get resolved, they turn into a wraith."

"I said that ghosts turn to wraiths if they lose hope. I haven't yet. And it's not all about unfinished business, remember? I refused to die being owned by vampires. My dying wish is to kill the vampire who did to me."

"Why do you train Hunters? Why not go out and find the other vampire?" Kyle asked him.

"I have over a hundred years of experience. There's a lot of useful information I can give. I'm still here because I simply wish to keep helping. Maybe one day I'll finally try and find that vampire, but that might be a while down the line."

Another werewolf emerged from the tree line. It was heading towards the group. Carlos reloaded his gun and was about to fire when Adelaide pulled his gun down.

"Don't!" she exclaimed. "It's Marcus!"

Marcus slowed down and stood upright.

"Hey, guys! Why are you standing around for? We need help!"

"We got a lot going on right now, Marcus. Also, did you know Aaron was a ghost?" Carlos asked.

Marcus laughed. "Damn, can't believe you finally got through a group of recruits before one of them found out. Anyway, let's go people!"

Carlos and Ivan took the ammo box and ran into the woods to help fight. Aaron and Adelaide remained with Kyle. Ivan left the flare gun for Kyle to use.

"Stay here Kyle, I'll go find help. If you need anything, shoot the flare," he said, putting the flare gun in Kyle's hands.

"Like I have a choice," Kyle scoffed. He grasped the flare gun and stood at the ready, keeping it held in the air. He knew why Carlos had gotten it. It was the middle of the night – not only would this be an advantage to the Hunters, but it would help them find the Bunker in the dark.

Kyle could hear the other werewolves in the distance, along with gunfire. Adelaide was getting jumpy.

"*Rrrrgh*! I wanna see some action!" she said, literally jumping in place.

"Go on, then," Kyle said weakly. "I'll give you five minutes."

Adelaide didn't even say thank you. She immediately made a beeline towards the sounds of gunshots. Kyle looked up at Aaron, who sighed heavily.

"That girl never could keep her enthusiasm under control," he said, walking off to find her.

Kyle was left behind, stuck alone in the dark. His eyesight slowly adjusted. He could see the tree line properly now. His eyes felt heavy like someone was forcing them shut. Kyle knew that he was losing too much blood. He looked down at his hand and saw how pale he was. Even lifting his arm was getting hard. The flare gun started to slip out of his grasp, but Kyle grabbed it with his other hand to keep steady.

There was howling from in front of him. Another werewolf. Kyle could see it galloping toward him quickly. He took a deep breath and readied his flare gun to fire at the werewolf when, suddenly, a gunshot rang out loudly from behind him. The werewolf immediately stopped, falling a few feet in front of Kyle.

Kyle turned around to see Neptune with a sniper from behind the Bunkhouse, who offered a friendly wave before immediately vanishing into the woods.

Kyle knew there wasn't much time left for him. It'd be better to signal a retreat now than die before anyone could get back. He mustered all his strength to hold the flare gun in the air and shot it up into the sky. Bright red light lit up the area. He could even hear the remaining werewolves wail from the sudden flash. Then, Kyle saw

Aaron return with Adelaide from the woods. Her hair was stained with blood.

"Nice to see you still alive!" she said, approaching Kyle and pulling him upright.

"Still can't believe a werewolf snuck in. How you holding up?"

Kyle leaned on Adelaide, who walked him down into the Bunker. "I'll live. For now. How about you – you get hit in the head?"

"Oh, this?" she said pointing to her blood-stained hair. "Not mine. Got a werewolf in the guts with my shotgun. Very messy."

"I guess being short really works out for you, huh?" he joked weakly.

"Keep it open!" a voice called. It was Ivan. He ran towards the Bunker with Carlos and Neptune, fleeing the woods. Neptune looked injured, as he carried his limp arm. It seemed like the attack was over.

Adelaide took Kyle into the med bay and laid him on the bed.

"I'll be right back, honey," she said, immediately running out of the room. Kyle heard her calling out to Ivan to hurry up and get inside.

Nick walked in through a door behind his desk, rubbing his eye.

"How bad is it?"

Upon seeing Kyle, he immediately rushed into work without saying another word.

He stuck Kyle with an IV drip and cut through his shirt with a pair of scissors. Adelaide returned with Ivan and Carlos.

"What happened?" Nick asked.

"Werewolf attack," Ivan replied. "We have it under control now. Just focus on him."

Kyle's sight slowly faded into darkness.

Chapter 11

When Kyle woke up, his bandages had been changed. His chest felt tight, and he was dizzy. The bright lights and sterile white walls of the med bay were blinding. He could see Ivan, Carlos, and Neptune talking across the room, near the door. He tried to signal them, but his arms felt heavy. He mustered some strength to talk.

"H-Hey." It was a weak whisper.

Kyle's throat felt dry. He tried to speak again but to no avail. He felt too frail. He let his head fall back onto the bed, making the metal frame rattle. The sound got the attention of everyone in the room. Ivan and Carlos ran over.

"You're awake! Glad you're not dead!" Carlos sounded ecstatic.

Ivan put his hand on Kyle's forehead, keeping him laying down.

"Stay still, don't talk. You took a real beating. There are over fifty stitches in your chest. The doctor didn't think you'd make it. You lost a lot of blood."

Kyle gave a weak smile, before drifting into unconsciousness once again.

When he woke up the next time, no one was in the room. His head was no longer dizzy. And his mouth was no longer dry. Kyle decided to get up and try to walk around. His chest still felt tight from the stitches, and he grabbed it with his hand. He looked around and saw no one else in the room. Kyle walked out of the medical bay and went to find someone to help him.

Carlos was sleeping in a chair at the back of the room, next to Marcus, who was also sleeping.

Probably tired from transforming again, Kyle thought to himself as he walked over to them, and nudged Carlos awake by kicking him lightly.

"Hey! How are you, man?" Carlos said, springing upright.

"Good, Carlos, just a bit sore. How are you holding up?" Kyle said weakly. He was still hurting pretty bad. Even standing felt like a challenge.

"I got clawed on my arm, but it wasn't that bad. Ivan's doing okay as well. Didn't get a scratch on him. And all the werewolves are dead. Neptune ended up getting a bunch with his sniper and Marcus did a lot of damage, too!"

"Where is everyone else?" Kyle asked.

"Well, they're trying to figure out what to do next. There's a meeting that Ivan's in right now. We lost everyone in the Bunkhouse ... which means we're the only recruits who survived."

There was a short silence. Kyle's mind flashed back to the night before, seeing the dismembered bodies of the other recruits – everyone who had died that night. The only reason he was alive right now was because he'd slept in the Big House due to his being drunk. Part of him felt relief that he'd come so close to death and survived, but the other, greater, feeling was one of shame.

Kyle's mind went back even further to the night he met Ivan, waiting in his apartment after Damien had been killed. That was catalyst. First Damien, then Travis, and now ... all those dead recruits. *Friends.*

He felt sick, his mouth went dry, and his head was light.

"You get back into bed. I'll grab a doctor," Carlos said. Kyle didn't put up a fight. Carlos helped Kyle back to the medical bay and got him into his bed.

Kyle noticed the bandages on his chest had loosened from him getting up and decided to see how bad the damage was. He made an opening with his fingers and peered inside. Looking at his wounds, he could see three large slices across his chest. They were still red, and the stitches were fresh, protruding from his skin. Kyle decided to lightly poke at it; it didn't seem to hurt.

"Don't do that. You'll make it worse."

Carlos was back with a doctor. This one was different from Nick. For one, it was a woman. She was dressed head to toe in white and had a mask on. Her dark brown hair was tied back to avoid getting in her face. She walked up to Kyle, slapped his hand away from his chest, and cut open his bandages to examine the stitches.

"Hmm. It's healing well, mostly closed up. No sign of infection."

Kyle just sat there, eyes darting wherever the doctor's fingers poked.

"Is there any other pain anywhere?" the doctor asked.

"My chest is a little tight."

"That's the stitches doing their job. Does this hurt?" The doctor prodded around the wound, giving a few presses before moving to another part and doing the same.

"No. I don't feel any pain."

"Good. You're a fast healer. I can't clear you for going out until the stitches dissolve. But that should only take a few weeks. Now, stay here and get some more rest. I'll return in the morning."

The doctor then immediately left the room.

"I better go too, man. I'm helping Ivan rebuild part of the Barn." Carlos gave a friendly wave and walked out.

Kyle was stuck there, alone once again. He felt pretty worthless, all things considered. He had no choice but to drift off to sleep.

When Kyle woke up, he looked to the clock on the wall to check the time. Five o'clock. The doctor was back, sitting on a chair at the only desk in the room. She was looking at some documents when she saw Kyle awake in the mirror on her desk and turned around.

"Good evening. How are you feeling today?"

"Evening?" Kyle asked.

"Yes, it's evening. Day after you got clawed. How are you?"

"Pretty alright. Apart from the gaping wound in my chest."

"That's mostly healed. You should be able to leave soon"

"And go where exactly?"

"We need to rebuild. Those wolves practically destroyed the Barn and the Bunkhouse. You can help around here. By the time everything's back to normal and built back up, you should be good to go. Now, hold still."

The doctor pulled Kyle's sheets back and looked at his wounds.

"The bruising has started to go down, and your chest is looking better than last night. You should be able to leave for now. Just wait here for a second."

The doctor went to a cabinet and grabbed a large box. She came back and opened it.

"We just need to clean up the wound, disinfect it, and wrap it up in some fresh bandages. I'll also give you some antibiotics. Just so you won't get an infection. And make sure you don't do any heavy lifting, or those stitches will tear. Try to not let anything get on your chest."

The doctor grabbed out a roll of bandages and placed them on the bedside table, along with a pair of scissors. Kyle laid back down as she cut open his bandages and removed them. He never saw how long the scars were before, but they reached just below his ribs. He also noticed something interesting.

"Um, my right nipple ..." he said worriedly. One of the claws seemed to have run right through it.

"Gone, I'm afraid," the doctor said bluntly.

"Oh, guess I didn't really need it."

There was a fine red outline around the stitches like a fresh sunburn. The doctor put some disinfectant on a rag and lightly dabbed his chest. It stung pretty badly, but Kyle didn't complain. She gave him a new set of bandages and wrapped them over his chest. It didn't feel as tight as the bandages before.

"There you go," the doctor said, packing everything away into the box and putting it back in the cabinet.

"You know, I never caught your name," Kyle said. "And what happened to Nick?"

The doctor laughed. "My name is Tracy. Nick and I switch shifts here every few weeks. We both work at small medical centers nearby.

Kyle nodded along as the doctor, Tracy, cleaned him up. Once everything was done, Tracy gave him some privacy to get dressed. Some clothes were sitting on a chair to the left of his bed. On top of his clothes was a note.

> Kyle
>
> Your clothes were too badly damaged to be repaired. I got you some fresh ones. You would've been given some new ones anyway. Enjoy.
>
> Ivan

Ivan had given Kyle a pair of black boots, dark blue cargo pants, a gray t-shirt, and a black denim sherpa jacket.

When he put the clothes on, they were a perfect fit. He thought the jacket was a little oversized upon first wearing it – the cuffs reached past his wrists and almost to his knuckles. When Kyle moved his arms around to get a feel for the fabric, he saw why: the denim's tightness meant it could be restrictive, with the cuffs pulling upwards when he stretched his arm. With them past his wrists, they wouldn't drag too far up his arm.

He opened the breast pocket of his jacket and put Ivan's note inside, along with his antibiotics in his cargo pants pocket. Kyle then thanked Tracy upon leaving the med bay and headed for the surface. When he walked outside the Bunker, the sun was low. Almost night-time. People were running all over the place; a lot more than Kyle has seen in the past month. He walked up to the Bunkhouse and saw some people in white coveralls, cleaning up the blood with hoses and extended sponges. There was a stack of body bags outside the Bunkhouse, laid out neatly in a line. Kyle caught a glimpse of Travis, in his human form, before he was zipped up – the bullet hole in between his eyes still agape. As he walked around, he saw the extent of the damage. The Big House's bottom floor was almost destroyed. The workshop had almost burned down, with a large burn to the roof. The Bunkhouse looked like a bulldozer had gone straight through it. Kyle looked and saw Ivan and Carlos repairing the workshop in the Barn. They were knocking down a wall. Carlos was dressed differently. He wore a blue plaid jacket with a black t-shirt. He also had on green cargo pants and brown boots. Ivan was dressed as usual, except his jacket was zipped up. Kyle walked up to them.

"Hey," Kyle said, opening his arms, expecting a hug from Carlos.

Hey! You're up!" Carlos walked up to Kyle and gave him a bear hug.

"Stitches! Not too tight!" Kyle yelped, pushing Carlos away.

Carlos immediately let go. "Oh yeah, sorry man."

"How's the damage?" Ivan asked, walking up and patting Kyle on the back.

"Should be good in a few weeks. Can't lift anything heavy."

"Ha! Lucky you. Now grab a sledgehammer and help us tear down this wall," Ivan said, picking up his own.

"You're not repairing it?"

"No, we were planning on expanding it anyway. Guess we were lucky it almost burnt down."

"What about Adelaide's stuff?" Kyle asked, picking up a sledgehammer and whacking away at one of the walls. "Doesn't she live up top?"

"She already took out all her stuff that wasn't burnt and packed it up. It's all in the Big House," Carlos answered.

All three of them chipped away at the giant wall. It was quite difficult for Kyle to get a strong swing in; his chest still hurt, and he didn't want to go back to the med bay again. Though, he was able to swing downwards, breaking down any large pieces. The job was hard, but eventually, the three of them cleared the wall. It gave the workshop a very large new doorway jutting out the side.

"Okay, good. Now, you two go to help somewhere else. We have a lot to repair around here. And we also need to bury all the bodies. I'll stay here are clean up all this mess," Ivan said, dropping his sledgehammer to the ground with a thud.

W

Carlos walked to the Graveyard, while Kyle went to the Big House. Adelaide was in the kitchen, alone, sweeping up rubble. She wore a leg brace. And she was humming to herself a happy tune.

"You seem too happy," Kyle said as he entered. "What happened to your leg?"

Adelaide looked up. "Oh hey! Good to see you up! I broke my leg when the wolf threw me. Didn't feel it until everything died down," she said, leaning on her broom.

"I know it may seem weird to be all happy after all that, but why shouldn't we be? We won."

"Yeah, but what about everyone we lost? Carlos and I are the only recruits who survived."

Adelaide shrugged. "That is a real shame, but we can't do anything about it. That's something you need to learn in this field: stay happy. Don't feel bad about every death on our side. If you can't do either of those, then you're as good as dead. Even Carlos isn't as shaken up as I thought he'd be. He's starting to get that ingrained in his head. Anyway, I'm good here. Most of the damage has already been cleaned up. But you can start up the table saw over there and make some planks so we can get that hole fixed."

Kyle looked to where Adelaide was pointing, just to her right. There was a stack of wood bundled in the corner of the Big House, opposite the kitchen, next to a small table saw and some protective gear.

He walked over to the table saw, put on the equipment, and powered the saw up. He grabbed some wood and fed it through. Kyle found woodworking calming. He used this time to reflect on the night before, and what Adelaide had said to him. Kyle had seen every recruit slaughtered, then he was mauled by a werewolf and almost died from blood loss in less than ten minutes. But he didn't feel like complaining. He was actually glad about the mauling. It gave him some sense of courage; more than when he first met Ivan. He'd had to toughen up more. Both he and Carlos. If he was like this, then what was the ever-nervous Carlos going through? He seemed fine, just like Kyle. But maybe he was suffering inside. This was the life they chose to lead. Adelaide was right. She always was. They couldn't bring back all those people who died, nor could they have stopped the attacks from happening. All they could do was be thankful they had won and made it through the night.

Adelaide walked up to Kyle and tapped him on his shoulder.

"Okay, that's enough for now. I'll grab the hammers and nails and you can help me patch this up," she said, pointing to the hole in the wall where the door used to be. Kyle turned off the table saw and put away his equipment. He picked up the planks and moved them over, closer to the hole. Adelaide arrived back with a toolbox.

"Let's get to it!"

The pair got to work on patching up the hole in the wall. Travis had made a real mess when he tore through it. Kyle was amazed at how strong werewolves were. He peeked at the Bunkhouse to see how badly it had been damaged. But the wreckage seemed minimal. The two people in hazmat suits were gone and there were others inside. He turned his attention back to the task at hand.

"Can I ask you something, Adelaide?"

"Sure, what is it?"

"Why are you always in such a cheerful mood?"

Adelaide laughed. "Why not? You can't just be sad all the time – it's boring! Being happy is great."

"It's because of your parents, isn't it?"

Adelaide looked glum. "Yeah, it is."

"Oh, no, I didn't mean it like—"

Adelaide stopped him. "It's fine, Kyle. I was born into this, but that doesn't mean I wasn't scared. My dad taught me to always face everything with a smile – that way, the monsters will be scared, and not me."

"Your dad sounded interesting."

"He was. I remember when he first started telling me about all this. I was just so amazed, like most people who first learn about it. He and my mom made sure I was capable of surviving."

The two continued to fix up the hole. It was starting to look fuller.

"We're friends now, right?" he asked.

"We've been friends since day one, dummy!" she said playfully.

Eventually, the hole was patched up, save for the space left for a new door. There was a packet of hinges and nails on a table nearby, left for when the new door was put in.

"Nice work, Kyle! You got a real gift for handiwork."

"Thanks. I guess it just comes naturally to me. It's calming, you know?"

Adelaide grinned from ear to ear. "It is! I love working in the workshop. Makin' weapons is great!"

Adelaide high-fived Kyle. "C'mon. There's still more to do. Check the Graveyard and see if they need help digging. I'm staying here to make gravestones."

"I've try, but I've still got fresh stitches. Have fun, Adelaide." Kyle waved goodbye and walked out.

"I always do!" she said, grabbing a large stack of plank and a chisel.

Kyle walked over to the Graveyard. He looked over to the eating area next to the Bunkhouse and saw Carlos stacking up bricks with some of the others. Kyle turned back to the Graveyard and saw Marcus and Aaron there. Marcus was digging some graves while Aaron looked on. Since Kyle now knew he was a ghost, he had an excuse as to why he couldn't help all that much. Marcus carried out body bags and piled them up in front of the Graveyard. A few grave markers had been made out in tape.

"Marcus!" Kyle called out, waving to get his attention.

"Oh hey! He's alive!" Marcus motioned Kyle to come over. "How's the chest?"

"Should be fine. I did want to ask though – you can't turn into a werewolf from a cut, can you?" he asked worryingly.

Marcus laughed. "No, it has to be a bite. Anyway, the window for the bite to take effect is only an hour, so it would've happened by now. You got nothing to worry about."

Kyle let out a sigh of relief. "By the way, where have you been hiding all those other guys?" Kyle asked, pointing back to the eating area where Carlos was.

"There are other Hunters, Kyle," Marcus said. "They're just not here all the time like we are. We called in who we could to help us clean this place up. Go and say hi when you can."

Kyle looked to Aaron.

"Still uneasy about my little revelation?" Aaron asked him, smiling.

"No. I'm just thinking. Marcus said you finally got through a batch of recruits before one of them found out you were a ghost. Do you two have some kind of bet going on?"

"Yeah," Marcus answered.

"Just a fun little wager to see how long it took people to figure it out. It's usually the fact that everyone always opens a door for him that tips them off. You should've seen Adelaide's face when she realized." Aaron and Marcus laughed.

"Anyway, grab a shovel. We need a few more graves dug," Aaron said to Kyle.

Kyle grabbed a shovel and walked up to one of the grave markers. He started to dig.

"How deep? Six feet?"

"Yes. Shouldn't take you long." Marcus called out. "Maybe five or six hours."

"Six hours?" Kyle asked, surprised. "It's gonna take *days* to bury everyone!"

"No, it's not," Marcus said. "I can dig the rest by myself. I'll just transform again and do it by hand."

"Why aren't you half-dead like you were the other time?"

"I drank a lot of coffee and painkillers. I'll crash hard tomorrow. But this needs to be done so I'm happy paying that price."

Kyle began to dig. He looked up and saw the black body bags starting to pile up at the front of the Graveyard. There were too many to count at a glance. There were the twelve recruits who had been killed by Travis, and then Travis himself. Thankfully, none of the veteran Hunters at the Farm were killed. Travis' body bag was blue, and there were a few other blue ones, too – the other werewolves, most likely.

There had been a good number of graves already dug, so Kyle didn't have to make that many. He saw Adelaide running across the field and into the Barn, then she ran back out with two boxes under her arms and into the Big House.

Soon, it was night-time, and Kyle had only dug half of one grave. Lights were set up and a few of the other Hunters had started to help. Marcus had transformed just after the sun set and helped Kyle by digging the rest of his grave in a matter of seconds.

"You really are fast in this form, huh?" Kyle said.

Marcus laughed. "Maybe one day you'll see me in action." As he walked off to help the others, he stopped for a second and dropped a knee. Kyle walked up to him.

"Coffee and painkillers wear off?" he asked.

Marcus huffed for a few seconds before slowly rising. "Yeah, people here know the drill. I'll drop the second I change back. I'll see you probably the day after tomorrow. I'll likely be out all of tomorrow." Marcus walked off to help with the other graves.

Kyle planted his shovel in the ground and started to walk off to the Bunkhouse when Adelaide burst out of the Big House in front of him.

"Oh good! I need a hand carryin' these." She grabbed his arm and pulled him inside.

There was a large pile of wooden crosses on the table and sawdust covering the whole floor.

Each cross had someone's name and dates engraved, which Adelaide had made personally. She had burned a personal pattern into each cross, including Travis'. He had a large wolf arching over his name.

"How'd you know everyone's birthdates?" Kyle asked, examining the crosses.

"When we brought y'all here we swiped your stuff. I went through and wrote them all down."

"Huh," Kyle said. "So, you know everyone's birthday off the top of your head?"

"Yes, I do!" she said proudly. "You were born in Maine on the 22nd of March, 1985. And I know your middle name is Maxwell. Carlos was born on September 19th, 1990. Ivan on December 2nd. Marcus, January 7th, 1984. Mine is May 5th, 1982. I can go on if you want."

Kyle chuckled. "No, it's fine. Just don't tell anyone my middle name, okay?"

Adelaide gave a warm smile. "Don't worry, silly." She winked. "Now c'mon. Help me carry these."

Kyle picked up a heap of crosses and followed Adelaide to the Graveyard. She stopped him every few feet to grab one and place it in front of a grave.

Each grave already had a black body bag inside, and each bag had a name on it.

"Hey, Marcus," Kyle said. "What are the blue body bags for?"

"Blue is for enemies. Black is for our own. We don't bury our enemies here – it's just for easier to bag them for transportation."

Hmm. Interesting, Kyle thought to himself. "Where are you buying the blue ones, then?"

"Somewhere else."

"What about the black ones – why not remove them?" Kyle asked. "Stick them in caskets?"

"Because," Aaron told him. "There's not enough of them to keep together. Travis tore them to pieces."

"We do usually bury them in silver caskets," Adelaide interjected, "but there's nothing holdin' these guys together."

Carlos and Ivan eventually showed up to help bury the dead, along with the other Hunters. Kyle's chest groaned in pain from the shoveling, and he eventually had to stop while everyone else continued. Kyle sat down and gave himself a few seconds to catch his breath, letting the pain subside, when Aaron walked up to him and Carlos.

"I'm glad that you two survived and took down the alpha who infiltrated our Farm. As long as someone survived this attack, it makes me happy to know the training didn't go completely to waste."

"Thanks, Aaron," Kyle said bluntly, wiping the sweat from his brow. "And thanks for helping us dig all these graves," he joked.

Aaron shrugged. "There's nothing I can do about that. I can't interact with anything. It's not my fault."

Kyle watched as the remaining graves were filled in. The fresh wooden crosses stood out in the Graveyard, as the others were all made of stone. But it was a short-notice job. Adelaide had taken care to put each cross in evenly so they wouldn't stick out to one side.

Everyone stood silently, giving a minute's silence for the dead. The minute ended when Aaron spoke up. "Thank you everyone for your help. I hope to see you here again for a happier reason."

Everyone disbanded; most of the new Hunters who had shown up went into the Bunkhouse to get some rest.

"At least we get some new roommates in the Bunkhouse," Kyle said to Carlos.

Carlos smiled. "I'll sleep better if they're gonna be with us. They're the pros."

Kyle noticed all the blue body bags being loaded onto a large white van parked at the exit to the Farm.

"Are they taking the others to be buried?" Kyle asked Marcus.

"Yeah. Maybe they'll be buried in some other woods. Or they could be dumped in the nearest city. Anywhere but here," he answered.

"Get some rest, everyone," Aaron said. "We have more work to do tomorrow, then we can get back to our lives. Kyle, Carlos – I have an assignment for you two once we're done."

Chapter 12

One week after the attack, everything was seemingly back to normal. Kyle had grown accustomed to living at the Farm. He'd been staying in the Bunkhouse with Carlos until they were ready to leave. All the repair work had been completed, and the few Hunters who stayed were on high alert, changing guard shifts constantly. Kyle had taken a few night watch shifts himself, which mostly entailed checking the woods every hour, checking each trap that had been placed, and playing cards with Carlos, Adelaide, or whoever he'd been paired with. He'd gotten good at poker and had beaten Ivan more than once, to his chagrin.

The other Hunters stayed in the Bunkhouse as well. Kyle had a chance to chat with a few of them over the week. He'd gotten along particularly well with one man called Smith. Smith was slender and lanky, wore a tight-fitting black suit, and parted his receding black hair to the right; but he almost always kept it covered with a porkpie hat. He looked like one of the Men in Black.

He was a reclusive man living by himself in New York, monitoring a possible demon.

Kyle was on the night shift with Smith again; they had just finished checking the traps and were heading back to the Bunkhouse.

"You see," Smith said to Kyle in a weak voice, "pride demons are the worst. They simply get out of control too quickly. And, unfortunately, I am not equipped to handle an outburst. Too big. Too messy. So, I have to watch from afar until the time is right. I have a friend, you see – he is the one who takes care of these demons. His name is Charles. My apartment has such a good view, so I'm using a telescope to monitor the demon for the time being." Smith was very soft-spoken and erratic. And he had a terrible habit of rubbing his hands together whenever he talked.

"I must get back home soon, you see." There was a slight worry in his tone. "It must not get out or find a new host. I will not be able to track it down otherwise."

Kyle put his hand on Smith's shoulder.

"I'm sure you'll be outta here by tomorrow, Smith," he said with a smile tugging at his lip.

Smith gently brushed Kyle's hand off his shoulder.

"Yes. That does sound good. You can speak to Ivan for me. I must pack immediately." Smith quickly scuttled away into the Bunkhouse.

Kyle followed him in. Their shift had ended. Smith sat on his bed, neatly packing his belongings into a black briefcase.

Kyle went to the kitchen and fixed himself a cup of coffee. There was another Hunter in there, as well. Her name has Katie. She was taller than Kyle and more well-built. She was dressed in a plain green shirt and blue jeans. Her red hair was tied into a ponytail.

"Hey, Katie," Kyle said.

"Shift change?" she asked. Her accent was English.

"Yeah, you're with me until sunrise. But before we go, can I ask you something?"

"Yeah, sure. What's up?"

Kyle looked back at Smith; he was writing down in a notebook.

"Smith. Is that his first name or his last name?"

"Got no bloody idea."

"Does *anyone* know a thing about him?"

Katie thought for a second. "Well, I heard when he first showed up, he was already pretty odd. He's just not a people person. But he gets results, so he sticks around."

Ivan walked into the Bunkhouse and approached Kyle.

"Evening, you two. What shifts you got?" he asked.

"I'm doing an all-nighter with Katie. Just came in to drop off Smith."

"How are you holding up? Wounds healed?"

"I'm alright. My stitches are almost dissolved. It's all fine now. It'll still take a while before the tenderness goes down," Kyle said, rubbing his chest lightly.

"Good to hear. Where's Carlos?"

"With Marcus. They're at the shooting range." Kyle paused and looked into his coffee cup.

"Can I ask you something?"

"Sure."

"How many Hunters are there?"

"In America? I don't know the exact number, but I think it's close to four or five thousand. Sounds big but the supernaturals outnumber us at least a hundred to one. Why do you ask?"

"Just curious. It feels like no one's here."

"Well, this is just one hideout," Ivan explained. "There's one on the east coast in San Diego and another on the west coast in New Jersey. The San Diego hideout is a bit livelier – last time I was there, anyway. You also need to remember that there are Hunters in places other than America."

"Ah. Right."

"Now," Ivan went on, "the reason I came here was to tell you that you're getting your first assignment tomorrow morning. Meet me at the Big House at six o'clock. Second floor."

Kyle nodded and went back to drinking his coffee. Ivan promptly left.

Kyle talked to Katie, pondering about what the assignment could be. It could be something dangerous or even a follow-up on the werewolves that attacked.

They spent the remainder of the night playing card games on the porch of the Bunkhouse and chatting, regularly doing their perimeter checks – every hour. The night was long and boring. Carlos stumbled out of the Bunker and walked past Kyle, too tired to say anything, and went straight to sleep.

When sunrise broke, it signaled the end of their shift. Katie had fallen asleep at four o'clock and Kyle didn't want to wake her. He put a blanket around her and kept watch.

Kyle had taken a few spare sheets of paper out of the Bunkhouse and started to sketch. All those art classes he took weren't for waste; he was quite good at drawing. First, he sketched Aaron, with his hands behind his back and glaring menacingly. Then, he drew Katie, sleeping beside him. His art wasn't completely fluid; more like rough sketches. He drew the woods in front of him, and the Bunkhouse, and then a full-body picture of Adelaide standing next to himself to scale the height difference. Kyle folded his completed pieces away to touch up another time.

Adelaide emerged from the Barn early, carrying a stack of planks over her shoulder. The Big House had yet to be rebuilt fully. The wall had been repaired, along with the door. But the kitchen and table Travis had broken were still not finished. Adelaide waved to Kyle and waltzed into the Big House.

Kyle followed her in. She laid the planks down in the middle of the room. She had a table saw set up to cut the wood appropriately.

"Morning!" she said, ever cheerful. "How was your first all-nighter?"

"The coffee hasn't worn off yet, so I'm still happy," he joked.

Adelaide laughed. "Well, you best get upstairs. Don't let me stop you all the time."

Kyle walked up the stairs – he was excited to see what the rest of the house looked like. But he was left disappointed.

The second floor was very bland: a small hallway with a few doors on either side and very old paintings hanging along the walls. At the very end of the hallway stood Carlos and Neptune.

"Kyle!" Carlos called out.

Kyle walked up to them. "How was the shooting range last night?" he asked.

"Great! Luckily, nothing in the Bunker was damaged."

"Let's get this over with, yeah?" Neptune said.

Neptune opened the door and let them in. Kyle didn't know what he expected, but it wasn't this.

It was cramped with file cabinets in every corner, bearing giant labels on them like 'Arizona' and 'Michigan'. A giant corkboard at the back of the room had been filled with pictures of supernatural monsters and, papers filled with writing. There was a coffee table in the center with four lounge chairs around it. Ivan was already there, sitting down patiently. He wasn't alone; there was also Aaron, standing in the corner, and a third man staring at the corkboard.

"Good to see you made it in time," Ivan said. "This is Greg. He's the owner of this place." Ivan motioned toward the third man.

Greg turned around. He bore a striking resemblance to Aaron – they were almost perfectly identical, apart from Greg being visibly older. He also had a large scar across his neck, and his left eye was fogged over. He was bald, but his large beard was whiter than snow. Though, it looked even whiter due to his dark complexion. He wore a pair of denim overalls and a white shirt that was slightly torn around the collar. He certainly *looked* like the type of person who owned a farm.

He walked up to Kyle and extended his hand.

"Good to meet you, son." His voice was deeper than Kyle expected. "I heard you killed a werewolf. Made a mess of my table. Thank you for putting that mutt down."

Kyle shook his hand. "Thank you. Um, sir?"

Greg then looked over to Carlos. "And you," he said. "I've been told you're adept with long-range rifles. It's a good skill to have."

"I'm happy to help," Calos said enthusiastically.

Greg walked to the cabinet labeled 'Minnesota' in the back left of the room. He shuffled through the folders and picked one out.

"Now, usually I'd be standing outside to brief new Hunters, but those mutts are out there waiting for me. We're staying in here where it's safe. This is your first assignment."

Kyle felt excited. He was finally being put to use.

Greg placed the folder on the table and opened it for everyone to see. Inside were pictures of a lush green forest, a lake, a cave entrance, a map, and blurry shots of what looked like someone going into the cave. There were also photos of two people with names scrawled beneath them: 'Angus Macmillan' and 'Jesse Thompson'.

"You're to go to a wendigo den near Meeds Lake up in the Misquah Hills of Minnesota and clear out the den.

We sent another team." Greg pointed to the two photos. "These two were sent two weeks ago and we haven't heard anything since. You'll be accompanied by Neptune and Ivan. You may have completed training, but we need to see how you do out in the field. Your main priority is killing the wendigos, but finding out what happened to the other team is also something we'd like to know. Are there any questions?"

Carlos raised his hand. "What's with the overalls?"

Ivan facepalmed at Carlos' obliviousness. "About the mission, idiot."

"Are you and Aaron related?" Kyle asked.

"Yes. I can tell you about it later," Aaron said.

"When are we going?" Carlos replied.

"In about three hours," Ivan said. "Gear up and let's get going."

"Hey," Kyle said. "When I got here my stuff was taken from me. Can I get it back?"

"No. Not until you leave," Greg hissed. "Those mutts can track you from a phone signal. They smell the radio waves — that's how they got here before. Never bring *anything* like that back here!" he screamed, shocking Kyle and Carlos.

"We don't need any more problems! I've had enough bullshit to deal with this week." Greg grabbed the folder and threw it in Kyle's direction, sending the contents flying.

"I ... I ...!" Greg clutched his chest and slowed his breathing.

Aaron stood in front of Greg, looking at him sternly. Greg huffed and turned around, glancing back to the corkboard and leaning on a cabinet to catch his breath.

"I can explain later. But it's best if you all leave for now," Aaron said.

Kyle, Carlos, Ivan, and Neptune all walked out of the room.

"Ivan!" Greg called out. "Send in the next pair!"

"He's kinda weird, huh?" Kyle said to Carlos.

"He's insane," Ivan said.

"Go to the end of the hall. Last door on the left. I'll meet you all in there," Neptune said as he passed Kyle and Carlos and wandered off down the stairs. Ivan took the pair to the room. It was a small library. Bookshelves lined the walls, with two desks on either side.

"In here," Ivan explained, "you can find more information on supernaturals. Everything from weaknesses to behavioral patterns."

"So, we're here to get some books on wendigos?" asked Kyle.

"Yes, just one or two. The wendigo section is over here," Ivan said, moving towards the back of the room to browse through the bookshelves.

Kyle and Carlos stood there while Ivan searched for books. When he found what he was looking for, he passed it over. After five minutes, Kyle had two books in his hands and Carlos had only one. They all sat down, crowding over one of the desks, and started to go through the books. Kyle grabbed the first titled: *Wendigos: What You Need to Know*. It felt old and smelled like dull vanilla. Inside, there were detailed pictures of wendigos' various shapes and sizes, anatomy breakdowns, and their strengths and weaknesses. With every turn of the page, Kyle had to be careful not to tear the thin paper.

Wendigos were thick-skinned. They had sharp claws and fangs, enhanced senses, vocal mimicry, and intelligence. According to the book, their only weaknesses were fire and silver. The fire would have to constantly burn so their skin wouldn't regenerate. Then, silver would be able to finish them off. And once it was dead, the book recommended cremating the body.

There were some loose sheets of paper and pencils sitting neatly at the back of the desk. Kyle picked up one of the pencils, grabbed a sheet of paper, and started to write down notes.

Fire — must always be burning to stop regeneration

Silver — kill

Body — cremate after death (recommended)

Headphones — they scream loud

Cremate after death. Make sure they're dead.

Of course, this was just the list of what they needed to know. If they were all to venture into the wendigo den, they also needed guns. Which meant their next stop would be the armory in the Bunker. Carlos and Ivan packed up the books and sorted them back onto the shelves. Kyle pocketed his notes and took off to the armory ahead of them.

When he opened the Bunker, Neptune was already there, standing in front of the shooting range door, talking to Marcus.

"Hey, Neptune," Kyle said as he walked up to him. "Quick question: what do you look like under that mask?"

"Does it matter?" Neptune said bluntly.

Kyle didn't bother to say anything else. Neptune was very guarded about anything personal. Maybe he was just a little paranoid.

Marcus kept talking to Neptune about this upcoming assignment about what weapons to take.

"Did you have to put them in order of size?" Neptune asked, pointing at the guns hanging up along the left-hand wall.

"I like things to be ordered correctly. It looks nice," Marcus said.

"Let's cut the chit-chat, guys," Kyle interjected. "We're going after wendigos. So, we need silver bullets and flamethrowers."

Marcus smiled. "Look at you! All grown up! Asking me for guns like a proper murderer!" Marcus sounded all gushy.

Kyle stared at him blankly. He didn't like being called a murderer. Neptune probably was staring at disapprovingly Marcus, too.

"What? Can't have a little humor?" Marcus sighed. "Fine. If you want to go after wendigos, you need more than a flamethrower and silver bullets. What you need are dragon's breath rounds – they're shotgun shells that shoot sparks and flames out to about a hundred feet. Very intense and super dangerous if you're on the receiving end. I'm gonna have to insist that you try a few rounds out on our firing range before you take them," Marcus said, opening up one of the many shelves behind his counter and looking through the boxes inside. He finally took out a small box labeled 'Dragon's Breath' and placed it on his desk. The box had a drawing of a red dragon breathing fire on it.

Kyle picked up the box and took out one of the rounds. It looked like an ordinary shotgun shell.

"It wouldn't hurt to see what you'll be dealing with. And that's what it's there for, anyway," Marcus said, taking the shell out of Kyle's hand and placing it back into the box. He then turned his attention to Neptune. "Neptune, can you go ask Adelaide to get some silver-coated daggers made up?"

"Sure thing. Don't waste too many bullets. We need all we can get."

Neptune walked off while Marcus guided Kyle to his shotgun rack.

"What type do you want? Since you're heading into a den, I suggest going with either the sawed-off or the Vepr-12. The sawed-off is good for close and tight corners. The Vepr-16 is a semi-automatic that just came in from Russia. It's got a twenty-round drum magazine. This thing is a beast."

Marcus picked a Vepr-12 shotgun off the rack and handed it to show Kyle. "Here, see how it feels."

Kyle accepted the gun and examined it carefully. The thing was heavy; he had trouble holding it at eye level. It was able to hold more rounds than a sawed-off, but the disadvantage would be reloading the large drum magazine. He fiddled with it, trying to switch drums as fast as possible – removing it and then placing it back on again, practicing.

Marcus handed Kyle a sawed-off as well. "Here," he said.

This gun felt a lot lighter. Kyle practiced swinging it, pretending to hit a wendigo over the head.

"I'll take both. Never can be too cautious. The sawed-off is good for one or two on their own and I can use the Vepr for groups."

Marcus smiled. "Good choice. Let's load up and get to the range." Marcus went back to his desk and took out a box of shotgun shells. He was about to open the shooting range door when Carlos and Ivan stepped into the Bunker.

"Ah, great timing, you two! We're about to test out some guns."

"Fine by me," Ivan said.

Marcus opened the door. The firing range looked slightly different. The targets were brand new, so no bullet holes. There were now spring-loaded targets on the floor and a zip wire running along the roof for targets to whip around.

"When did you have time to fix this up?" Kyle asked, astonished.

"I've had these for a while. Didn't get the time to pull them out while you guys were training. I set everything up while you were all busy rebuilding. But for now, let's just use the stationary targets," Marcus said.

Kyle gave Carlos the sawed-off and he used the Vepr. Ivan and Marcus stood behind them. Kyle loaded up ten shells. He aimed and fired. The kickback from the shotgun hurt his shoulder slightly. He winced and rubbed it. Kyle quickly regained himself and shot again, exhausting the rest of his rounds.

Carlos was faring well with the sawed-off. He made the mistake of only using one hand to fire and the kickback knocked him in the head, but otherwise, he knew how to reload it correctly and quickly.

"Try the dragon's breath," Marcus said to Kyle, pointing at the box next to him.

Kyle took out two rounds and put them in the drum. He didn't want to use them all up. "Want some?" he said to Carlos, throwing a shell towards him.

"What's in it?"

"Put it in and see for yourself," Marcus said.

Kyle waited for Carlos to load his shotgun and fire. When he did, a bright flash shot from the barrel, setting his target on fire. The dragon's breath. Carlos tried to hide the excitement on his face, but it was no use, as he giggled with joy.

"That was insane!" he exclaimed, jumping up and down on the spot. "Give me another!"

Kyle fired his, but he missed the target because he was closing his eyes, afraid the flash would blind him.

"That'll teach you to close your eyes, idiot," Ivan said, smirking.

Kyle opened his eyes and fired again. The flash wasn't as blinding as Kyle thought it would, and the sparks flew out of his shotgun like someone put a firework in it.

Carlos walked over to Kyle and grabbed some shells to "test", and then aimed at the target again.

"Not a toy, Carlos," Marcus said, taking a few of the shells off him and putting them back in the box. "Two more, that's all you get."

"Aw, damn," Carlos said, frowning while looking down at his last two shells.

"Pretty bright, huh Carlos?" Kyle said.

"These are insane! I can't wait to use them," Carlos said, grinning from ear to ear.

Ivan started to walk off. "I'm checking in on Neptune. See what he's grabbing us."

Kyle waved goodbye to Ivan and put his gun down. He'd tested the rounds and was happy with them. He gave the box of shells over to Marcus.

"Can you pack these guns, along with twenty dragon's breath and twenty regular rounds?"

"Sure thing. Carlos, you want the same?"

Carlos looked down at the sawed-off shotgun and fiddled around with it for a few seconds.

"No. I think I'd do better with a regular shotgun. I'll also take a machete if you got them."

"Can do. I'll give you ten of each round as well. I suggest taking the machete over to Adelaide and having it lined with silver."

"I was planning on doing that, don't worry, Marcus," Carlos said, handing Marcus the sawed-off. Marcus took the pair back into the main room of the Bunker. He put the Vepr and the sawed-off on his desk, then walked over to the left side of the room to take a pair of machetes off the wall.

Kyle decided to follow Carlos to the workshop, since Marcus was busy gathering all the guns and ammo, but they were stopped by Aaron just outside the Bunker.

"I feel I must apologize for Greg's actions when you first met him," he said. "He's not exactly all there these days."

"How long have you known him?" Carlos asked.

"His whole life. He's my great-great-grandson. I was here when his father, George, built this farm. I was here when *George's* father, Arthur, purchased this land. And I was here when my son, Nathaniel, was hiding in the tree line behind you from the vampire slave owners that killed me."

Kyle took a moment to take the information in. This place had been in one family for nearly two hundred years. "Was he always like that?" Kyle asked. "He talks down to werewolves like they're nothing."

"No. For a time he was radicalized. But he was a boy then. I had him brought home and taught him a lesson in humility, which straightened him up. His dementia is getting worse each day, and I fear he has not long left. But as much as it pains me to see him slowly degenerate, I still love him so very much." Aaron's voice broke. "He reminds me of Nathaniel."

Aaron quickly turned around. "Forgive me, I have some ... duties to attend to." He strode off into the Big House.

Kyle looked at Carlos. "He's surprisingly emotional when he's not training us."

Carlos agreed. "I like him better this way. He's a lot more fun to be around."

They continued walking until they arrived at the Barn, where they found Neptune chatting to Ivan and Adelaide showing off a weapon rack she'd made. After repairing the damage, Adelaide had taken it upon herself to renovate the whole Barn. It was larger now – there was a new room made from the hole in the wall, which led to a big storage area. An entire wall had been remade, and the singed roof had been replaced. There were large buckets of paint sitting at the entrance, most of which had been emptied.

Unlike Marcus' weapon racks in the Bunker, Adelaide's new room was filled with only melee weapons: knives, stakes, swords, and an assortment of blunt objects. It looked like something a medieval dungeon would have. Carlos pointing out a machete on the wall.

"Marcus is sending over a machete," he told Adelaide. "Can you line it with silver, like that one?"

"Absolutely! How about you two — need silver machetes?" she said to Ivan and Neptune.

"I'm more of a ranged attacker," Neptune said.

"I'll take one." Ivan looked over and saw that Kyle had walked in. "You want one, too?"

Kyle scoffed. "Who wouldn't? That thing could slice through a wendigo like butter if it had silver on it."

Ivan interrupted. "Kyle. Machete. Want one or not?"

"Obviously," he said plainly.

Adelaide's face lit up. "Brilliant! I'll get to work melting the silver. You can all go now. I got lots to do."

Adelaide shooed everyone out of the workshop and shut the doors. Kyle, Carlos, Ivan, and Neptune were all standing outside.

"Is that everything? We got the guns, the notes, and the silver," Kyle said.

"Yeah, that about does it," said Ivan. "I'll go back in and talk to Adelaide; I need to tell her to drop off the machetes in my room, among other things. I have a few errands to run after that. You two get some more practice at the range. Get some food, too, and revise. We leave at midday."

"Before you go," Kyle said. "Could you also take Smith out? He said he wanted to leave."

Ivan scoffed. "That freak is getting nowhere near my car."

Chapter 13

"You wouldn't mind if I asked you about what you saw that night, would you?" he said, taking out a small notepad from his coat.

Kyle thought for a second. There wasn't much for him to do. And Smith might have been a little eccentric, but he seemed to be good at heart.

Kyle shrugged. "Might as well."

Smith beamed with delight. "Oh, brilliant! Please, from the start," he said, edging closer as Kyle began to tell him about what had happened that night.

He started with the night before, when Andrew tried to get him to leave, and how Travis and Andrew were werewolves sent to scope out the Farm and get back to their people, but Greg had confiscated their phones – meaning they were forced to play along for the whole month of training. Kyle ended his account with being brought into the Bunker before passing out, since that's when he stopped experiencing it, too.

Smith almost wrote down Kyle's story word for word, pressing him for more information once Kyle said he was done.

"Sorry, that's it. Try asking Carlos or Adelaide."

"Ooh, that is a good idea. Thank you, Kyle." Smith made a quick exit from the Bunkhouse, already reviewing his notes and mumbling about what changes to make.

Kyle knew there was no point in staying in there alone, so he got up and decided to go check with Adelaide on the progress of the machetes. Something caught his eye as he headed over to the workshop: Ivan had brought his car into the open field. He parked it just in front of Kyle and got out.

"Where have you been hiding this?" Kyle said, running his hand along the bonnet.

"There's a small parking lot near the entrance."

"Huh. Where is the entrance?"

Ivan pointed to the right of the Big House. There were two trees far enough apart for a car to drive through, leading onto a dirt road. Debris and track marks had cleared the foliage, creating an opening onto the Farm – likely from the werewolf attack. It made the road look more visible than it was probably supposed to be.

"It's that way, you just need to follow the dirt path past those two trees."

"Hey. Since, you know, I'm actually in the 'Hunter club' now, can I know where we are?"

"We're still in Illinois. A very secluded part down south."

"Really – I never left Illinois?" Kyle sounded surprised.

"It's a big state. Now, you want to help me load up the car? Marcus said he's got everything ready for us. We have a lot of bags to pack."

"Might as well." Kyle shrugged as he followed Ivan down into the Bunker.

Marcus had prepared two large duffel bags, which were sitting in the center of the room.

"Got everything the four of you asked," Marcus said, sitting behind his desk, arms folded while he leaned back on his chair.

Kyle picked up the larger bag, not realizing how heavy it was. "What's in this one, Marcus?"

"You can look if you want to," Marcus replied, smirking. Kyle set it back on the ground and unzipped it. Inside was the guns they had asked for – four of each – as well as boxes of ammunition.

"What's in the second one, then? Everything we asked for is in this one."

"Extras." Marcus winked.

Kyle picked the bag up again and left the Bunker with Ivan. "Should we maybe keep this one in the back seat instead of the trunk?" he asked.

"No. Just throw everything in the trunk. It'll be too cramped otherwise. We're going to the airport, and I'd rather get there sooner than later."

"Are you sure they'll let us through with all these guns?" Kyle asked, rightfully concerned.

"Do you remember what I told you when we first met? The supernatural are everywhere. That means we have to be, too. We have Hunters working in airports all across the globe. Pilots, security, and the like. All we need to do is tell them we have a meeting with Mr. Hyde and they'll slip us through security and onto a private plane. It's makes traveling internationally a lot easier. Usually, we would get to our destination by car, but for this, we'll need to take a plane. This mission is too urgent and air travel's faster." Ivan opened the trunk of his car and tossed the duffel bag in. As he did, Kyle caught sight of something on Ivan's right arm.

"What's that?" he said, pointing. "That mark on your arm."

"Oh. It's a tattoo. Nothing special." Ivan rolled his sleeve back and showed the tattoo to Kyle. It was hard for him to make out – two words written in an unconventional, almost gothic, font.

"What's it say?"

"*Memento Mori.*"

"What's it mean?"

Ivan rolled his sleeve back down. "Not important. Now get in the car. I'm fetching Carlos and Neptune."

Kyle didn't bother pressing the subject further and complied. He sat in the passenger seat and waited calmly for Ivan to return. He took out his notes on wendigos to kill time. It seemed like a few seconds had gone by when the passenger door opened again.

"Get in the back." It was Neptune. Kyle simply nodded and got in the back seat with Carlos. Kyle saw that Neptune was carrying his jet-black bag with him.

He didn't part with it, but instead placed it on his lap when he sat down.

"By the way, Carlos, I sorted this out for you." Neptune reached into his bag and pulled out a folder, handing it to Carlos.

When he opened it, he saw an American birth certificate, along with a driver's license and other documents.

"Wow. You got all this for me?" Carlos asked.

"I was getting them sorted out for everyone you arrived with, but you know what happened there. Those are good, so no one will know they're fake. Congratulations on being an American citizen since birth."

Carlos took out the ID and looked at it admiringly, before his face quickly changed into a sour expression.

"Why did you put my real birthdate?"

"Didn't say I'd make you old enough to drink, mate. You get it and that's it."

Carlos scrunched his face. "Oh well, thanks anyway, buddy!"

"Everyone ready?" Ivan asked. All three nodded.

He started the car and slowly pulled out into the woods toward the exit. But he was stopped by Smith, who had run out of the Bunkhouse and stood in front of the car. Ivan stopped and honked his horn. "Out of the way!" he shouted, swiping his arm.

Smith walked up to the back door and opened it calmly, pushing Kyle aside as he stepped in. "Very sorry. You see, I have to leave. And I know you are going to the airport, so I decided to join you all."

"Get out, right now," Ivan said angrily, gritting his teeth.

"Oh, just let him, Ivan," Kyle said. "It's not like he's gonna be here long."

"My car, my rules. Out."

"Just fucking go, mate," Neptune said.

Ivan grumbled and begrudgingly started to drive again.

Kyle looked back through the rear window. He was leaving this place for the first time in what felt like forever. He was glad to finally put all his training to use. Unlike last time when he was trapped in a room with a werewolf who had a vendetta against him, he'd be fighting monsters. Real monsters.

The car slowly made its way through the woods. Kyle could see the clearing, past which point there was nothing but trees and a dirt road. The road stretched far into the distance. At the end was a mesh gate. Ivan had to get out and manually open it, then close it once they passed. The gravel path continued still, but was shorter than before.

"I can see a road!" Carlos blurted out from the back seat. The gravel path led onto a concrete road with lanes going left and right.

"We're a little outside of Farina, Illinois. We have an hour and a half drive to the airport," Ivan said.

"Farina? Never heard of it," Kyle said.

"It's in the south of Illinois. The nearest city is St. Louis in Missouri. We're going to the airport in downtown St. Louis," Neptune interjected.

"Wait. Carlos, you told me Neptune found you trying to cross the border. Why are you here and not somewhere close by, like the hideout in California?"

"Because I had business to attend to here," Neptune said. "Most Hunters will usually train people personally, unless there's a big group or some other situation. Plus, the Farm is the one hideout that's completely hidden. Rest are just fancy houses on large blocks of land."

"What about you, Ivan – what place did you train at?" Kyle asked.

"Not one in America." Ivan seemed to be disinterested in the conversation. No one pressed him further. Instead, Kyle took to looking out the window and the trees as they went by. The trees slowly turned into vast corn fields with wire fences. The road was straight, with no traffic in sight. Kyle had never left Aurora before; this part of the state was alien to him. He was used to the bustling cityscape and suburban neighborhoods.

"This place looks cleaner than what I had back home," Carlos said.

"Your house in Mexico?" asked Kyle.

"Yeah. It was horrible there. I lived in the outskirts of Ciudad Juárez. This tiny little orphanage I was in with my friends. I tried to apply for a work visa, but it never got approved. That's why I tried to get in illegally. I met some guys who said they'd smuggle me in for a fee, but they turned out to be vampires. Neptune saved me, and that's how I got here."

"What were you doing in Mexico, Neptune?" Ivan asked.

"I got a tip that vampires were posing as people smugglers in Mexico. Just saved him in time."

"What about you, Ivan, what were you doing Aurora the night we met?" asked Kyle.

"I was tipped off about a werewolf ring that was forcefully turning humans to boost their numbers. The guy I killed, Damien, was one of the werewolves I was keeping tabs on."

The rest of the ride was mostly quiet. Kyle asked Ivan to turn on the radio, but he insisted it was broken. Smith was in his own little world, muttering to himself while writing in his journal. Kyle kept looking out the window. He watched the scenery as they passed by. Trees and grass. Just that and the straight road. They did eventually get to a small town, but this was just to pass through. It was a nice change of pace, seeing some form of society, but then it went straight back to trees and grass.

"Are we—"

"Twenty minutes. Just wait a little longer," Ivan said. Kyle looked to see what Carlos and Neptune were up to. Carlos was staring out his window and Neptune was sitting still, looking forward. He could've been asleep, but it was hard to tell. Kyle just looked forward and watched the road. He took out the small bottle of antibiotics and read the label; it was surprisingly interesting to read what was in it.

Eventually, they reached St. Louis. Kyle felt relief. He was back to civilization.

"You won't get used to it," Ivan said, looking at Kyle and Carlos in his rear-view mirror. "Now that you two are Hunters, you won't be able to see the world the same again. That, and sometimes assignments will take you to uninhabited places."

It was an unwelcome statement, but it had to be said. It felt like it was just hitting home for Kyle. This was his life now; endlessly traveling to deal with supernatural threats. But he kept his chin up and put that in the back of his mind. For now, he could at least enjoy not having to look at the trees and grass, and, at the very least, living a life filled with adventure. He watched as the road became livelier and the buildings became more abundant. He wound down the window next to Smith and took a deep breath. The city air smelled different, and Kyle welcomed it.

"There's the airport." Ivan pointed to his left.

"Finally!" Carlos exclaimed, seeming exhausted with boredom.

Ivan pulled into the airport and found a parking space. It took a while, as there were a lot of cars and they ended up a fair way away from the airport itself. Everyone got out. Ivan opened the trunk of the car and gave everyone a bag.

"Wait," said Kyle. 'What about Neptune? Isn't it gonna be weird for someone to walk into an airport looking like that?"

"I'll be going on ahead. Don't worry about me." Neptune picked up his bag and left the three, heading on into the airport. Kyle could see him removing his mask and pulling off his hood before entering, but since his back was turned, he couldn't see his face.

"What are you looking at? Take a bag and let's go." Kyle turned as Ivan put a bag into his hands. Ivan then put the trunk down and locked the car.

"You can make your way from here, Smith. See ya," Ivan said bluntly.

"Oh yes," Smith said, smiling. "I must check the departure times for New York flights. Hopefully, I will not have to wait for long."

Smith started to scuttle away before stopping and turning around. He walked up to Kyle and pulled out a business card from his breast pocket. "Please do keep in touch. You see, this wendigo situation could make a good story."

Kyle looked at the card. It read 'Smith's Novella and Antique Emporium' with a number and address written at the bottom. Kyle pocketed the card next to his antibiotics.

"I'll call you when I can. See ya, Smith." He went to shake Smith's hand, which Smith reciprocated happily.

"Be seeing you, Mr. McManus." He smiled and walked off.

Ivan looked worriedly at Kyle. "You know he's gonna make a skin suit out of you?"

"He's not that bad. What do you have against him?" Kyle said accusingly.

"He just ... gives me the creeps. Let's just go." Ivan led Kyle and Carlos into the airport.

"Follow me closely," he explained. "It's easy for us to get pegged by one of the regular security guards here. Just act like you're not carrying a bag full of weapons through and airport. Look straight forward instead of looking at every single person you walk past."

Kyle and Carlos glanced at each other, concerned. Was he being sarcastic? They followed Ivan, walking through the airport. Kyle kept looking ahead while Carlos' eyes darted around. Kyle nudged him. "Calm down. Okay?"

Carlos nodded. "Yeah, just, uh … It's—it's just hard." Carlos kept his eyes fixed on Ivan. There was a very visible gleam of sweat on his forehead.

Once they got to the baggage screening area, Kyle saw there was a door to the right guarded by two security guards. Ivan led them to it. One of the guards stepped in front of the door and held his hand out, stopping them.

"This area is off-limits," he said.

"We have an appointment with Mr. Hyde. He's expecting us," Ivan said.

The guard put down his hand and laughed.

"I know. It's good to see you again, Ivan. Now get in quickly. The big guy already boarded."

Ivan gave the security guard his keys.

"Can you take my car back to the Farm for me?"

"Yeah, I'll drive back after my shift ends." He smiled and the three walked through. It was a small hallway, all white, with nothing but a door on the other end. Like a secret passage.

"By 'big guy', he meant Neptune, right?" asked Carlos.

"Yeah, but I doubt he knew it was him. Mask was off."

Ivan opened the door at the end of the hallway. It simply led to the other side of the security checkpoint, allowing them to bypass it. Ivan pointed out the window to a small plane on the runway.

"That's our ride." He led Kyle and Carlos through the airport and to a door that led outside. Standing there was another security guard.

"Nice to see you again, Ivan. New recruits?"

"Yeah, first assignment. Anyone else boarded?"

"Just one. Already on."

"Good."

The security guard opened the door to the runway. The door to the private jet was already open, waiting for its passengers to board. Ivan, Kyle, and Carlos all walked to the jet and got on.

It looked like the inside of a mansion.

A gray plaid carpet lined the floor. The seats were lined with fine white leather, with fancy pillows and blankets folded neatly on top. At the back of the jet, there was a couch and a table, with two chairs at both ends. Sitting there was Neptune, his mask back on. Ivan put his bag next to his chair and sat opposite Neptune. Kyle and Carlos sat together on the couch.

"Ever flown on a private jet before?" Ivan said to Kyle.

"First time on a plane," he replied. "What about you, Carlos?"

"Same." Carlos was looking around the plane, mesmerized by the quality of everything around him.

"How can you afford this?" Carlos asked.

"It's not mine," Ivan replied. "But some Hunters made a few good investments in the past. We've also got a few people in the right professions to help us out."

The pilot's voice came over the speaker. *"Afternoon, everyone. We'll be arriving at the Grand Marais Airport near the Misquah Hills in one hour and fifteen minutes. Please remain seated while we take off."*

The plane moved along the tarmac and picked up speed to take off. As it started to elevate, Kyle fell to one side, as he was still sitting on the couch. Carlos fell on top of him. They picked themselves back up as the plane gained altitude.

"You'll get used to this in due time," said Ivan. "Going through airports is going to be a big part of your job unless you want to settle down in a single city."

"I'd imagine there are a lot of Hunters who have settled down, right?" asked Kyle.

"Yes. Most do tend to stay grounded or travel across the country by car. But some get called out somewhere and they need to take a flight. Like us. The wendigo problem was urgent, but if it wasn't, we could've driven the whole way. That would've taken about twelve hours."

"I don't think spending twelve hours in the car would've done us any favors, Ivan. No offense mate, but it's seen better days," Neptune said.

"I bought that thing when it was new. I'm aware of how beat up it is but it's a lot cheaper to keep it than replace it."

"How very sentimental of you, Ivan," said Neptune. "The first car I bought was Fiat Cinquecento. Had it for two years. It was run off the road by a werewolf. Written off."

The pilot came over the speaker again.

"We're approaching cruising altitude, people. You can start any preparations now."

"Preparations?" asked Kyle. "What preparations?"

"We can prep our weapons for when we land." Neptune rifled through his bag. "Get those bags you carried on onto the table. We need to take inventory and load up everything."

Kyle and Carlos complied and took their bags out. The four of them placed everything on the table. All up, there were: two silver-tipped machetes, four sawed-off shotguns, two Vepr-12 shotguns with four twenty-round drum magazines, two Remington 1100 shotguns, four Molotov cocktails, eight twenty-four-round shotgun shell boxes, four ten-round dragon's breath shotgun shell boxes, four lighters, four holsters, four flashlights, four pairs of earplugs, four body vests, and four bandoliers.

"Looks like Marcus got ahead of himself when he was packing everything up for us," Kyle said, picking up one of the Molotovs.

"Why do we only have four boxes of dragon's breath rounds but eight boxes of regular rounds? And there's less in the dragon's breath boxes," Carlos noted, immediately unboxing a dragon's breath box. He'd only wanted to use the dragon's breath.

"We didn't have a lot of the dragon's breath on hand," Neptune said, swiping the box away from Carlos. "We were given what we needed. A regular shotgun round can wound a wendigo, but a dragon's breath will slow it down more – even kill it if you aim it right. There's a good chance we can get through this without using any dragon's breath rounds," he added, stopping Carlos from asking any more questions.

"Okay, but what about the other shotguns? I thought we were all getting the Veprs," said Kyle.

"The Remingtons were my idea," said Ivan. "They're slower than the Veprs but easier to reload. Just slot the shells into them – you need to detach the drum on the Vepr, then place another one in there. Under pressure, there's a good chance you can mess up with the Vepr more than with the Remington."

"And the vests I assume are for protection?"

"Yes. Wendigo claws can cut deep, and you're still healing from the werewolf attack, Kyle. You could use as much protection as possible."

Carlos pointed to the Molotovs. "Do we use the Molotovs on the wendigos to kill them, or to destroy the bodies?"

Either or," Ivan said. "Whatever the situation calls for, but preferably to kill 'em." Ivan picked up a Vepr-12 and a Remington shotgun and held them outwards. "Now, what are you going to pick? You two have to choose between these as your primaries."

Carlos and Kyle looked at each other.

"What do you prefer, Carlos?" asked Kyle.

"I, uh, don't really have a preference."

"Mind if I take the Vepr?"

Carlos shrugged. "Go for it."

Ivan threw the Vepr at Kyle and the Remington at Carlos.

"Time to load up, you two. We have all these rounds to split and organize into the drums."

The four of them split everything evenly into small sections on the table. Kyle and Ivan had the Veprs; they ended up with one hundred and twenty-eight shotgun rounds between the two of them. Sixty-four each. Carlos and Neptune had the Remingtons. They had one hundred and four total, or fifty-two each, including the forty dragon's breath rounds. They all got to work with loading their bandoliers. Kyle and Ivan had to load up the drum magazines for their guns, which took significantly longer than the Remingtons. Meanwhile, Carlos and Neptune only had to load up their shotguns once, and all of them needed to load the sawed-offs. Ivan looked into his bag to see if he had forgotten anything, and sure enough, he had. He placed the two items he missed onto the table. There were satchels.

"These are for holding the Vepr drums, Kyle. Take one and put your extra magazine in it."

Kyle complied and took one. He put it next to his gun as he loaded his drums. He only had ten dragon's breath rounds, so he split them between his two guns. He put four rounds in each drum, every fifth shot, and the remaining two were placed in his sawed-off. If he was going to use his sidearm, it would be as a last resort.

He then placed his first drum into his Vepr-12 and the other one into the satchel Ivan gave him. He stood up and slung it around his shoulder. Then, he grabbed his Vepr-12 and flung that over his back, making an 'X' with the straps on his front. He turned to Ivan.

"How do I look?" he asked.

"Like a proper Hunter," Ivan said, with a faint smile.

Kyle took off the bag and gun sat back down to get to work. He loaded the sawed-off and put it in his holster. He had just started to work on his bandolier when he spoke up.

"You guys want to sit in silence or actually talk? I really hope this isn't going to be the norm."

Neptune looked at him. "I'm not one for small talk, honestly. Not much to talk about."

Kyle turned to Ivan. "What about you, Ivan; got any good stories to pass the time?"

Ivan was working on his bandolier.

"A few. I could tell you about the time I almost killed Dracula."

Carlos piped up. "You met him? What's he like?"

"Yes Carlos, I met him. He's a dick. Now." Ivan cleared his throat. "It was twenty years ago ..."

Chapter 14

North Las Vegas, 1988

Ivan pulled over, looking at the large mansion that lay at the end of the road. Smith was in the passenger seat, giving Ivan some last-minute advice.

"You see, Vladimir will be on the top floor. I suggest making sure you can get out as quickly as possible. I have the transceivers all sorted out. Make sure to switch it on so we can communicate. I will be standing by with your car, ready to leave post-haste. You must not take your time. Please be efficient as possible. You only have one chance."

"Yeah, yeah. I get it. Be fast. Just keep my car running. Have you got your end sorted out? I doubt it's gonna be an easy escape."

Ivan got out of his car. His muscular frame was encapsulated in his tight gray t-shirt. His head was full of graying hair that had been combed back, and his salt and pepper beard was neatly trimmed. He opened the trunk and took out a large duffel bag. Smith walked up behind him.

"One last gift. Joshua made it just before we left." He handed Ivan a green messenger bag.

"Is this what I think it is?" Ivan asked, shaking the bag to gauge what was inside. "I thought he couldn't make it in time?"

"He put her training on hold to make it. He said the girl could wait one extra day."

Ivan scoffed. "Adelaide's gonna be pissed tomorrow. Pretty feisty for a six-year-old."

Smith got into the driver's seat. "I will be waiting until it is safe to plant the explosives. Please do not make me wait too long."

"This is gonna take maybe ten minutes. The second I walk in, start."

Smith nodded and waited patiently in the car. Ivan began to walk, examining the contents of his duffel bag. He had a shotgun with two bandoliers, a Walkman with a cassette and headphones, a spray bottle, and a large cross-shaped silver stake – an MVK.

"Let's hope the holy water hasn't worn off yet," he said to himself, pulling the MVK out and twirling it around, getting used to its weight. Lights from the upcoming mansion illuminated the night sky. As he got closer, he could hear the party in full swing. He saw the guests inside, vampires, eagerly awaiting their guest of honor.

Ivan took out his transceiver and turned it on. "You hearing me okay?" he asked Smith.

"*Yes. Yes. Perfectly,*" Smith replied.

"Good. I'll be keeping this on. Once it's safe, get out and do your part."

Ivan tucked the transceiver into his belt and continued walking. As he neared, he looked around to see if anyone was lingering around. Thankfully, there wasn't.

Ivan stopped just before he got to the house and geared up. He put his headphones and Walkman on. Strapped his bandoliers around him; the shotgun slung over one shoulder, his satchel over the other. And his MVK, which was too bulky to hold, he kept in the duffel bag. He could reach in and grab it easily. He had everything he needed. His shotgun shells had silver dust mixed in with the gunpowder, which would give the vampires a severe burn in addition to the wound. His Walkman was to help dampen the damage he would get from the vampires' screeching and the blasts of his gun. The MVK was to finish off the only vampire Ivan was there for: Vladimir Dracula.

"I must again remind you to be efficient as possible," Smith said from the transceiver. *"You will only have one chance at this."*

Ivan grumbled and ignored him. He scoped out the mansion. It was vastly larger compared to the rural houses of the surrounding area, secluded in a street with only five other houses. Ivan guessed that all these houses were owned by Dracula and his vampires.

Ivan snuck around the back of the house carefully, hoping that no one saw him. He took out his transceiver and whispered into it, "Now, Smith."

Smith didn't respond, but Ivan saw the car slowly approaching. He knew that he didn't have much time to distract the vampires. If any of them saw Smith, then Ivan would have to bail early.

He got lucky; the back door was wide open. But the bad news was the backyard *wasn't* empty. There was a group of vampires mulling around an empty pool, chatting. Ivan was too far away to hear, so he kept his focus on the door. He didn't know if anyone would be coming in or out of that door. He had to move fast. With no intel on the house's layout, knowing what was just inside that door was a complete guess.

Just then, his window of opportunity presented itself. A woman came through the back door.

"Everyone, get ready!" she announced to the group. "It's speech time!"

The group immediately got to work. There was a large water tank behind them, which they began to drain into the pool.

It was blood.

Ivan ignored this – he had to get inside. Knowing they were preoccupied, he wasted no time and snuck in through the back door.

Thankfully, the back door led into the kitchen, which was empty.

He could see everyone congregating in the main living room up ahead. Ivan took this time to double-check his equipment and take a deep breath.

"Okay," he said to himself. "Five minutes. That's all I need."

Ivan got into position in the kitchen, right next to the living room. Once he turned the corner, he would be in the open. Fully exposed. He had to take it slow. He waited to hear the voice. Dracula wouldn't take long to start his speech.

"I'm so glad you all turned up tonight!" Ivan heard Dracula speak. His fake British accent always annoyed him – it sounded too posh and pompous. But his supporters thought differently. They cheered, whooped, and applauded every single word out of his mouth.

"I have a special treat for all of you. Momentarily, that delectable pool out back will be drained and filled with the blood I've been saving up since the beginning of the year. We will bathe in our delectable wine!"

The crowd roared. Ivan knew that enough was enough. He didn't have the time left. Dracula was there, which meant it was now or never.

He took one last breath and walked out into the open, amongst the cheering crowd.

The living room was much larger than he thought; larger than that of a regular house. Filled to the brim with vampires. And, at the top of the grand staircase, Dracula.

"That's enough!" Ivan roared, stepping out into the middle of the room. He made eye contact with Dracula only. He was dressed splendidly in tight black trousers and a white shirt. He had on a red paisley vest with a matching tie. His thin black hair was tied up neatly in a ponytail, showing off his sharp facial features.

Every eye immediately turned to him, before reaching a sudden realization of who he was.

"Of course," Dracula said blandly. "You Hunters always ruin the fun."

There was a wave of hissing from the surrounding vampires. Ivan dropped his duffel bag and cocked his shotgun.

"No talking. Let's just get this over with." Ivan pressed play on his Walkman. Thankfully, the correct tape was inserted. It was his favorite song; Don McLean's 'American Pie'.

"Kill him," Dracula said, waving a hand without care.

The first vampire that came close to Ivan was stopped when Ivan grabbed it by the neck, and his skin started to burn.

"I came prepared," Ivan said, aiming his shotgun at the vampire's face and putting the trigger, blasting him away immediately.

Just then, a stampede of vampires lunged at Ivan. He ducked and rolled out of the way, shooting anything that got nearby.

He backed up against the wall. It wasn't the best strategy, but at least he wouldn't be taken by surprise. He took out his spray bottle and started to mist the air around him. A few vampires walked through it, only for their faces to burn. Ivan took this opportunity to shove them, knocking down those behind them. He vaulted over them, trying to desperately get closer to Dracula. He shot his way through the crowd, not even stopping to reload. A vampire grabbed him by the neck, ignoring the sizzling of its skin, edging closer to sinking its teeth into Ivan. Ivan quickly filled his barrel and cocked the gun, turning his head to aim just behind him. He pulled the trigger, momentarily deafening himself.

"Ah, shit!" Ivan cried. "Knew I shouldn't have done that!"

Ivan slung his shotgun around his shoulder and took out the item tucked away in the satchel: a bullwhip, with the end made of small silver strings.

He spun it around, the vampires around him keeping their distance. He targeted a vampire in front of him and cracked his whip in its face. The vampire dropped to the ground, screaming in pain, with a large part of its face burning away.

Ivan smirked. He wound up and cracked his whip in a frenzy. Any vampire hit would be in severe pain. Each crack of the whip was like a bolt of lightning striking the vampires. He managed to hit one of the vampires in the heart, evaporating it in an instant. His accuracy wasn't the best, but Ivan didn't stop. He needed this window to have some breathing room from the outnumbering vampires.

He continued to use his whip, taking out a good number of the vampires around him – at least twenty by his count.

A vampire lunged at him from the second floor, toppling Ivan and knocking his whip out of reach. Ivan kicked the vampire off him and pulled his shotgun out again, shooting the vampire and killing it.

Ivan got back up and ran towards his duffel bag, unzipping it and pulling out the MVK, then spinning it around to show the other vampires.

"Back off right now!" he said, flashing the cross around him. The vampires kept their distance, trying to find a way around his defenses.

"I only need to use this on one of you," Ivan said, pointing his MVK towards Dracula.

Dracula scowled. "Enough of this! Kill him *now*!" he bellowed, almost shaking the ground with just his words.

The vampires all attacked at once. Ivan knew that this was it. He had only one chance. He had his shotgun in one hand, and the MVK in his other.

But the vampires were closing in on him. He dashed the stairs, only to be bitten on his wrist; a vampire smirking at him as it started to drink. Another grabbed his other arm and also began to drink, ignoring all pain. He felt himself being pulled back into the crowd by hungry vampires – he would be drained in an instant. Ivan looked up and saw a chandelier right above him. He shrugged the vampires off his arms, took aim, and fired.

The chandelier came down on the vampires, knocking Ivan free and giving him enough to time regain himself.

"*Ivan? Ivan?*" Smith's voice came over the transceiver. "*I am ready.*"

Ivan could barely hear him. But he knew that Smith calling meant time was almost up. He made one final sprint up the staircase towards Dracula, ignoring everything else around him.

Dracula remained standing at the top of the staircase, surrounded by a group of loyal vampires. He looked down and Ivan, disinterested in his attempt to kill him. He merely smirked. "Better luck next time." Then he waved and walked off with his group.

Ivan flared up, mustered all his strength, and threw the MVK at Dracula.

The MVK went soaring through the air on a direct path towards Dracula, but it was grabbed by another vampire before it could reach him.

The vampire's hand began to burn badly, immediately dropping the MVK to reveal bright red flesh.

Dracula looked at his savior, tutting as he examined the wound. "Shame. This will take some time to heal. You've earned a reward, Arthur."

The vampire bowed his head. "Thank you, Lord Dracula."

Dracula and his group proceeded to leave.

Ivan screamed in anger. He shrugged off the vampires feeding on him and dashed the stairs. He picked up his transceiver. "Smith. Do it! Now!"

Smith didn't respond – not with words, anyway.

The ground floor erupted in explosions, killing a vast number of vampires as they rushed Ivan. The second floor gave way and collapsed, and Ivan fell into the rubble.

Ivan picked himself up as fast as possible. He first tried to find his whip, with no luck. Nor could he find the MVK he'd thrown. He still had his shotgun and Walkman, which had stopped playing.

Ivan wasted no time in leaving. He escaped through the front door, which had been blown open from the explosion.

He was dizzy. The effect from the various vampire bites and the drained blood was starting to hit him as the adrenaline wore off. Ivan had no choice but to leave; the mansion was crumbling and would give way soon, and he didn't want to be caught in it.

Smith was waiting patiently by the car.

"How did it go?" he asked. Ivan didn't reply. He threw his shotgun and Walkman in the back seat and got into the passenger side.

Smith got in and drove away. Ivan looked at the mansion in the rear-view mirror.

He started beating the dashboard and screaming. "*Fuck*! Fuckfuckfuckfuck*fuck*! *FUCKKKKKK*!"

He took a heavy breath and passed out.

Chapter 15

"Wow," Carlos said, astonished. "That was awesome!"

Ivan scowled at Carlos. "No it wasn't, Carlos. I had my chance and almost died because of it."

Carlos' face dimmed and he looked down at his gun.

"Hey, how'd you find the place anyway?" Kyle asked.

"Well," Ivan said, "He holds these yearly festivals and I managed to find out where it was. I had no idea he owned a bunch of houses in Vegas. Got a tip from an old friend about it. I honestly didn't believe it at first. Seemed too bland for Vlad."

"Vlad?" Carlos asked. "Why not call him Dracula?"

"I'm on a first-name basis with him," Ivan said sarcastically.

"Okay, that's cool. But why couldn't the vampires touch you?" Kyle asked.

"Easy. I bathed in holy water before I got there. Didn't know how long it would last so I had to be quick. It started to wear off just before the explosion. So, it lasts about an hour if I'm remembering correctly."

"What about the cross?" Carlos asked.

"The Master Vampire Killer. MVK. A silver stake shaped like a cross and covered with holy water. If you kill a master vampire with one of those, then everyone they've turned will become human again. Everyone inside that mansion of his was someone he'd turned. I was trying to save them and wake them up from the delusions Vlad promised. I had to deal with at least two hundred vampires."

Kyle and Carlos looked shocked. "Two hundred vampires?" Kyle asked. "How'd you survive?"

"Smith. After we escaped, he took me to the nearest hospital. I was still turning from the bites, so we couldn't stay long. He brought me back to the Farm, where I was locked in the attic for three days until I became human again."

Kyle and Carlos were awestruck. It sounded almost impossible. One man against two hundred vampires and he got out almost unharmed.

"Still, I didn't get off lightly. Greg told me not to go since he needed me for something else, and I couldn't pass the opportunity off. My punishment was that I had to stay at the Farm and couldn't leave the state. This is the first time I've been allowed to leave Illinois since then."

"Why didn't you just leave?" Carlos asked. "It's not like he could find you."

"Actually," Neptune said, "Greg said that if Ivan left, he would put a hit on him. Greg still has lots of connections."

"What about others?" Carlos asked. "Have you ever met the Devil?"

"Yes, Carlos, and he's an asshole. Here's a tip. If you ever get the chance to meet him, just tell him to fuck off. Don't listen to anything he has to say. Way too charismatic for his own good. Literally. He'll find a way to try and get you to sell your soul to him."

"What happens if you do?"

"I don't exactly know. I do know that Satan gives you one wish if you do sell him your soul. And that wish can be fulfilled as long as it meets his criteria. Then you'd be indebted to him in some way. Just don't do it." Ivan got back to finishing up his bandolier. Carlos looked like he had a lot more questions to ask but didn't want to bother Ivan any longer, so he continued with his preparations.

The four finished up their preparations and started to outfit themselves. Everyone had body armor and bandoliers under their shirts, which they then buttoned up. The machetes were strapped to their legs, with the sawed-off shotguns holstered to the other. Kyle was left-handed, so his shotgun was strapped to the opposite leg than everyone else's. Kyle and Ivan had the Vepr-12 shotguns strapped over their shoulders, as well as the spare barrel in a satchel across their other shoulder. Carlos and Neptune had the Remington shotguns over their shoulders. They all had spare ammunition and the lighters and flashlights on their belts. Kyle stuffed his Molotov in his jacket's inside pocket. All but Carlos had an inside pocket, so his was on his belt next to the lighter. Kyle placed his earplugs in his right front pocket.

The four of them looked like they were hunting a pack of bears, which would've been a lot easier than what they were actually facing.

"Damn," Carlos said. "We look awesome!" He beamed with excitement.

"Okay. Looks like everything's all prepped. Now let's pack all this away, apart from your body vests – we don't want to alarm anyone when we land," Ivan said, starting to take everything off.

"Wait," said Kyle. "What was the point of gearing up if we're taking everything right off?"

"We're just checking to see how it all fits. We do this now rather than on-site in case you need anything adjusted. Kills less time," answered Neptune.

Kyle sighed and took everything off. He got it. It was necessary to make sure everything was good beforehand, but he still felt down. He'd gotten pumped up and was immediately deflated. He packed everything carefully into his bag and zipped it up.

"What do we do with the cartridge boxes?"

"We can leave them here," answered Ivan. "The cabin crew will make sure they're disposed of." Kyle placed the bag next to his side of the couch and sat back down.

There was an eerie silence on the plane. Kyle sat on the couch, playing with his thumbs, and occasionally looking out of the window to see what was below.

"So, how much longer?" he finally asked.

"I don't know. Go ask the pilot if you want," Ivan said.

At that point, the pilot's voice came over the speaker.

"I hope you've finished with preparations. We will be arriving within twenty minutes."

Ivan smiled and threw his hands in the air. "There, you have your answer."

He sat back, pulled a small book out from his jacket pocket, and started to read. Carlos looked out the window, and Neptune practiced idly with his machete. Kyle decided to clean up the cartridge boxes into a neat pile on the table. Then, he got up and went to the bathroom to clear his head.

The bathroom was a lot different to a normal airplane cubicle. This was a private jet, so it looked more like the restroom of a fancy hotel. This didn't just mean more space, but more items inside. The sink had cabinets underneath it, there was a shower in the corner, and a large circular mirror above the sink. Kyle opened the cabinet to find a first aid kit and a hairdressing kit tucked in the corner. He took out the hairdressing kit and opened it up. Inside was a pair of hair clippers, a small bag of hair ties, and an electric razor; along with extra batteries. He looked at himself in the mirror. He hadn't seen his reflection at all during training – there was no mirror in the Bunkhouse. When he thought back, there hadn't been a single mirror at the Farm at all. His stubble had gotten long enough to be a scruffy beard. He hated that Travis' nickname for him had been accurate. He felt his beard, examining its length and gently stroking it. He turned on the razor and started to trim. His facial hair fell into a small pile in the sink.

Once he was done, his beard was a lot shorter. It wasn't quite the stubble he had before, but it was still nice and trimmed. After taking a few minutes to make sure everything was straight on both sides, and cleaning up the sink, he walked back out and sat back on the couch.

"Back to normal, I see," said Carlos.

"You should probably get yourself cleaned up, too, Carlos. Your hair's starting to get a little long. And that goatee of yours screams 'Satan'." Kyle joked. "He does have the goatee, right?" he asked Ivan, who replied by sighing in annoyance.

"Yes, he's got the goatee. He gets mad when you point it out."

Carlos got up and walked to the bathroom. "I'm cutting my hair, but not my goatee. I like it," he said, shutting the door.

"Have either of you two hunted wendigos before?" Kyle looked at Ivan and Neptune.

"No," said Ivan.

"Once," said Neptune. "It was a few years ago, but it was only one. A survivor of a previous attack by Hunters. I was sent to finish it off. Simple work. One is easy, but this is a full den we're facing. My advice: don't believe the screams. Since they can mimic voices, it's easy to be lured in."

Kyle nodded in agreement and laid back on the couch, silently waiting for the jet to land. After about a minute, Carlos walked out of the bathroom. His hair looked worse than before. It was all chopped unevenly. He looked ridiculous. He walked up to Kyle.

"What do you think? Be honest."

"It's horrible. Honestly," Ivan said sarcastically. "Have you ever cut your hair before?"

"Well, no. But I thought I did well for a first try."

Neptune sighed. "I'll clean it up."

He put his arm around Carlos and brought him back to the bathroom. Kyle decided to look out the window. He could see the airport they were heading toward. It seemed very small and surrounded by a thick tree line. The ground getting closer. They wouldn't be in the air much longer. The pilot's voice came over the speaker once more.

"Everyone please get seated, as we're beginning our final descent."

Neptune and Carlos came out of the bathroom and got into their seats. Carlos' hair looked better now. It was much shorter. Neptune had buzzed his sides and the hair on top was brushed towards the left. His patchy facial hair had been cleaned up; his goatee was now visibly smaller.

"Much better," Kyle said, giving Carlos a thumbs up.

They could all feel as the plane started to go down, and hit the runway with a bump. The plane slowed until it came to a halt. The pilot emerged from his cabin. He was a short and slender man with platinum blond hair and clean-shaven.

"Hope you all had a great flight," he said with a smile. He opened the door and the stairs flipped out onto the ground. Everyone got up with their bags and left the jet.

"Have a nice day," the pilot said as they left. Sitting closely to the jet was a black Jeep Wrangler; the car Ivan had organized before they left.

Standing next to the car was a clueless valet, holding the keys.

"Mr. Winters?" the valet sheepishly asked.

"Yeah, that's me," Ivan said, snatching the keys out of his hand. "We got it from here."

Ivan unlocked the car.

"Get the bags in the trunk, Neptune. Kyle – you and Carlos in the back."

Kyle nodded and opened the back seat and climbed in. The car smelled new; it probably *was*, considering how clean the inside was. Neptune put the bags in the trunk and got in. Ivan got in the driver's seat and turned back to talk to Kyle and Carlos.

"To get from here to Meeds Lake is about an hour away. Hang tight, you two." Ivan fiddled with the rear-view mirror.

"When we get there, stick close to us. And try not to die. It'll look bad." Ivan started the car and drove out of the airport.

The ride would've been pretty boring if it wasn't for the radio working in this car. Kyle looked out of the window. The Misquah Hills were thickly forested. Much more than the Farm in Illinois. A perfect shade of green trees dotted the landscape. The mountains on the horizon looked like an oil painting. And the vast lakes they passed by shimmered in the sunlight. Everything looked like a picture on a postcard.

Kyle and Carlos passed the time by playing I Spy and talking excitedly about the mission. Neptune and Ivan seemed to be more reserved about the trip.

After what felt like forever, Ivan turned off the road and into a forest.

"Why are you going off-road?" asked Carlos.

"Because we can't get there without going off-road," Ivan explained. "Unless you want to walk there. We won't be arriving until the sun sets. So, visibility will be low. It's also going to be cold – keep your jackets buttoned up."

The off-road journey to Meeds Lake was bumpy. Kyle knocked his head against the window three times in five seconds before moving to the middle seat. The forest was dense, but it was easy to get through with the Jeep. Kyle could see the light slowly start to fade. It was getting close to sundown. They'd be there soon, hopefully.

Ivan cleared the forest and parked in front of a lake, besides which a sign read 'Meeds Lake'.

They'd arrived.

Chapter 16

Everyone got out and took the bags from the trunk to unpack. As they were putting on their gear, Ivan spoke up.

"Alright. There's a small cave close by. That's most likely the den. Kyle, with me. Carlos, with Neptune."

"Are we splitting up?" asked Carlos.

"Once we get into the den, yes. I want to scope out the surrounding area before we go in, though. Search for any clues. Once I'm sure we're in the right place, then we can proceed."

Kyle finished up first. He looked to Ivan for reassurance, spreading his arms out, showing off his outfit.

"Yes, you look fine," Ivan said while finishing up himself. Kyle had strapped his Molotov to his belt, opposite his sawed-off shotgun, with the lighter in his right front pocket. The flashlight he had placed in his jacket's inside pocket. He felt like hunting a wendigo would be easy with everything he had on him.

Once everyone had finished, they all put their empty bags into the trunk of the car. Ivan locked it and put the keys in his pocket.

"Now. Before we head out, I need to talk to you two." Ivan pointed at Kyle and Carlos. "I need to know you won't freeze up and get yourselves killed." The pair looked at each other, then back at Ivan.

"Well," Kyle spoke up. "We don't have a choice, right? It's kill or be killed with this job, right?"

"I'm not happy about killing," said Carlos. "But I'd rather not sit back and watch."

Ivan smirked. "Good. Just think of it like they're bugs. Everyone kills bugs. You'll get used to it." Neither of them replied, but simply nodded in compliance.

"Now come on, let's get to the den."

Everyone followed Ivan as they walked through the forest. The sunlight was almost gone. Kyle saw traces of an orange sunset reflected in the clouds above starting to fade into the dark. The woods thinned out. Ivan stopped the party every few minutes to look for clues on the ground. Neptune, who was at the back of the group, also looked around behind them in case Ivan missed something. Since Kyle and Carlos didn't know how to track properly, all they could do was stand in place until Ivan told everyone to move on. Kyle didn't mind this because he liked the stillness of the forest – the air felt thick amongst the trees.

As the group continued to walk, Kyle noticed that some of the trees had long scratch marks on them; something Ivan also saw.

"They're definitely close," Ivan said. He walked up to the tree and looked around its base.

"There aren't any more scratch marks. This could be a signal." Ivan studied the nearby trees to see if they had any scratch marks as well. Kyle looked up. The sunlight finally faded away and the forest darkened.

"So?" Carlos asked. "What were the scratches about?"

"It looks like a wendigo marked it to show the cave is nearby for the others to find. The cave should by up ahead," Ivan replied, readying his shotgun. He led the group into a clearing against a small mountain with a cave. It was surrounded by broken trees and leaves strewn along the ground.

"Alright. This looks like it could be it. We'll search the outside first. Kyle, with me." Kyle nodded and followed Ivan as they walked to the left of the cave's entrance.

"What are we looking for?" he asked.

"Anything someone would've left behind if they were dragged off. Wendigos don't leave anything that we can track. So, we need to look for something that shows us that they're here. A body they ate, some clothes, anything."

Kyle got to work, rummaging around bushes. There was nothing apart from berries. It was frustrating. Not a thing in sight. Kyle could see Carlos and Neptune searching around the other side of the cave entrance. Kyle looked up and turned to Ivan.

"What happens if we can't find anything here?"

"We find some other cave. Wendigos will always leave something outside their caves to let the others know it's their den. We just have to find it," Ivan said, studying the trees around him.

"Would they leave an indicator this far from the den?"

"Yes, like a bread crumb trail. They leave certain things around. Stuff that most people will just look at but leave alone. Maybe a boot or a glove. Scratch marks like before. Just gotta find the right thing."

A boot or a glove. That's something Kyle could focus on trying to find. He decided to start looking up in the trees as well to see if something was up there. Carlos walked over to Kyle and Ivan.

"Hey, we found something. Looks like it could be important. Neptune sent me to get Ivan to check it out."

Ivan nodded. "Okay. Kyle, stay here and keep looking. I'll call you over if it's important."

Kyle shrugged. "Yeah, that's fine by me. I'll keep searching the trees."

Ivan gave an approving nod and left.

Kyle watched as Carlos and Ivan slowly faded into the darkness. He searched between bushes and rocks for anything out of the ordinary. He looked up at the trees occasionally. He decided not to stray too far, as he could get lost, so his search area was limited.

And then he found something: a pair of hiking boots. Tied up and tossed across a tree branch. Kyle thought about climbing the tree to examine them further, but Carlos called out before he got the opportunity to.

"Kyle! Get over here!"

He could tell it wasn't a good sign. Something was wrong. Kyle sprinted over to them and found Carlos and Ivan standing outside the cave.

"What's wrong?" he said, huffing. Trying to catch his breath.

"It's Neptune. A wendigo got him," Ivan said.

"He's dead?" Kyle asked worriedly.

"No. Taken." Ivan held Neptune's mask in his hand, showing it to Kyle. He then pointed to Neptune's gear on the ground at the entrance to the cave. "Check it out. They disarmed him and took him into that cave. So, this is it. We need to get him and everyone else in there."

"How many people *are* in there?" Carlos asked.

"Hard to say. All I know for sure is Neptune and possibly the two missing Hunters."

The missing Hunters. *That's right.* Kyle remembered that the only reason they were all here was because two other Hunters tried to clear out the den but hadn't been heard from since.

"Okay. So, what's the plan, then?" asked Kyle.

"We can't split up anymore," Ivan said, with his hand balled in a fist and pressed against his mouth. "We'll have to go together. We can take Neptune's gear and get it back to him. It might be harder to move around with the extra weight, so we'll have to split it. I'll take the bandolier and Remington. Kyle, take his Molotov. Carlos, you got his machete and his sawed-off."

"Wait," said Kyle. "How is this even? You have his guns and ammo. We have his backups."

"When we get close to the heart of the den, I'm gonna find Neptune as fast as possible. I'll be getting to him while you both lure the wendigos away. Trust me." They didn't really have a choice. The three all readied their weapons and made their way into the wendigo den.

Ivan took the lead, with Kyle in the middle and Carlos bringing up the rear. The den looked amazing. The tunnels were carved into the mountain in perfect cylinders. For every passageway, there were five intersections leading to other passageways. This was a maze meant to confuse intruders.

"Do wendigos dig these?" asked Kyle.

"Sometimes, yeah. If they don't dig the caves themselves, they usually live in abandoned mines and 'renovate' them. But this one, it's all wendigo. There'd be some minecart tracks if it wasn't. Just makes this all harder," Ivan replied. "Now, can any of you remember the way for me?"

"I might be able to," Carlos said.

"Good, there's a good chance we might have to leave while being chased. So just keep focused and memorize our path, okay?"

Carlos nodded.

"Okay, get your lights out, it'll only get darker from here."

Everyone took their flashlights out – they'd been given angle head flashlights, meaning they were able to place them in their pockets and keep moving. Kyle put his into his left breast pocket. It slid in smoothly. Ivan continued to lead them into the den. It all looked the same. Just one long tunnel with side passages, and then those side passages had side passages. How was anyone meant to navigate this place?

"Hey Ivan, do you know where to go?" Kyle asked, shining his torch along the walls and down the passages they walked past.

"A little. The center of the den is where anyone would be taken to. So, for now, all we can do is follow the path that goes down."

The caves were slowly getting darker the further they went in. Eventually, the only source of light was from their flashlights. Kyle could barely see the walls in front of him without it. Ivan slowed down, going heel to toe to stay silent, keeping his gun aimed and ready for an attack. He had one arm always on the wall. Carlos glanced back, just to see if a wendigo was tailing them. Kyle held his flashlight outward so Ivan could see better. The three pressed up against each other, making sure not to stray. There was a sound of shuffling and some rocks dropping from up ahead.

"Lights out!" Ivan said in a loud whisper. Kyle tuned his off and hugged the wall. Carlos bunched up to Kyle. Kyle heard Carlos' heavy breathing.

"Calm down," he said. Carlos started to breathe through his nose, taking deep breaths. Up ahead there was a clicking noise, followed by a snarl. There was a wendigo very close. The clicking got closer. And Carlos' breathing got faster.

Kyle reached over and pinched his nose and whispered, "We can kill it if it gets close."

Kyle heard footsteps approaching before they suddenly stopped. The clicking faded away and the footsteps ceased. Kyle let go of Carlos' nose. Ivan turned his light back on.

"Hopefully, that means we're close. Stick to whispering for now."

"What was with the clicking?" asked Carlos.

"They can use echolocation, which means they can see the outlines of things around them. Easier for them to hunt at night."

"Why wasn't that mentioned in any of our bestiaries?" asked Kyle.

"Those books at the Farm are old and outdated. Let's just focus on this for now."

Suddenly, a voice screamed out, "Hey! Over here! They got me!"

Kyle swung his head to the source of the voice. It was Neptune's voice, no longer muffled from his mask.

"Don't!" Ivan said. "A wendigo. But this means we might be close to the center. Let's keep moving this way. We're also only using one light from now. Kyle."

Kyle hastily turned on his flashlight and pointed it down the dark tunnel. There was nothing there, except for some large footprints a few feet from where they stood. They looked like large human footprints, apart from the claw marks at the end of each toe. Ivan grabbed Carlos by the shoulder and pulled him in close.

"You're sticking with me. Kyle, you're up front. I'll tell you where to go."

"Got it."

Kyle took the lead now. There were a few more footprints along the way. The cave got colder the further they went in. Carlos and Ivan hung back, making sure there was nothing following them. Ivan would occasionally give Kyle orders on where to shine his light or which passage to take. They wandered for a few minutes, inching slowly down deeper into the caves. Kyle started to feel claustrophobic. He hadn't been keeping track of where they were going and would get lost in a second if he was alone.

"Hey Carlos, you been keeping track of our route?" he asked.

"Yeah," Carlos replied. "Three rights, a left, right, left, left, right, left. I remember how many passages we walked past before we turned down each one."

Kyle breathed a silent sigh of relief.

"Nice memory, kid," Ivan said approvingly.

After a few more turns, they found something. A light poked out of a nearby passage, along with a putrid smell in the air. Kyle was close to retching from it.

"What the fuck is that smell?" he asked Ivan.

"Corpses," Ivan replied, not even covering his nose.

"Did we find the center?" asked Carlos.

"Could be. Stay here with Carlos while I check it out." Ivan walked up to the end of the tunnel and peeked through. Kyle was able to just make out his silhouette from the light at the end. He saw Ivan waving at them to come over.

It was the center of the den. This part was much larger than the other passages, exposing a large open area. The ceiling was a thirty-foot-high dome with holes all over it. They looked like other entrances. Small torches scattered all over the dome to provide a light source, with a small bonfire in the center. There were no wendigos in sight, but there were people. Twelve, Kyle counted, all tied up and on the floor near the bonfire with blood pooled around them. Ivan took out two photos from his pocket and studied them.

"Angus Macmillan and Jesse Thomson. Nice to know they're alive." He showed Kyle and Carlos the photos and then pointed up at the pile of bodies. The photo of Angus depicted a tall, fair-skinned man with a big red beard. Jesse Thompson was a dark-skinned woman with straight black hair and a scar across her left cheek. When Kyle looked back at the pile of bodies, he saw them. They looked a lot worse for wear. Angus had a black eye swollen shut and blood dried on his head. Jesse had a bloodied bandage over her torso and her right leg.

"I'm going in to find Neptune. You two guard this entrance and don't make any noise unless you have to." Ivan walked into the heart of the den quietly and up to the bodies. He checked the pulses of each one before landing on Angus.

Angus opened his good eye and groaned.

"Shhh!" Ivan said.

"Ivan, what you doin' here?" Angus asked. He had a light Canadian accent.

"Saving your ass. Can you fight?"

"Yeah, just give me something to cover my eye and a gun. And check on Jesse for me."

Ivan went to Jesse and tried to stir her awake. She wasn't moving. He checked her pulse and returned to Angus.

"Her pulse is weak. She might not make it."

Angus sighed. "Shit. Just untie me."

"Hold on, they also got Neptune. I need to find him." Ivan got up and looked around the bodies. He found one slumped over the top of the pile, wearing a white parka with black accents.

"There you are," Ivan said as he pulled Neptune down. His face was still concealed to Kyle and Carlos from where they were standing, his hood hanging over his head. Ivan returned his mask before the others could catch a glimpse. But before Ivan could pull Neptune to his feet, a rock flew from one of the other entrances and hit him in the back of the head. He immediately fell forward onto Neptune, unconscious.

The wendigo that threw it was about to emerge from the cave, but before Kyle and Carlos could act, there was a loud snarling from behind them. Kyle was too panicked to turn on his light, but he could see the outline vaguely. He pushed the wendigo, grabbed Carlos' hand, and sprinted away. Carlos wasn't complaining, but he *was* panicking. Kyle took him down some random tunnels to see if they could lose the wendigo. He heard muttered growling behind them. After running for a good minute, he let go of Carlos to grab his light. He turned it on and shone it behind them. There was nothing there, thankfully. Kyle turned around and saw a long passage with left and right exits.

"Which way?" he asked Carlos.

"Umm," Carlos said. "We went a different way. I don't know where we are. Just go right."

As they darted into the right passage, they heard the wendigo behind them catching up, galloping through the tunnel. They kept rushing down the paths as Carlos called out directions. The sounds of the wendigo somewhere behind them started to fade. Kyle put his arm out to stop Carlos. Both were panting heavily.

"Why'd you stop?" Carlos asked through breaths.

"It's useless. We'll just get caught if we keep trying to run. Best we stand ground."

"So, we wait here and shoot it?"

"No. It's too early to use our guns. We should use our machetes for now." Kyle threw his flashlight on the ground to illuminate their current whereabouts and then took out his machete. Kyle and Carlos got close to one of the walls and tried to make out any noises. It was hard to do while they were recovering from all the running. But they eventually caught their breaths and fell silent. They could hear the crunch of the ground getting louder as a wendigo approached. It growled in a low voice.

"Where are you?" That was Ivan's voice. "It's safe."

Kyle looked at the flashlight he'd thrown and saw it being picked up, then shone in his face.

"Don't. Worry. Being a wendigo is fun."

Kyle couldn't believe what was happening. Was he really about to have a conversation with this thing?

"Is it, though?" he asked sarcastically.

The wendigo snarled. "You don't. Have. A choice."

The wendigo threw the flashlight at Kyle, but he dodged it. He still couldn't see what it looked like, and the dim cave didn't help. Kyle felt a cold and clammy hand wrap around his throat and pin him against the wall. The light provided Kyle an outline bright enough to see the wendigo's shape. And to see it raise its hand to slash him.

But Carlos ran over and swung his machete, cutting the wendigo's arm off.

The wendigo screeched and fell back. Carlos picked up the flashlight and shone it onto the wendigo. They were finally able to get a good look at it.

Its skin was pale; its arms and legs elongated. Its torso was emaciated. Claws on the tips of its thin fingers. The face was unnaturally smooth, its lipless mouth showing sharp, yellowed teeth. The eye sockets were hollowed, with eyes clouded over, completely milk-white. What little hair it had on its head was long and frayed. What little clothing it was wearing seemed to be the remnants of a hiker's pants, now torn to shreds and barely long enough to reach its knees. The wendigo stood up tall, reaching the top of the cave ceiling. It looked and Kyle, then turned around.

"*Heeeeeeerrrreee!*" the wendigo screeched.

Kyle and Carlos had to cover their ears. The two swung into action to silence it with an attack. Carlos thrust his machete into its abdomen as Kyle cut off the other arm to stop it from grabbing them. Carlos then got behind the wendigo and kicked it in the back of the knee, making it drop to eye level.

Then, Kyle swung his machete down at its head. But its skull was tough and the machete slid to the side. The wendigo looked at Kyle, took in a deep breath, and screamed as loud as it could, calling out to the others. Kyle had to step back and cover his ears again. Carlos punched it in the throat to shut it up. He then took his machete out of its abdomen and thrust it into the wendigo's jaw. The machete jammed, and the wendigo's screams faded. But it was still alive.

Carlos leaned the machete forward, punching the wendigo's head back, and hit the butt of the handle, forcing it in further. With each hit, the machete inched in deeper. The wendigo's screams were fading. Carlos thought he must have killed it by now – the machete was almost completely inside its head. Kyle pulled Carlos aside and kicked the wendigo in the face to shut it up for good. The body toppled to the ground, lifeless. Kyle slowly walked over and kicked its corpse lightly. It was dead.

Kyle took the machete out of the wendigo's head and handed it back to Carlos. "Thanks for that," Kyle said.

"I didn't think I had it in me, honestly. That was a lot worse than I thought it'd be."

Kyle picked up the machete he'd dropped when the wendigo screamed in his face and sheathed it.

"We need to keep moving."

"Wait." Carlos walked over to the dead wendigo. "We should cut its head off. Make sure it's fully dead."

Kyle nodded. He walked over and put his foot on the wendigo's head to stabilize it.

"Hack away."

Carlos went for it with full force. It took about ten swings to cut through the neck. But eventually, he was able to decapitate it. Carlos got to his feet.

"I guess cutting the heads off is out of the question," Kyle said, picking up his flashlight. "We should move. It called out for the others. I'm surprised they haven't already arrived." Kyle put his machete away and took out his Vepr-12 shotgun.

"We should put our earplugs in. The blast from this is gonna kill our ears."

Carlos cocked his Remington. "So, where to?"

"Back to the center," answered Kyle. "We need to get everyone out of here."

"You know where that is?"

"No, but it shouldn't be hard to find, right?"

Kyle and Carlos had little time. They needed to find their way back to Ivan and the others without being seen by the wendigos. They were coming, but how many? And from what direction? Kyle was on high alert, checking every passage they passed before quickly moving down.

"We can still get there without being seen. We just need to keep quiet," Kyle said to Carlos.

"But why have we got our shotguns out if we want to be quiet?"

"We've been made. There's gonna be a lot of them coming down on us. If we run into one, we run into all of them."

"How do you know so much?" Carlos asked.

"It was in the books in the library. I spent a lot of time reading over wendigos. Didn't you?"

"I was mostly looking at things to bring along with Neptune."

Kyle's flashlight led the way. Unfortunately, they'd gotten lost. In this maze, it was almost impossible to find your way once you lost it. They could hear scuttling all around them. There were wendigos nearby. But they couldn't afford to slow down. Navigation was pointless. There were running down the first path they saw, as long as no sounds were coming from it. Every tunnel looked the same. It felt like there was no point in trying to find the center or the exit. But Kyle wouldn't give up. It was either find everyone and save them or die. And he didn't feel like dying right now.

Kyle continued along with Carlos, making sure he didn't fall behind or get sprung upon by a wendigo.

"Is there a chance you know where we are, Carlos?" Kyle asked.

"No," he replied.

"I really hope we haven't just been running in circles the whole time." Kyle slung his Vepr-12 back over his shoulder. "What if we let them catch us?"

Carlos looked confused. "What makes you think they won't kill us?"

"They had ample opportunity to kill Ivan and Neptune when they got them. Why are they keeping people instead of killing them?"

Carlos shrugged and gave a quizzical look.

"They're stocking up. This is a den. They could be hibernating soon. You saw how many bodies there were back there. What if we let ourselves get captured and fight our way out from there?"

Carlos looked shocked. "You're insane."

Kyle smirked. "No, I'm just an optimist." He knelt and pulled up his left pant leg. He took his machete and sheath and strapped it to his leg. "If they get us, we can just use the machetes to cut the ropes and get Ivan and Neptune too."

Carlos started to panic. "This isn't going to work!" he said in a loud whisper. "They'll just kill us when they—"

A wendigo jumped out of the shadows and tackled Carlos to the ground. Kyle felt another wendigo tackle him from behind and he hit the ground hard. The wendigo wrapped its arm around his neck and started to choke him. Its hands felt icy cold. He tried to pull them off, but the fingers were locked around his neck. Kyle could just barely see Carlos' struggle as well. He felt his heartbeat slowing. His eyesight dimmed. The last thing he saw was Carlos reaching out to him.

Chapter 17

When Kyle woke up, he was back in the center of the den. His arms and legs were bound with rope and his flashlight was broken in his pocket. He looked around and saw Carlos, Ivan and Neptune. Carlos was still passed out and Ivan was sitting there, talking to Neptune and Angus.

"How long have I been here?" Kyle asked Ivan.

"About twenty minutes," he replied. "Glad you two are still alive."

Kyle propped himself up and tried to lift his pant leg to get to his machete. But the rope was stopping that from happening. He was about to try and take his pants off to get to it when he heard a familiar voice from behind him.

"Looking for this?"

That was *his* voice. The wendigo had copied him. It was holding Kyle's machete, dangling it in his face and smirking at him.

"We. Hear. Everything."

It threw the machete into a pile of weapons. All of theirs. Including the weapons Angus and Jesse had brought. The wendigo got up and walked over to Kyle.

"You could. Join us."

Kyle looked concerned. "Why would I do that?" he asked.

"You're strong. We need more. Eat with us."

Kyle stared down the wendigo, smirking. "I'm gonna enjoy killing you."

The wendigo picked up Kyle by his collar, holding him high in the air. He could see how tall a wendigo was compared to him now, and it was frightening. At least eight feet tall. Its lanky frame made its arms look like twigs.

The wendigo pulled Kyle in and stared *him* down now.

"I'm. Gonna enjoy. Eating. You," it said, snarling at Kyle. The wendigo then threw him back down and crawled away into an exit tunnel.

"So, what now?" asked Angus.

"We could try and crawl to our weapons," suggested Neptune. "But there's another wendigo watching over them." He pointed up. Just above the cache of weapons was another tunnel with a wendigo crouched down, looming over the den's center, waiting patiently.

"I can't fight," said Ivan. "My head's still not good from that rock."

"And my eye's gonna cause trouble," said Angus.

"So, no one can fight?" questioned Kyle.

"I can," Neptune said. "Just get me out of these and I can help."

The wendigo watching them snarled.

"It's pointless," said Angus. "Just accept that we can't win." He was being overly animated with his hands. "When Jesse and I came in, they choked us out immediately." He motioned towards his throat. Then he pointed with his thumbs to the wendigo behind him – signaling to Neptune and Kyle to choke it out.

Kyle crawled over to Neptune to help him up. The wendigo kept snarling, like a rabid dog, slowly getting louder. Once Neptune was on his feet, the wendigo had had enough and jumped down.

"Get! Back! Down!" it yelled in Angus' voice.

"Make us," Neptune replied.

The wendigo lunged at Neptune. Because of his size, Neptune was a lot harder to pin than the rest. Neptune was close to the size of the wendigo. He pushed it back and stood his ground. Having his hands and legs bound was a handicap, but he seemed to have somewhat of a grasp on how to handle the situation. He waited until the wendigo tried to attack him again, then he punched it in the gut with both his hands, which was enough to make the wendigo double over and stop for a few seconds.

Neptune then hopped behind and put his arms over its neck, pulled back – using the rope to choke the wendigo. Kyle took this opportunity to hop over to the big pile of weapons and pull out a machete. He was able to get one quickly and started to cut through the ropes on his legs first. He kept looking up at Neptune to see how he was going. The wendigo dug its claws into Neptune's arms, but he was shrugging off the pain.

"Quickly, mate!" Neptune said. "It's starting to hurt pretty badly now."

Kyle cut faster. The ropes were tough. He was eventually able to cut through and get his legs free. Although he could have tried to cut the ropes around his hands, too, he decided that helping Neptune was the more pressing matter. He got up and ran over to Neptune, thrusting his machete through the wendigo's torso. He pulled it back out and swung downwards into its head.

"Go for the neck," Neptune said as he pulled the wendigo's head back.

Kyle took a swing and slit its throat. Blood poured down its front onto the ground. The cut was about two inches deep. Kyle backed up to avoid getting blood on his shoes.

"Good enough," Neptune said. "Let me finish this one."

Neptune then grabbed the wendigo's head and started to twist.

Kyle heard the wendigo's bones snapping, and the muscles and skin tearing, the more its head was twisted. Neptune managed to twist its head a full three hundred and sixty degrees. The wendigo, amazingly still alive, made a few gurgling sounds. Neptune then forced the wendigo down to its knees, dug his hands into its now-frayed neck, and yanked its head upwards as hard as he could. The muscles finally tore from the strain. The wendigo's body slumped to the floor, leaving Neptune holding its head, as the blood poured out from its neck like someone had left a faucet on.

"Well, I guess that's one way to decapitate something," Kyle said, slightly shocked Neptune was able to do that. But then again, Neptune was nearly seven feet tall. And he was wearing baggy clothing. He could be complete muscle underneath all those clothes.

Neptune dropped the wendigo's head. "Get me out of these, will ya?" he said, holding up his bound hands. Kyle walked over and cut the ropes.

"Are you gonna be okay?" he asked, pointing to Neptune's bloody arms.

"I'll live, but I won't be able to fight. I don't think we'll have long anyway. We need to get any survivors to the surface."

"What about the wendigos?" asked Kyle.

"I brought gasoline canisters with me," Angus said, trying to stand up. "They should be in the pile of stuff over there."

Kyle handed his machete to Neptune. "You untie everyone, and I'll get the weapons."

Neptune walked over to Angus. Kyle started to pull weapons out of the pile, searching for the gas canisters. He could see them at the very bottom of the pile. All the guns his group had brought, as well as presumably what Angus and Jesse brought with them, he put into a smaller pile. There were two more Remington shotguns and two sawed-offs after he'd gotten all their gear back. There was also a bag filled with glow sticks.

Kyle pulled the gas canisters out. There were two and both were full. He heard the gasoline sloshing around as he picked them up.

Kyle decided to gear up again. He took two bandoliers and put them on. The Vepr-12 drum bag was back over his shoulder and the sawed-off was on his hip. He took the remaining weapons and moved them closer to the group. Neptune had cut off everyone's ropes by the time Kyle got there.

"Right. This is all we have. Everyone else is dead." There were seven people in total. Kyle, Ivan, Carlos, Neptune, Angus, and two other survivors. Jesse, unfortunately, died from her injuries shortly after Ivan discovered her. The two other survivors were still unconscious. But breathing. A man and woman.

"Did you check their pulses?"

"Yes. Faint, but still alive. They might've been here as long as us," Angus said, double-checking the pule on the unconscious woman. "I think we should bring the dead as well."

"Why? Wouldn't it just slow us down?" Neptune said, who had started to bandage his arms.

"These are missing people. It's better if we take them outside, put them in a mass grave, and call the authorities. That way their families get closure."

Kyle looked puzzled. "That sounds like way too much work. Lots of people go missing and are never heard from again."

"It's better than not knowing," Angus replied despondently.

Kyle didn't want to argue. Luckily, any argument was cut short by groaning – the unconscious man stirring awake. He was dressed in mountaineering gear, as was the woman. He had a scruffy brown beard and his hair was dried and stuck together with blood. He had nicely tanned skin. He pulled himself up and looked around, dazed.

"Wh—What's going on?" he said, looking at the group worriedly.

"Shit," said Ivan.

Neptune walked over and helped him up. "First thing. Calm down. Take some deep breaths and close your eyes." The man looked around slowly, squinting. "Who are you?"

"Someone who can help," Neptune replied. "I need you to keep calm and lower your voice."

"Why?"

"Because we're all going to die if you don't."

The man looked more confused than ever. Kyle walked over. "You're scaring him."

"Fine." Neptune put his arm around the man. "What's your name?"

"It's Anton."

"Okay, Anton. I'm Neptune. I need you to listen very closely. You were knocked out and kidnapped. We're here to help get you out safe."

Anton looked around. "My wife, she—"

"Is that her?" Neptune pointed to the woman next to Anton.

"Yes, it's she alright?" he asked, concerned.

"She's alive. We don't have time. I need you to carry her out with the rest of us."

"What about the wendigos?" Kyle asked.

"You're going to have to deal with them for us, mate," Neptune said.

"Wendigos?" Anton asked.

Kyle sighed. "No time to explain, Anton. Long and short of it is supernatural monsters exist and they kidnapped you. Neptune can explain on the way."

Kyle helped Ivan and Angus to their feet. Ivan took one of the shotguns and a bandolier.

"I thought you said you couldn't fight," said Angus.

"I can't, but I might be able to get a good shot in. Neptune should be able to get us to the surface safely."

"And you, Angus?" questioned Kyle.

"I can try, but with one eye I'll only be good with close range." He bent down and picked up a sawed-off and a machete. Kyle looked over at Carlos. He was still unconscious. Ivan walked over and kicked him lightly to wake him up. Carlos wasn't as dazed as Anton and quickly regained consciousness. Ivan helped him to his feet.

"Still good to fight?"

Carlos rubbed his head. "Yeah, just give me a second."

"We don't have a second. We're leaving." Ivan handed Carlos his sawed-off. "You're coming with us. We need to get these bodies to the surface." Ivan walked to Kyle and put his hand on his shoulder. "We're counting on you. I'll make sure Carlos doesn't die."

Kyle smiled. "Thanks man. Don't die on me."

Kyle picked up a Remington and put it over his shoulder. He was more loaded up than before: two bandoliers forming an 'X' over his chest, the Vepr-12 over one shoulder and the Remington over the other, a sawed-off shotgun strapped to his left thigh, and a machete on his right. He carried an extra Vepr-12 drum, too. He couldn't carry anything else even if he wanted to.

Neptune picked up the gas canisters. "I'll drench this place. Can you find a way to lure the wendigos here? You can light them all up if you make it back here."

"Sure," Kyle said, cocking his Remington.

Neptune handed him a Molotov. "The others got broken. You have one shot."

Kyle took it and stuffed it into his jacket the best he could. Anton picked up his wife, Ivan picked up Carlos, and Angus dragged the dead bodies out to an exit.

"Give us about five minutes. Then go wild," Ivan said.

Kyle smiled again. "Oh, don't worry. I can do that."

Kyle watched as everyone dragged bodies out of the den. He picked up the bag of glow sticks and walked out of the opposite side.

He got to an intersection, took out a glow stick, cracked it, and left it on the ground. That way he could find his way back to the center. He kept this up for every side passage he went down. There were only twenty glow sticks, so he had to use them sparingly. As he was making his way through the maze, there was an unnerving quiet. Where were the wendigos? He couldn't hear anything. Not even the scuttling of feet he'd heard earlier. His heart pounded from the fear. He took some deep breaths and tried to calm down. The only thing he was afraid of was a surprise attack.

He continued to plot his path with glow sticks, going slower with every turn, until he was down to only five. He stood at a four-way intersection. He threw one down each path, apart from the one he came from, dropping the last at his feet. He hadn't come across anything during this entire time. His heart was still thumping. The only thing that would calm him down was risky and stupid. But it had to be done.

Chapter 18

"I'm here! *Come and get me!*" Kyle screamed as loud as he could, his voice echoing down the passageways and all around him. He held his Vepr-12 shotgun and aimed down the barrel, keeping it at the ready for any wendigo that would inevitably be coming for him. He turned into each path slowly, waiting for something to appear. Kyle slowed his breathing. His heartbeat slowed down. He fell silent so he could hear something, anything.

And then there was the scuttling. It was coming from every direction. His gaze kept darting to the source of the noise, waiting for a wendigo to attack. And he finally saw one – charging at him fast down one of the tunnels. He waited until it was close enough to open fire.

The first shot was a dragon's breath round. It immediately lit up the entire cave, momentarily blinding him. It was enough to blow the wendigo back as it shrieked in pain. Kyle took a few steps toward it and fired three more rounds at its body. The wendigo desperately tried to crawl away, but Kyle stopped it by stomping his foot down hard on its back.

Kyle pointed the gun directly at the wendigo's skull and fired, blasting a good chunk of its head off. He took out his machete and stabbed it a few times to make sure it was dead. Kyle stepped back to the intersection and looked around. Surely that wasn't it.

Two more from different directions; his left, and his right. Kyle waited for them to get close and fired again, one for each to knock them backwards. He then switched to his sawed-off and ran to the one on his left. He jumped on top of the wendigo before it could get back up and shoved the sawed-off into its mouth, firing immediately. He turned to the other, which had recovered and was within arm's reach. He only had enough time to fire into its chest. He couldn't reload in time and wouldn't be able to unsheathe his machete.

The wendigo lunged at him again. Kyle kicked it right in the gun wound, which was healing quickly, making the wendigo stop and grunt in pain. Kyle responded by getting up and punching it in the face, then kicking it to the ground. He stomped on its face to stop it from getting up. At the same time, he reloaded his sawed-off. With each stomp, the wendigo would gurgle as its mouth filled with blood. It scratched at Kyle's leg, managing to sink a claw in.

"Ahh! Shit!" Kyle said, grabbing the wendigo's hand and tearing it free from of his leg.

After clicking the barrel back into place, he stopped stomping and shot the wendigo to finish it off.

Kyle heard more wendigos coming down the tunnels around him. The glow sticks he'd scattered illuminated their skeletal bodies as they rushed towards him from every direction, which included blocking the way back to the center.

A wendigo jumped out of the shadows and tackled Kyle to the ground. His Vepr-12, Remington, extra magazines, and sawed-off flew off him like he was a cheap piñata. The wendigo tried to bite his neck, but Kyle held it back with one arm pressing against its chest and the other on its head. The wendigo was overpowering Kyle and getting close – it drooled onto Kyles's chest, snarling.

Kyle reached for his sawed-off, which had been knocked out of his hand when he was tackled. It was only just out of reach. He tried to pull himself closer without letting the wendigo sink its razor-sharp teeth into him. Kyle was close, so he punched the wendigo to give himself some room and wiggled himself out enough to grab the gun.

When he turned around, the wendigo was back on top of him, angrier than before. It was so close to biting him when he turned around that he wasn't able to shield himself in time, and the wendigo managed to chomp into his right forearm.

"*Aaarrghh!*" Kyle screamed in pain. It felt like the wendigo had bitten right down to the bone. He ignored it as best he could, put his sawed-off to the middle of the wendigo's forehead, and fired.

BANG!

The wendigo immediately unclenched its jaw and fell next to Kyle.

Kyle dropped the gun and grabbed his right ear. The gun being so close to his face meant the shot was too loud for him to handle. All he could hear now was an incessant ringing, like someone had struck a bell and jammed it in Kyle's ear.

He didn't have any time to stop. Kyle got himself up as quick as he could – his right arm was now no longer able to do anything. He held the arm tightly to his chest and picked up his guns, hurling them over his back, and looked around. No other wendigos had appeared. He could still hear them scuttling around, and now there were voices following them.

"Help me, Kyle!" Ivan cried.

"We're over here! They got us!" Angus shouted.

"Please!" Carlos pleaded.

Kyle could tell it wasn't his friends who were calling out.

"Cut the shit!" he yelled back into the darkness.

The scuttling immediately stopped.

"If that's how you want it, then," a wendigo imitating Kyle said, in a very flat tone.

Suddenly, Kyle was surrounded by the wendigos' shrieking. The scuttling changed into thunderous gallop. Kyle turned and saw a group of wendigos running toward him. He looked into the tunnels around him and saw wendigos streaming in from every direction.

"Ah! Fuck it all!"

Kyle took his Vepr-12 and started to fire at the wendigos. A dragon's breath shot out and flooded one tunnel with fire, lighting the cave and giving Kyle a brief second of sight, showing him just how bad his situation was. Too many wendigos to count. Certainly enough to kill him in an instant if they managed to grab him.

He didn't have time to stop. He turned toward another tunnel and fired again. Kyle made sure not to move too far down any one tunnel. Even though he was out in the open, it was a good spot to keep eyes on the enemy.

After exhausting his rounds, he decided to switch to his Remington. He didn't have a chance to reload his Vepr-12, nor *could* he with one arm. Even though it was slower, reloading the Remington was his best option. With it strapped around his shoulder, he could hold in against him and load it when he ran out.

Kyle had to move, so he ran down the tunnel that would lead him back to the center and came close to the wendigos coming out of it. Taking out his machete, he hacked away at them, making sure not to slow down, and stuck to the walls. He had to get past them, so he focused on evading rather than fighting.

A wendigo grabbed his bad arm and tugged it, causing blood to spurt out and drip to the ground.

Kyle yowled. He kicked the wendigo back, forcing it to let go.

He felt the blood starting to drain from him. He threw his machete to the ground and pulled his Remington back out.

Now backing up into the tunnel, Kyle kept firing at wendigos as they came to him, counting his shots and inserting shells when he was close to empty. He'd used almost all of an entire bandolier when he saw something out of the corner of his eye. More wendigos. A never-ending horde surrounding him. He saw them rushing at him with greater force than before, out of every tunnel direction.

Kyle had no choice but to head back to the center. No more fighting. It was useless. He was thankful the wendigos hadn't picked up the glow sticks. He ran down the tunnel that led back to the center. He fired wildly at the wendigos coming after him. Kyle didn't have any time to stop and make sure to kill them – he simply had to get back to the center. He'd run out of shots with the Remington, so he threw it around his shoulder and continued to sprint.

Kyle glanced over his shoulder at the group of wendigos closing in – they looked like spiders running through a drainpipe. All he could do was run as fast as he could. His gear slowed him down, swaying wildly while he ran. He had to drop something.

"Fuck!"

He dropped the Vepr-12 and the satchel with the spare magazine. They were too bulky to run with. He grabbed his sawed-off and turned back to fire. He couldn't tell if he'd hit one or not. He didn't even know how many were chasing him anymore. The mass of wendigos was so dense that it concealed most of the light from the glow sticks.

Kyle kept darting down the tunnels, following the glow stick trail he'd left. If he could get to the den, then he might be able to burn them all. Hopefully, Neptune had doused the center room with gasoline and gotten everyone out by now. The wendigos behind him were shrieking, almost able to grab him. He'd forgotten all about the earplugs in the stash, so he had to ignore the noise hurting his ears.

Kyle ran as fast as he could, hoping that the den's center was near. He'd forgotten how long the trail was – he'd made sure to get as far away as possible to give everyone a chance at escaping. He could see the faint light of the bonfire at the center peeking out of an upcoming tunnel. He was so close.

Kyle didn't dare look back, fearing that there was too many to fend off in the tunnel. He used the last of his stamina to make one final sprint toward the light.

Chapter 19

He finally got back to the center. The ground was wet, with the smell of gasoline pungent in the air – thankfully covering up the lingering smell of rotting corpses. There were still at least ten corpses in the center, but all the weapons had been taken. Next to the bonfire, which was the only dry spot left, was another Molotov and a Vepr-12 shotgun. Kyle dropped his Remington and picked up the Vepr-12.

He stood his ground in front of the bonfire, panting heavily, desperately trying to catch his breath. When he saw the wendigos chasing him arrive in the center, there were a lot less than expected. Only three. But then Kyle looked up: wendigos dropped from the tunnels in the ceiling and slowly crept towards him. They came out from every opening, stopping Kyle from any way of escaping. There were now at least fifty of them surrounding him, like a plague of hungry rats. At that moment, Kyle practically lost all hope of escaping.

At least I'll die in a cool way, he thought sadly.

Being out of breath from running, mixed with the air being filled with gasoline, made it hard for him to breathe. The wendigos surrounded him in a circle, looking ready to tear him apart. Then, one of them stepped forward.

"We. Need food. You're not enough." This one sounded like Ivan.

"Well, I'm sorry to disappoint," Kyle replied dryly through deep breaths. "Couldn't you grab everyone on their way out or were too focused on me?" He smirked.

"You will do. We. Will. Make. You. Suffer."

The wendigo ran at Kyle. He aimed for its legs and fired. The wendigo tripped from the blast and Kyle grabbed it.

"I'm not really in a suffering kinda mood, ya know?"

He threw the wendigo onto the bonfire and watched it burn to death. He could feel the heat from the flames grow as the wendigo started to burn, shrieking out in pain as it slowly died.

He grabbed the Molotov on the ground and used the fire to light it. The wendigos didn't move.

"Come any closer and I'll torch this place!" Kyle warned. "I'll kill us all."

The wendigos all stared at him, not moving a muscle.

"No. You won't," one said as Carlos.

Another stepped forward. "You. Are afraid," it said as Neptune.

The pack of wendigos slowly inched toward Kyle. Taunting him with snapping and snarling.

"You. Will. Die."

"We. Are hungry."

"Slow. Death."

"Give. Up."

Kyle panicked; the Molotov shook in his hand. He backed up closer to the bonfire until he felt its heat all over his back. Kyle lowered his arm and started to shoot. But none of the wendigos flinched, even if they got hit. They were gaining confidence, now no longer creeping towards Kyle, but standing up tall and walking casually.

He was backed into a corner. He started to hyperventilate, trying to think of a way to escape this situation alive. He looked at the tunnels – all of them were blocked by more wendigos. He could try and run, but he was wildly outnumbered. He'd have to think of something else.

Shooting his way out? Could be possible. He didn't know how many dragon's breath rounds he had left. If Kyle could shoot one at the ground as he was leaving, he had a chance to escape. But without knowing where the round *was*, he couldn't confidently go through with this plan.

The wendigos were now in front of Kyle. Standing still, waiting for him to give in.

One of them stood forward and leaned down to Kyle's face.

"You are surrounded," it said as Ivan. "You've lost."

Kyle took a deep breath. "Nah."

He shoved his shotgun into the wendigo's mouth and pulled the trigger. Its head crooked back with the blast. Kyle then grabbed the wendigo and threw it onto the fire.

The wendigo flopped around like a fish out of water. Kyle turned and saw the other wendigos not moving at all. Another stepped forward.

"You've lost," it said as Kyle. "There is no point in fighting. Please. Give up."

Kyle looked around. No matter what he did, there would be another wendigo to replace the last. More than enough to end this immediately. They were toying with him.

Kyle looked around again, desperately seeking a solution to get out of the den. There was only one that would give him a real chance of escape.

With no other option, Kyle threw the Molotov. It hit the wendigo directly in front of him, which burst into flames immediately. The fire spread to the two wendigos beside it, then caught the den floor and set the center alight. Kyle had to cover his eyes from the brightness.

It seemed that Neptune didn't quite have enough gasoline, as the fire – albeit bright and engulfing the center – was too spaced out to engulf the surrounding space.

That was the final straw, as the wendigos charged at Kyle. He shot a few of them back, but he wouldn't be able to kill them all. Kyle was thinking about accepting his death and turning the shotgun on himself, but luckily, he didn't have to.

Carlos emerged from one of the caves and opened fire on the wendigos. "Back away from my friend!"

He shot wildly at any wendigo close to Kyle, creating a passage for him to escape.

"Come on! I can cover you!" Carlos waved frantically for Kyle to follow him.

Kyle took his final Molotov out from his bandolier, lit it, and sprinted for the exit. As he passed Carlos, he threw the Molotov on the ground in front of the tunnel. It was a big enough spread to stop any wendigos from following them. Their shrieking in the center was unbearable.

Carlos grabbed Kyle and pulled him away. "Let's get out of here!"

Carlos held onto Kyle's arm tight. Pulling him through the caves, leading him by the small flashlight he was holding. Kyle looked back – a wendigo was chasing them. Charred from the fire, and still burning in some places. This one was mad. Kyle cocked his gun and fired but it was hard to aim while he was being pulled. He managed to blast a piece of the tunnel off, the debris sprinkling over the wendigo.

"Carlos, stop! There's one behind us."

"All the more reason to run!"

Carlos wasn't slowing down. Kyle eventually shrugged him off and fired again, blasting the wendigo backward.

"I just need a sec," Kyle said, panting heavily. "Wasn't exactly easy running from these guys."

The wendigo pulled itself up and lunged at Kyle. He used his right arm to shield his face again instinctively, completely forgetting the earlier incident.

The wendigo bit down hard into his arm. Kyle screamed in agony as its teeth sunk into his skin.

Carlos stabbed it with his machete. He pulled it off Kyle and tried to take it on, but the wendigo slapped him to the ground and simply continued.

Kyle was losing strength, and when the wendigo attacked again, he was helpless. He used his hand to shield himself, but the wendigo bit through it, making a loud *crunching* noise.

Carlos stabbed the wendigo again in the back, pulling it off Kyle again, and then shot it to make sure it was dead.

"Are you okay?" he asked Kyle.

Kyle looked at his right arm. His arm had three large puncture wounds, along with several smaller bite marks. His hand had a large bite mark along his palm and ring finger. All of which were seeping blood.

Too much blood. Kyle was starting to lose feeling in his arm, and he felt lightheaded. He fell to his knees, using his left arm to keep himself from completely collapsing.

"I'll live, but we should hurry," Kyle said, trying to control his breathing.

Carlos pulled Kyle back to his feet, then used his empty bandolier as a makeshift bandage, wrapping it around Kyle's bite wounds.

Kyle gave Carlos his Vepr-12. "I don't think I can use this anymore. You should take my bandoliers, too."

Kyle clutched his arm tightly to slow the bleeding. He could feel it throbbing. Carlos took only one of the bandoliers and put it over himself. "I think we're close."

He led Kyle again through the passages.

"Do you know where you're going?" Kyle asked.

"Yeah, this way is mostly a straight line. Too bad we didn't know about this when we came in."

It may have been a mostly straight line, but it was long. Neither of them looked back to see if any wendigos were chasing them. But from the lack of sound, Kyle guessed they were relatively safe. Most probably burned in the fire. He could see a light from ahead.

"We used a few glow sticks to mark our way," Carlos explained. He took Kyle down the illuminated path. There was a wendigo waiting for them up ahead.

With no hesitation, Carlos aimed his Vepr-12 and fired. The wendigo was knocked back and hit the ground. Carlos unloaded four more rounds directly to the head.

"Since when were you the confident one?" Kyle said, astounded.

"I guess Ivan made some good points." Carlos laughed it off.

Carlos continued to navigate their way out. This way was faster than the way in. They'd only taken two turns and they could see the moonlight shining into the entrance of the cave. Kyle started to trip over himself. The blood loss was getting worse. He could barely feel his legs as they thumped the ground. Carlos pulled Kyle's arm over his shoulder and carried him the rest of the way.

Blood was dripping on the ground, leaving a neat exit trail through the cave. Kyle faltered, his steps becoming looser and weaker. He almost gave up on using his legs altogether; they were that useless. The cave exit was about thirty feet ahead. All he had to do was hold on for a few more seconds and he'd be out of this nightmare.

"Carlos?" Kyle said weakly.

"Save it!" Carlos shouted. "You're not dying! We're almost out of here!"

Carlos dropped his gun and pulled Kyle with all his strength, as he finally led Kyle out of the cave.

The cool breeze of the night was a welcoming one; better than the stuffy and toxic air inside the cave. Carlos stopped as soon as they were outside to take deep breaths of the cold, midnight air.

Kyle fell to his knees, exhausted and close to passing out. He looked at his arm to inspect the damage properly. He had lost a lot of blood – his arm looked as though he'd reached into a bucket of red paint. Ivan rushed over to him.

"Shit. How bad was the bite?" he said as he took his jacket to wrap around the wound.

"Pretty bad. You can't turn into a wendigo from a bite, right?"

"No. Only bites that turn you are from vampires and werewolves," Ivan reassured him. "You will be fine. We need to get you a medivac. Now sit down."

Kyle wasn't going to argue with that. Ivan picked him up and slumped him against a tree.

"I'm going back to the car and bringing it here," Ivan said, making sure that the makeshift bandage was tight. He then walked off, back to the car.

Ivan took out his phone. Kyle could hear him asking for a medivac and giving their location. Kyle looked around and saw Anton beside his wife. Carlos was sitting with them. Anton's wife had regained consciousness.

Angus was with the bodies that had been dragged out, neatly stacked in a small pile. He was kneeling, putting his hand on Jesse's lifeless body; a final goodbye to his friend. Carlos walked up to Kyle and sat beside him.

"Neptune's checking the area for any wendigos that weren't in the cave. Should be back soon," he said, heaving a heavy sigh. "We were gonna get all the bodies out, but we ran into a ton on wendigos halfway through and Neptune decided to give up on the rest. At least we got a few out."

Kyle managed a weak smile. "Not bad for our first day on the job, huh?"

Carlos stifled a laugh. "You think we can ask for an office job instead?" Carlos joked, wiping blood off his cheek. "I hope there's at least a company baseball team."

"How's the new guy and his wife?" Kyle asked, curious about the couple.

"Well, he's shaken up and she's unaware of the situation. Neptune said he's gonna talk to them."

"I really hope they're gonna be okay."

"Me too. Anton seems like a good guy." Carlos fiddled with his fingers, trying to distract himself.

Kyle took a deep breath. His head felt light. He wanted to fall asleep but was afraid he'd never wake up if he did. Carlos knocked his chest to keep him awake.

"Don't fall asleep on me, Kyle. I'm not losing the only friend I got."

"Only friend?" Kyle asked. "What about your friends back in Mexico?"

Carlos scoffed. "I doubt I'll ever see them again. Most of them were trying to get across the border with me, so—" Carlos stopped himself. "I can make new friends. I already got you."

Kyle looked over to Neptune. He had arrived back and had sat down next to Anton. Kyle overhead the conversation. He was explaining everything to Anton and his wife. The wife's expression bore a mixture of fear and confusion. Anton pointed to Kyle and Carlos. Carlos responded by giving a quick wave. Neptune looked back at them and continued to talk to Anton's wife. Anton got up and walked over.

"He said you saved us back there," he was talking to Kyle. "I just wanted to thank you. Both of you."

The moonlight exaggerated how pale Kyle was. "I'd, uh, shake your hand, but I'm losing quite a lot of blood." Kyle mustered a smile.

Anton just stood there, not knowing quite what to say for a moment. Finally, he spoke, "Um ... so, is everything he says true? The wendigo thing? I mean, it all sounds insane."

"Sorry, but it's true," Carlos said.

"Um, how long have you been doing this, then?"

"First day on the job," Kyle managed to say. "Well, after a month at training camp. Which was attacked by werewolves about a week ago. But this is our first official mission. I hope it doesn't end like this every time."

Anton looked worried.

"I know it's a lot to take in," Carlos said. "But, honestly, it's kinda fun. Maybe you could take some kinda other job. Neptune was telling me about how there are people who aren't Hunters but help us out with things like finances, and run gun shops. You can talk to him about it if you're unsure."

Anton seemed to think it over.

"You know, I love all this stuff. Werewolves, vampires, everything. I loved all those stories growing up. And now I know they're real ... it feels like an opportunity too good to pass up."

"Same thing I thought," Kyle said.

Carlos smiled. "Well then. Welcome to the club. I just hope you're prepared to give up your old life. What about your wife, though?"

Anton looked back at his wife. Neptune was squatting down, talking to her. She seemed calm, just listening to what he was saying.

"She might need some convincing. Alyssa is an outdoors type. This trip was her idea. I won't be mad if she's against it."

Then, something caught Anton's eye, as he turned to look at the cave. A surviving wendigo.

The wendigo was badly charred, its skin almost completely blackened. But it was still alive, just barely. It was struggling to walk properly – its left leg seemed to be hanging on by a thread. It saw Neptune and lunged at him, tackling him to the ground.

Alyssa backed up in a panic and pressed herself close to a tree behind her. She hadn't been conscious when they were in the cave, so this was her first time seeing a wendigo.

Anton saw the Vepr-12 at the cave entrance and ran over to pick it up. He went over to the wendigo. Neptune was holding it at arm's length – it was incredibly weakened, and Neptune could've easily dealt with it. But then he saw Anton approaching.

Anton aimed the gun at its temple and fired, finally killing the last wendigo. Neptune threw the body off him and got up.

"Thanks for that, mate," he said, brushing the charred skin flakes off his jacket.

Anton looked astounded at what he'd done, immediately dropping the gun.

"Don't worry, happens all the time." Neptune patted him on the shoulder.

There was a horn honk from behind Kyle. Ivan had returned with the Jeep. He parked it right in front of Kyle and got out.

"I heard the gunshot, everything good?"

"The new kid killed a wendigo that got out," Angus said.

"Hmm. Nice job," Ivan said to Anton, who gave a nervous wave.

Ivan walked up to Kyle. "Carlos, get up and help me get Kyle in the car. I called a medivac, but this place is too dense for them to get in. We're driving back to the lake where we parked."

"How'd you guys afford a medivac?" Alyssa asked.

"Can't. It's a regular one. I said he was attacked by a bear. I called Nick as well to help take him back to the Farm once we get back to Illinois."

Carlos got up and pulled Kyle off the ground, holding his good arm. Kyle's legs felt like they were feathers. He was having trouble standing upright, or even feeling his lower body at all. Ivan held him up by pressing up on his chest. They helped Kyle to the car and sat him in the passenger seat.

"Neptune. Call into the locals and report the bodies," Ivan said as he walked to the opposite side of the Jeep and got in. "Kyle needs to get out of here now."

"What about me?" asked Carlos.

"I suggest staying here. Help Angus with grave digging and keep an eye out for any more wendigos, if any survived."

Carlos nodded. He patted Kyle on the arm.

"Don't die on me, okay?"

"I'll try my best." Kyle managed to grin. Carlos shut the passenger door and walked over to Angus to help dig graves. Ivan pulled out and went back to the lake.

Ivan tried to make the ride as tolerable as possible. But the bumpiness was inevitable.

"Shit! Just hang in there, okay?"

Kyle was struggling to stay awake, so the constant thrashing actually helped.

"Don't worry about me, just focus on driving."

The dark forest was lit only by the headlights of the Jeep. The moonlight was barely able to break through the dense tree line.

"How's your head?" Kyle asked.

"Ah, hurts a little. You're in a worse state than anyone. You're the priority."

Kyle felt the throbbing of his arm slow. He struggled to stay awake even more than before.

"I—I can't last … much … longer …"

The forest evened out as they finally cleared it and made it back to the lake. Ivan could see the helicopter close by.

"Medivac's here! Just stay awake!" Ivan punched Kyle in the leg to keep him up. Kyle groaned. Ivan honked his horn and flashed his lights, hoping the helicopter saw them. He stopped the car and got out, then walked over to Kyle's side and opened his door. The medivac had seen them and was starting its landing.

"Hey, you did good today. Now stay alive so I can thank you properly."

Kyle looked over at Ivan. And then he slipped into unconsciousness, finally giving in to his body's demands.

Chapter 20

When Kyle regained consciousness, he was in the medical bay at the Farm once again.

Nick was there, talking to Tracy. Kyle looked down at his body. His right arm was wrapped tightly in bandages and suspended at an angle with thin wires attached to the ceiling. Luckily, there were no other major injuries on him – other than the stitches in his chest, which thankfully were unharmed. He saw Angus sitting on the bed next to him with a bandage over his left eye. He was reading a book.

Angus looked up and saw Kyle awake.

"Hey, Nick! He's up!" he said loudly.

Nick saw Kyle and walked over to him.

"Thanks, Angus. Please remember to keep it down."

Angus shrugged and got back to his book.

"Never, in my entire stay at the Farm, have I had so much trouble from one person, Mr. McManus," Nick said calmly. "I wouldn't be surprised if you came in here with a hole in your gut. And you'd probably still manage to live through that!"

"Surprised to see me again so soon?" Kyle joked. He was feeling much better than before.

"You need to be more careful in the future," Nick said. "I don't want any of my patients winding up dead, and you've almost died three times since arriving here."

"Anyone come close to my luck?" Kyle decided to ask. Grinning as he did so.

"You'd be surprised how many people are in here more than once. I've treated everyone at the Farm at least five times." Nick started to unwrap his arm. "That was a pretty big bite you got from the wendigo. And I was told you were almost pronounced dead-on-arrival when you got here. You were taken to a local hospital and rushed into the ICU. After they stitched you up, we had you brought back to the Farm under the guise of being moved to a private hospital, which is technically true." Nick chuckled.

"Even once your arm heals, the scarring will probably be more pronounced than the claw marks on your chest. And you will need physical therapy to make sure your arm heals properly."

Nick finally finished unwrapping Kyle's arm. The stitches were still fresh and there was some dried blood, along with a yellow tinge around the wounds. His arm felt tight, and he could see that the stitches made small concave dents in his arm. His ring and pinkie fingers were taped together. He couldn't even feel them. Kyle wiggled his pinky and index finger to test his hand. It felt painful and tight.

Nick examined the stitches. "Hmm, if I'd been able to see you straight away, I might have been able to do a better job. I'm sorry, but this is a little shoddy. The doctor probably rushed because of the blood loss. The damage will heal, there's just going to be some mild deformity."

"Mild?" Kyle asked.

"Just from the scars healing. You see ..." Nick slowly lifted Kyle's arm so he could see the underside. There were also stitches on his palm and forearm. "You have a few wires in your hand. Wendigo chipped one of your metacarpals. Luckily, that was the only bone that was damaged. The bite marks were wide, so stitching it up meant pulling your skin together more than usual. But don't worry, it shouldn't affect your day-to-day life." Nick put Kyle's arm back onto the cast.

Kyle scoffed. "What exactly is 'day to day' here?"

Nick examined the stitching on the upside of Kyle's arm.

"I guess, if you're out there, then 'day to day' would be a lot like what happened to you." Kyle winced as Nick raised his arm again. "Okay, seems like it's mostly in working order. I'll get you in a cast to keep your arm in as well as some fresh bandages. And I'm ordering you to stay here for rest and observation for six to eight weeks."

"Six to eight weeks?" Kyle was shocked.

"Oh, it's not so bad, is it? At least you'll be spending Christmas here. That's always a fun day."

"I kinda wanted to see my parents for Christmas."

"You'll have to settle for calling them from here, I'm afraid."

Kyle was puzzled. "I thought we couldn't use phones here. Greg said."

Nick smiled. "He'll never find out. Spends all day in the Big House."

Nick finished rewrapping Kyle's arm with fresh dressings. He then went to get some plaster to make Kyle a temporary cast.

The new cast was a bit bulky. Kyle's arm was at an L-angle across his chest. His ring and pinkie finger were still taped together, and his remaining fingers didn't have a lot of wiggle room.

"Okay," Nick said. "You're all good to go. I'll give you some privacy to get dressed."

He slid the curtains around Kyle's bed and left.

Kyle got out and started to get dressed. Like the last time, a set of new clothes had been neatly placed on the chair next to his bed. He was given a near-identical outfit: a pair of black boots, dark blue cargo pants, a white t-shirt, and a dark blue denim sherpa jacket. Putting his new clothes on took effort with one good arm, but he managed. He didn't bother to put his new jacket on over his cast; just his left arm.

Nick came back with a sling and helped Kyle with his shoes since he couldn't lace them up with one hand. Once he was finished, Nick wished Kyle luck and excused himself. Kyle looked at Angus.

"How's the eye?"

"Eh. It'll heal, not the worst I've had," he laughed.

"What about everyone else? What happened after I left?"

Angus put his book down. "Well, Ivan had a mild concussion and Neptune had claw marks in his arm. They're both fine now. Those two kids we picked up are recruits and probably going through training as we speak. The bodies we put in a shallow grave were *'anonymously'* reported and have been claimed as victims to an unknown serial killer."

"And Jesse?"

Angus sighed. "Yeah, she's with the bodies. Couldn't take her with us. I'm gonna miss her."

"What about Carlos?"

"He was the only one to get out without a scratch. Lucky guy. He said he was at the shooting range."

Kyle thanked Angus and walked out of the medical bay. He was still a little dizzy, but he felt better with every step. He walked out of the Bunker and stood at the top of the entrance. He was starting to reminisce. He'd only been there a month during training, but it felt longer.

He walked through the field, where Travis had beaten the living shit out of him and given him his first visit to Nick's medical bay. Not something he particularly wanted to remember. He saw a window on the second floor of the Big House, where the library was. Where he'd spent a few hours researching wendigos, studying like he had an exam the next day. He saw the workshop, where he'd met Adelaide and had a heart-to-heart with her one morning.

Most importantly, he walked up to the Bunkhouse. The doors were shut, so he couldn't see inside. He didn't feel like seeing what was inside, anyway. He couldn't help but recall the mutilated corpses of his friends. It had been cleaned since then, but that image remained in his head.

The Bunkhouse was the last stop before he went into the Big House. He walked in and looked around. The first thing he saw was Ivan talking to Aaron on the couch.

"Sad I wasn't gonna join you in death, Aaron?" Kyle said as he walked over to them. Aaron laughed.

"It's not so bad after the first hundred years."

"Glad to see you've still got the arm," Ivan said.

"Yeah, Doc said I need eight weeks off for it to heal, so I guess I got off easy."

"Not bad for a first mission. Most get injuries, but you were thrown into the deep end with wendigos. I'm just glad you didn't die," Ivan said, placing his hand on Kyle's shoulder. "Nice job."

"Where's Neptune?"

"Got discharged a few hours ago. He's skulking about somewhere here. Carlos is—"

"At the shooting range. I know. I'm gonna see him now, you coming with me?"

Ivan smiled. "Sure. We'll talk later, Aaron." Ivan waved goodbye to Aaron and then he and Kyle walked over to the shooting range.

"How long was I out?"

"Not long. We were at the wendigo den five days ago. You were rushed to the hospital for emergency surgery. We got there about an hour after you."

"Okay. Back there, you said you wanted to thank me properly. What did you mean by that?"

"You saved me. Everyone. You were an inch from dying. I just wanted to thank you for that. Not bad for someone with next to no experience."

Kyle smiled.

"Since when do you get sentimental?"

"Heh, well. You're the only person I've recruited that's lived this long. All of them died on their first mission. I guess you're just special."

Kyle was surprised. "Really – they all died? How is that possible?"

"Couldn't handle it. Got cold feet when they had to kill something. I guess that werewolf attack might have been a good thing," Ivan joked to himself.

"You know, I feel like the high death rate of the job should be declared *before* signing up. I probably would've said no."

"Hmm. Maybe so, but it's not like everyone dies on their first mission. I just picked the wrong kids."

They arrived back at the Bunker and walked down the stairs. Ivan opened the shooting range door for Kyle. Carlos was at one of the stations, shooting a pistol.

"How's Carlos holding up?"

"Surprisingly well," Ivan answered. "I honestly thought he was gonna die in that cave. I almost had him held back here to wait for another assignment. Something less ... scary."

"He's not that bad, is he?"

"No, he's actually quite skilled. His problem is he's still scared. I thought we should probably train people in a more practical sense. I wanted to use real vampires for target practice. But they're hard to keep detained."

The two continued to chat, patiently waiting for Carlos to finish. He was there with Marcus.

"Well, look who's still alive!" Marcus exclaimed as turned around and saw Kyle. Carlos also turned around to see.

"How are you still alive?" he said with a smile on his face. He walked up to Kyle and hugged him.

Kyle groaned. "Stiches. Arm this time."

Carlos immediately pulled away and apologized.

"I thought you were dead, man! That's what they said when you got to the hospital!"

"You can probably thank the doctors for that."

"So?" Carlos said.

"So what?"

"What's the afterlife like?"

Kyle seemed puzzled. "I don't think I was far gone enough to die properly. It was just black and then I woke up in the medical bay."

Carlos seemed down. "Oh, I just thought it'd be nice to know where you were headed."

"I think you know we're all going to Hell, Carlos," Ivan said coldly.

That comment seemed to unsettle Carlos.

"He's right," said Marcus, patting Carlos on the back. "There's one thing we all have in common and that's going to Hell when we die. But don't think of that as a bad thing. Having friends in Hell could be a good thing."

"Could?" asked Kyle.

"Well, we don't know what Hell is actually like," Ivan said. "But there's a good chance that we could stick together and survive it."

It wasn't exactly the thing Kyle or Carlos wanted to hear. Especially Kyle, after almost dying. Carlos seemed especially uneasy. Kyle put a smile on his face.

"Could be worse. I could be unemployed, sitting in an apartment right now. I think I like this life better."

"Yeah," Carlos said. "I was gonna be killed by vampires if Neptune hadn't saved me. I prefer this to being dead right now."

"So how long are you out of action, Kyle?" Marcus then asked.

"Eight weeks."

"Ha! Lucky. You get a guaranteed break for Christmas."

"We don't all get Christmas off?" Carlos asked.

"Most do. All recruits do, so don't worry, Carlos. You'll be safe here over the Christmas break," Ivan said.

"You should come with us, Carlos. We need to see Greg. He wants to know how the mission went." Ivan pulled Carlos away from the shooting range and walked off with him and Kyle in tow. Carlos waved goodbye to Marcus.

"If we're going back to the house, what was the point of me coming here?" asked Kyle.

"I wasn't expecting you to wake up yet – I told the damn doc to keep you down there and tell me when you woke up. Fuckin' Nick." He muttered the last part under his breath, but Kyle was still able to hear it.

"Look, there's no point in being angry about it," Kyle said calmly. "Let's just go in and report to Greg."

Kyle and Carlos followed Ivan to the Big House and up to the second floor. Greg was in the same room he'd been in when he gave them the wendigo assignment. He was sitting on a chair at the end of a table, reading through folders. Neptune was in there too, looming over Greg's shoulder. Seemingly reading what he was. Ivan opened the door to let Kyle and Carlos in.

"Ah! Good to see you're back!" Greg said. He put the folder down, got up, and walked over to shake Kyle's hand. He went in with his left, as Kyle's right wasn't exactly in working order. He also shook Carlos' hand.

"I'm glad to see you awake! Neptune was just giving me a report of what happened. I'm glad to see you two survived. Come, sit." He waved them to the chairs around the table. Everyone chose a seat. Greg cleaned up the files on the table and folded them closed.

"Now, there's no need to tell me everything that's happened. Neptune has done that for you. Well done, you two. You've also managed to save two civilians and recruit them." Greg turned to Ivan. "Now Ivan, what's your opinion on these two?" He gestured to Kyle and Carlos.

Ivan cleared his throat. "Well, Carlos seemed to have a timid nature and some trouble freezing up. Kyle throws himself into danger with little regard for the results. But they saved us back at the den. With some proper guidance, they can both become very skilled Hunters."

The pair smiled.

Greg stroked his beard in thought. "Hmm. I see. That's good to hear. Now. Kyle, Carlos. You two have an important decision to make. Most of our Hunters live either here or close to here and do local assignments across a few states. Others travel the country and the world for work. I'd honestly like you two to remain local, as we do have a few assignments in neighboring states, but the decision is ultimately yours. I have some assignments ready for you both once you heal up and the Christmas holiday is over. I'd like you to think about where you want to go. As I said, you've both done brilliantly with your first assignment. Injuries notwithstanding. Please, have a good day and have some fun while you're both still here."

Greg finished speaking and got up. Then he seemed to remember something.

"Oh, that's right. Carlos. Would you and Neptune please remain behind? Since you're not injured, I'd like to give you some assignment options. You'd be heading out January 1st."

Carlos didn't say anything. He just nodded and remained seated. He waved goodbye to Kyle as he left the room with Ivan.

"So, what's the difference between being local and heading out?" Kyle asked.

"Simple. Locals get steady supplies, intel, and help. If you leave, you get what you need and go. Minimal help and few leads. I'd suggest going out, though. Better than being cooped up here."

The two left the second floor and headed to the kitchen on the first. Kyle sat down at the table while Ivan prepared them some coffee.

"Got any Christmas plans?" Kyle asked.

"I never do," Ivan replied.

"Does anyone have Christmas plans? It feels like this is a year-round job."

"It is, but Christmas is a calm period. Supernaturals have lives too, remember."

"Even the wendigos?" Kyle said jokingly.

Ivan didn't say anything, but Kyle thought he heard him laugh under his breath. Sitting at a table drinking coffee was a nice change of pace from the past few days. And with Christmas coming soon, Kyle had something to look forward to.

"Do you have my stuff – the box I took with me when we first met? I want to call my parents."

"Oh yeah. I kept everyone's belongings in my room when we got here. Just don't let Greg see you using it. He'll kill you."

After their coffee, Kyle left the Big House and decided to go to the Bunkhouse. He wanted to see the two people he'd helped save: Anton and Alyssa. They were sitting on their beds; the first two at the front, with water bottles in their hands.

"Nice to see you two," he said, approaching them. He sat on the edge of Anton's bed.

"You're Kyle, right?" asked Alyssa.

"Yeah, I guess we haven't had a real chance to meet. Same with you, Anton."

"Anton told me about the wendigo den you saved us from. I just wanted to thank you."

Kyle blushed and looked away. "It wasn't just me. You should really be thanking Neptune – he's the one who carried you out. I was just luring them away."

"Oh, don't be modest," said Anton, sipping his coffee. "You saved us back there. And we get to do this now. So, it's a win-win."

Kyle looked surprised. "You think this is a win-win? Didn't you have lives before?" he questioned.

"Well, yes. But we were never the 'stay in one place' type," Alyssa chirped up. "I've always been the outdoorsy type and I got Anton into mountain climbing when we first met. Our lives were starting to go a bit downhill with debt, so we decided to go exploring Misquah Hills to clear our minds and get away from the troubles. Our 'disappearance' kinda works out for us."

"Hm, what a great way of thinking about this." Kyle was a little impressed the couple was so willing to give up on their lives.

He got up. "Well, I should go. I'll probably check in on a few more people."

Anton got up as well and extended his hand. "Stay safe, Kyle. And thank you." Kyle shook his hand and smiled. He then turned around and left the Bunkhouse. "We'll see you around, right?"

Kyle turned back. "For the next eight weeks."

Chapter 21

Eight weeks of recovery felt a lot longer stuck in the middle of the woods with next to no technology.

Kyle was still in the Bunkhouse, as was Carlos. Kyle had read an entire shelf of books in the library, and he'd seen the new recruits; Anton and his wife, Alyssa; finish training. Anton and Alyssa seemed in high spirits. None of them got an assignment until after Christmas, which meant they could all relax.

Kyle's Christmas was uneventful for the most part, though. Adelaide had to leave a few days before and gave her presents out early. She had given Kyle a silver dagger, with the words 'THIS WAY UP' engraved inside an arrow on the dagger's blade. He'd been wearing the dagger on his hip since he got it.

Adelaide had also made Carlos a silver zippo lighter with 'Adelaide's Finest Miniature Flamethrower' engraved on its side. Something he found hilarious and made sure to show off to everyone the second he got the chance. Kyle was also able to call his parents and explain why he couldn't make it home for Christmas that year. He'd lied and said he was in Canada for a new job in software engineering.

Carlos had organized a small lunch for him, Kyle, Ivan, and Neptune on Christmas Day.

And New Year's had felt like any other night. Apart from Marcus transforming and howling at midnight. Kyle made a promise to himself at midnight to make sure his 2009 was going to be the start of a new life. Not just as a Hunter – he had been given an out to the monotony of his old job. He was going to make sure he would make something of himself.

On January 1st, Carlos and Neptune headed out. Carlos decided to stay around the northern states and so the two were stationed in Indianapolis, getting leads on a few demons running amok in the area. He'd left in the early morning. They both promised to remain in touch.

Kyle wasn't able to do much at the Farm with his arm in its injured condition. He'd taken his cast off just after Christmas and was put in a splint for his hand, which was still broken and had a few wires in it. His arm was wrapped in new bandages to keep the stitches from getting infected. He also had to spend half an hour each day with Nick doing therapy, making sure the muscles in his hand didn't atrophy.

He spent most of his free time with Adelaide in her workshop. He liked her company. She also had a nice view of the Farm from her window; something Kyle loved to look at.

He had shelves of books to study, and when he felt like sitting down and relaxing, he'd grab a book and learn more about the supernatural. He loved one book in particular; *Wraiths, Do Not Contact.*

The book explained various types of ghosts and their interactions. It reminded him of Aaron. Its main body of context surrounded Wraiths, which - as the book explained - were originally people who had become ghosts. Their unfinished business wasn't possible to fulfil. And as a result, they went insane, turning them into Wraiths.Wraiths were extremely dangerous, being able to manipulate objects and physically attack living beings. It was strongly advised not to fight one alone.

Kyle would also go down to the shooting range now and then, using only pistols. He'd gotten good at firing with one hand, and even managed to get a few bullseyes. Marcus had jokingly offered to turn Kyle into a werewolf, so he'd heal faster, but Kyle turned down his offer, as he didn't want to take the chance of dying from a werewolf bite over a broken hand that was healing quite well on its own.

Kyle went back into the medical bay a couple of weeks later to get the wires taken out of his hand – something he'd been looking forward to. This meant having to be put under for surgery.

"Are you sure it's okay to do this here?" he asked Nick worriedly.

"You think all this medical equipment is for show?" Nick said. "This isn't the nurse's office at school."

Nick put a needle into Kyle's arm to administer the anesthetic. He could feel it running up his arm as his eyes started to feel heavy.

"Can you count backward from ten for me?" Nick asked Kyle.

"Ten. Nine. Eight ..."

Kyle woke up dazed. His eyes hurt from the bright lights in his face. He squinted and looked down at his arm. No more bandages. He was finally able to see how badly the wendigo had bitten him.

The scars on his arm and hand were sunken. They ran across his forearm like he had bumped into someone with a paint brush, creating a wave-like pattern.

I could pass it off as a dog bite, he thought.

Kyle tried to move his fingers and make a fist, but it was too painful.

His chest felt a lot better. The scars no longer made the flesh feel tight. He used three fingers on his left hand and ran them along the scars as if to imitate Travis when he'd dug his claws into him.

"It looks like it healed nicely," Nick said, gesturing to Kyle's arm.

"Yeah? It doesn't feel like it," Kyle replied, slightly annoyed.

"It's not going to feel one hundred percent the second I remove the bandages," Nick chuckled. "Give it time. A few more weeks should make it as strong as it was before. But until then, go easy and no heavy lifting. Now,

Greg has something for you. Once you can get up and the anastatic has worn off, I'll help you to the second floor. I also have a sling and some fresh bandages for that arm."

"Still gotta wear bandages?" Kyle sighed.

"Just for another day or two. The stitches in your arm will dissolve in a week. Don't be such a downer." Nick always had a smile when talking to patients. Possibly to calm them down. Kyle felt it was weird. Like a customer service smile.

Nevertheless, he was discharged and given a flimsy silk sling for the next few days. Once that was off, he could finally start working again.

As Nick helped him walk out of the Bunker and toward the second floor of the Big House, Kyle thought about visiting the Bunkhouse. The front door was open this time. He could see Anton and Alyssa sitting on their beds talking. Kyle asked Nick to stop so he could duck his head in and say hello.

"Morning, you two," he said, smiling. He leaned against the door to keep himself up.

"Oh hey! You get your stitches out," Alyssa said.

"Yup. How are you two handling everything?"

"Well," Anton said, "a bit excited. A bit scared. I'm just worried about using a gun. It felt a little weird, just us two at the shooting range. It was like being given private lessons."

Alyssa put her hand on Anton's shoulder.

"What about you, Kyle?" she asked. "How was your group of recruits?"

Kyle hesitated.

"They're all dead. Carlos and I are the only ones left. A werewolf snuck in and pretended to be a recruit. Then he killed the rest of them while they slept."

He immediately regretted telling them that. But it also felt necessary.

"I shouldn't be bringing down the room. Don't worry. You guys did a whole lot better than me and Carlos."

Kyle gave them a thumbs up. "I should leave you two be. I have to see Greg and I don't want to keep him waiting any longer."

Kyle started to leave the Bunkhouse.

"We'll see you around, right?" asked Anton.

Kyle looked back one last time.

"I wouldn't count on it. But if we do, I'll treat you both to a beer." He smiled and finally went on to the Big House.

Ivan was waiting at the bottom of the stairs.

"How's your arm?"

"Could be worse. At least I've still got it."

Ivan took over from Nick and helped Kyle up the stairs and into the back room where Greg was waiting. He was where he always was, sitting in his chair with a file on the table. Aaron was also there. He saw Ivan and Kyle enter and waved to them.

"Please, remain standing. This won't take long," Greg said.

"I'll take my leave. I need to speak to the new recruits anyway," Aaron said as he walked through Kyle and the door. As he did, Kyle felt a cold shudder throughout his body.

"You know, you could've just walked *past* me," he said.

Aaron walked back through the door.

"I could've. But it's more fun that way." He grinned and left again.

Kyle turned his attention to Greg.

"I've prepared your next assignment," Greg said. "And I'm glad to see your arm is doing a lot better. Are you cleared for work?"

Kyle started to rub his arm nervously. "Not really; Nick said a few more weeks and no heavy lifting."

"Ah well, you won't need to do any heavy lifting where I'm sending you. It's more of a stakeout. A very long stakeout." Greg turned his attention to Ivan.

"Now, I've had you stay here twenty years because of your little adventure to Las Vegas. But I've now decided that you're competent enough to be given some freedoms. So, Ivan, you can go with Kyle on his assignment and look over him."

"Who was going with me if he wasn't cleared?"

"Marcus expressed a desire to go along with you. And Adelaide as well. But they're being given a different assignment. I was going to ask Akihito, but I haven't heard anything back from him."

"Who's Akihito?" Kyle asked.

"Old Hunter," Ivan said. "He retired a few years ago."

"Then who's running the shooting range and the workshop?"

"We have Hunters come and go all the time. We have the necessary teachers already here if more recruits were to arrive. Now, back to business."

Greg slid the file on the table toward Ivan and Kyle. Ivan picked it up and opened it. It was filled with a single page and some polaroid photos. The photos were of several women.

"This looks like a stalker's diary," Kyle said bluntly.

"You two are heading to California. There have been some cases of werewolf gangs starting to join together. We think there might be something big happening. Those women are possible targets for you. What we know of the west coast wolves is that they're led by someone under the alias 'The Wolf Queen'. We have the location of her operation – Los Angeles. We've set you two up in an apartment in Pasadena. And, so as not to arouse suspicion, you have jobs."

"Jobs?" Kyle asked.

"Yes, that old antique store of yours, Ivan. I believe you've kept it all these years?"

"Uh-huh," Ivan grumbled.

"Good. You can dust it off and move back in."

"Brilliant," Ivan said sarcastically. "How are we gonna get any info from an antique store?"

"It's not like you'll be working around the clock. You can sort it out yourself. And I'd suggest you leave as soon as possible. I don't want anything major to happen."

Ivan closed the file. "We'll leave now. Just give us our supplies and we're outta here."

"I'll make the arrangements," Greg said, shooing Ivan and Kyle out of the room.

Ivan helped Kyle down the stairs – he was still a bit dazed from the surgery.

"So, are we flying or driving?" Kyle asked.

"Flying. Easier and faster. But I'm getting my car shipped over with us. I'm not leaving it behind."

"Okay, that's fair. You ever gonna get that radio fixed?"

Ivan scowled. "Maybe. If I want to. Let's just pack for now."

Kyle walked off to his bed in the Bunkhouse to pack his things. There wasn't much; just a spare change of clothes. These clothes were almost the same as what he was wearing now: the cargo pants, the boots, and a gray shirt. The only thing different was there was a gray hoodie instead of the sherpa jacket. He picked them all up and left for outside. He caught up with Ivan, who was waiting at the entrance to the Bunker. Ivan had packed a full bag, filled with who knew what.

"I guessed you wouldn't have a lot of shit to pack. Probably a good thing."

Ivan set his bag down "I'll bring my car around. Just wait here. Someone will probably be out here to give us the rest of our supplies." Ivan walked off to grab his car.

Kyle was stuck waiting around with nothing to do. It was surprisingly torturous. Just sitting around waiting for Ivan's car to arrive. Luckily, someone was emerging from the Bunker with two large duffel bags. He was stocky and bald, with a short beard that had some small white spots in it.

"You Kyle?" he asked.

"Yeah, I am. Just waiting for Ivan to get here."

"Good. These are for you." He put the bags at Kyle's feet.

"You taking over for Marcus?" Kyle asked.

"Yeah, got a problem with that?" he said agitatedly.

"No, no problem. I'm just making small talk, man."

The stocky bald man grunted at Kyle and trudged back into the Bunker. Kyle definitely preferred Marcus to this guy.

Kyle heard a car engine in the distance. And then he saw Ivan's car pull up to him. Ivan got out.

"Good, we got the supplies. Pick one up and stick it in the trunk."

Kyle picked one of the bags up with his good arm and followed Ivan to the trunk. They placed the bags inside, as well as Kyle's clothes. And then, they got in to leave.

"So, California. Have you ever been before?" asked Kyle.

"Not for a long time. The last time I remember being there was in the seventies. I'll be good to go back."

Kyle was happy. It had only been a few months since Ivan saved him from that werewolf back in Aurora. He was still distant, but Kyle felt that Ivan was going to be a good teacher to him, and a good friend.

"Looks like we have a crazy werewolf to catch," Ivan said.

"Let's hope it doesn't go as badly as the wendigo cave," Kyle replied. "I'm ready to get back to society."

Ivan started the car and the two left the Farm one last time.

Kyle's Bestiary

Kyle

- Me
- Love the jacket (Thanks Ivan!)
- Impeccable hair

Ivan

"Do I look like I could care less? I hope so."

- Old
- Very old
- Grumpy
- Good tattoos though
- Good shot
- Terrible teacher

Carlos

*"I joined because Neptune said he thought
I could make something of myself."*

- Professional Wendigo killer
- Great sense of style
- Great kid

Neptune

"Go away. I'm not interested in chatting."

- Who is he?
- Seriously, who the hell is he?
- He's English
- Too tall
- Kinda scary

Adelaide

*"It's Adelaide, Adelaide Parker.
Try to remember it."*

- Bestie
- Signature look of superiority
- Smug
- Somehow older than me
- Don't give her caffeine!

Aaron

"I help so that other's can avoid my fate."

- Stoic
- Professional ghost
- Good choice of clothes
- Can he change clothes?
- Probably not, might ask him later.

Werewolf

- Weak to silver and wolfsbane
- Curse passed though bites
- Other Werebeasts originate from Werewolves.
- Can change whenever, but full moons force a transformation
- Left weak after transforming back to human.
- Scary fangs
- Scary claws (I have firsthand experience)
- VERY large
- Is a dick even when human
- Screw you, Travis!

Wendigo

- Lanky
- Horrifying
- Weak to fire and silver
- Voice mimicry
- Cannibalism forces change in Native American grounds
- Stocks up on victims for winter
- Don't wanna see these guys again

About the Author

Murphy O 'Reilly was born on May 5th, 1997 in-
    Look, does anyone really read these?
    Just read the book, yeah?
    There's nothing interesting back here.

WROUGHT UPON US